TARGET PART III
ABSOLUTE POWER

RICKY BLACK

MAILING LIST

If you want more information regarding upcoming releases, or updates about new content on my site, sign up to my mailing list at the end of this book - You'll even receive a novella, absolutely free.

CHAPTER ONE
MONDAY 6 APRIL, 2015

BEING a multimillionaire criminal engendered little community sympathy, yet as Lamont Jones stood on the tough streets of Chapeltown, he silently prayed for help. His eyes flitted from the bleeding man at his feet, to his burning building, as he tried desperately to think of a plan. He could hear the loud shouts of the firefighters and the screams of the people still brave enough to be standing there. The acrid stench of gunpowder stung his nostrils. Never in his life had Lamont felt more vulnerable. He didn't know if the shooter was still in the vicinity, or if there was more than one.

The gunman had given him a smile after pumping bullets into his bodyguard, Akeem. He couldn't take it. He was sick of all of it. As unnerved as he was, part of him wondered what that sweet release would feel like. He closed his eyes, ready for it to be over.

A second later, he opened them, feeling foolish. He needed to be strong. Now more than ever. Lamont pulled out his phone, and with only a split-second to decide between calling an ambulance or calling for backup, he made his choice.

'L, what's happening?' Asked Manson, one of his lieutenants, when he answered.

'There's a situation. The office got blown up. Trinidad is dead, Akeem got shot. I need people sweeping the Hood, looking for the shooter. He's skinny, short hair, light-skinned, wearing a black jacket and trackies. Question anyone you don't recognise. I need you to do this now.'

'Got it. Catch me up when I get there. I'll have people en route.'

Lamont hung up, again glancing down at Akeem before finally calling an ambulance, only to learn the firefighters had already called through. Akeem was unmoving, the pool of blood surrounding him growing by the second. He knelt down, trying to stem the bleeding. He didn't know what he was doing, or if he was making a difference, but he needed to try something. Marcus Daniels had died in his arms in a similar fashion two years ago, and he hoped history wasn't repeating itself. Giving the ambulance five minutes to arrive, Lamont called again, stressing that they needed to hurry.

He sensed the crowd growing closer and instinctively concealed his emotions. The idea the shooter could be watching meshed with the rage he felt. Lennox had caught him off-guard, and given Lamont yet another reason to hunt him down.

'You're going to make it,' he said quietly to Akeem, his hands warm with the man's blood. The wet body armour had done nothing to stop the bullets. The crowd's murmuring grew louder. A man had his phone out, recording. A glance from Lamont, and he put the phone away, mumbling an apology.

'Let me help you,' a woman he didn't recognise pushed her way through the crowd. 'I have medical training.'

He stepped away, overcome with dizziness. Nothing about the situation seemed real, but it was. This was life for him.

The sounds of screeching tyres announced Lamont's people arriving in two cars. Manson jumped out, along with half a dozen other men. They hurried over, most of the crowd dispersing when they noticed.

'I've got people sweeping the Hood now. Which direction did he run in?'

'He ran toward Nassau Place,' said Lamont. Manson shouted instructions, and four men peeled off, hurrying back to the car and

TARGET PART III

driving away. Manson looked from Lamont to Akeem, his face solemn.

'We need to get you out of here.'

'I'm not leaving him,' said Lamont immediately. He didn't know if the woman was helping, but she was checking airways, keeping one hand pressed to the bleeding area. She certainly seemed more composed than he was. Manson gripped his shoulder, stealing his attention.

'You're too exposed out here. Trust me, you need to go.'

Still dazed, Lamont was bundled into the remaining car and driven away.

―――

AT HOME, Lamont waited for news about Akeem. Several hours had elapsed. Manson had checked in, saying they still hadn't found the shooter, and he was racking his brain trying to work out who it was. Lamont had been right in his sights, and the shooter had left him alone. He couldn't work out what Lennox was thinking. The conflict that had escalated between them could have ended right there.

Was he toying with him?

The thought filled him with both dread and frustration. It struck him that he knew little about Lennox's organisation. Even his assault on Nikkolo had only been possible because of the information Stefanos's contacts gave him. It was something he would need to rectify.

A shooting in public would need an immediate police response and investigation. There was nothing in the building or on records that would negatively link Lamont to the business. The business he had helped Trinidad grow. Trinidad was dead, and it was all his fault. Nausea swam over him, and he took several deep breaths, trying to control himself. Trinidad had died for his stupidity. He should have warned him of the danger, rather than leaving him to suffer.

Lamont paced the room, his temples throbbing. Trinidad had a family, and someone would need to contact them. The phone rang, and he scrambled to answer it.

'Lamont?'

It was his solicitor, Levine.

'Yes?'

'I don't know all the details of what you're involved in, but the police want to ask you some questions in connection with two murders.'

Lamont's stomach plummeted. He knew he had heard correctly, but still needed to check.

'*Two* murders?'

'A second man died on Chapeltown Road, and witnesses placed you at the scene. I want you to come to my office, and we will draft a statement together.'

Lamont didn't respond. Akeem was dead, and it hurt to hear. He closed his eyes, his shoulders slumping.

'Lamont. Are you listening?'

'I heard you. I will come to your office tomorrow.'

'Time is of the essence here. The police aren't looking to arrest you at this stage, but if I'm going to protect you, I need to know the facts.'

'I said, I will come tomorrow. Or did you forget you work for me and not the other way around?'

The coldness of Lamont's tone reminded Levine who he was dealing with.

'Tomorrow will be fine. I'll be in the office from ten.'

Lamont hung up without responding. There was no reason for him to react to Levine like that, yet he couldn't help it. The police wanting to speak to him was nothing important. He wouldn't be giving them any information that would help.

Sitting back down, he rubbed his temples and closed his eyes.

What the hell was Lennox thinking?

LENNOX THOMPSON WAITED for news of his attack with no emotion. He had prepared his message with care. Teflon had located one of his hidden spots. He didn't know how, but it had rattled him, and needed answering in kind. The plan was simple. He would destroy Teflon's business. Everyone knew he owned the barber shop, and that Trinidad ran it for him. It would send a clear-cut sign that war wasn't a good idea. If he showed, his shooter, Sinclair, was to kill whoever was with him. He wanted Teflon to know he could get him whenever he wanted.

The spot Lennox was in was on Well House Drive, off Roundhay Road. He had several spots dotted all around, and after Teflon had located one, he had instantly moved. It was spartan, with a television, a lumpy grey sofa, and a simple table in the middle of the living room.

Soon, two booming knocks at the door alerted him. He slid into a seat and waited for a worker to let them in.

The pair traipsed into the living room. One was stocky, with straight brown hair, steely blue eyes, and rugged features. The other, Sinclair, looked like a kid. He was twenty-four years old, but had the build and features of a teenager. Lennox signalled for both men to sit.

'Is it done?'

'Yes,' said the stocky man. He was Mark Patrick, and had been elevated by Lennox after Nikkolo's demise. He had served time in the army and had connections and experience with explosives. 'The owner bit it too.'

Lennox straightened in his seat. 'You killed Trinidad?'

'By the time we realised he was in there, it was too late.'

Lennox glared at him. 'You messed up.' He wasn't pulling punches.

'You wanted a message sent, and I sent it. He was an old man, and he was down with Teflon.'

'He was a civilian.' Lennox continued to stare Mark down. 'Watch how you speak to me.'

'You should have let me drop Teflon too,' Sinclair added, bored with the conversation. 'His bodyguard went down easy. Never even saw it coming.'

Lennox ignored the boasting. 'We have a primary target in place. What happened today was payback, and Teflon will realise that.'

'Do you know how they found Nikkolo yet?' asked Mark. Lennox shook his head.

'I spoke with everyone connected with that hideout, and no one gave anything away. No one stands out either. It's possible they just got lucky, but I doubt it.'

'What's the next step then? Teflon and his people are gonna be gunning for you.'

'Set up a meeting with Nicky Derrigan.'

Mark and Sinclair exchanged looks. They knew Derrigan by reputation, and it wasn't a move they expected Lennox to make.

'Are you sure you want to go there?'

Lennox's stare only intensified, and Mark looked away.

'I'll make the call.'

―――

DETECTIVE RIGBY WAITED in an interview room as K-Bar was shown in. His solicitor was with him, and they both took seats opposite Rigby. K-Bar appeared well for a man on remand. His expression remained as guarded as it had during the initial interview. He brushed a stray dreadlock from his face, not taking his eyes from Rigby, waiting for him to speak.

'You wanted to talk,' said Rigby after a long moment. He hadn't started recording. The conversation was informal at this stage, but for anything to be agreed, they would need to have it on record.

'I want to know what's on offer.'

'Do you have something to trade?'

K-Bar evaded the question. 'What do I get if I did?'

'What do you want?'

K-Bar smiled. It was the first bit of emotion he'd shown since entering the room.

'I'm innocent. I want to be released.'

'If you were innocent, you wouldn't be behind bars, would you?'

K-Bar's smile widened. 'Wouldn't be the first time you lot got it wrong. You don't have a clue what's really going on out there.'

Ignoring the jab, Rigby pressed on.

'You're looking at serious time, Keiron. If you want to spend your time dicking around, I'm sure you would be more comfortable doing that from your cell. You killed people — men and women — to further your interests. You're not innocent, and your hands are not clean. So, you can help yourself, or you can go back.'

'Innocent until proven guilty.' K-Bar remained unruffled, though his smile had vanished.

'We have nothing but time. Time, and some key witnesses.'

'That saw me kill people? Can't be the case if I'm innocent, can it?'

Rigby shook his head. His temper crept up, and he couldn't stop it.

'Innocent? You've no shame, have you? You take away somebodies daughter, a lifelong friend . . . a life. Then you sit here giving it *innocent until proven guilty*. You'll see what we have when you're in court fighting for your freedom.'

Rigby was unsure how he expected K-Bar to react, but he hadn't expected his eyes to light up. A moment later, he was back to normal.

'I think I made a mistake. I changed my mind, and I don't wanna talk anymore. You're never gonna get what you want. That's a promise.'

'What do you mean by that?'

Shaking his head, K-Bar rose to his feet. His solicitor, who had remained silent throughout the exchange, followed suit. After directing an officer to take him away, Rigby headed back to his desk. Murphy immediately came over.

'What did he have to say then?'

'Nothing. He was fishing to see what he could find out.'

Murphy frowned. 'That's a shame. I'd have liked to stuff Teflon in the cell next to him.'

'We'll let K-Bar stew a while, then go for him again. He is the key to bringing down the whole crew.'

AFTER RIGBY LEFT, K-Bar asked to speak with his solicitor. The officer was hesitant, but allowed it after a glance over his shoulder to see who was around.

'What was the point of that, Mr Barrett?' the solicitor started. 'You overplayed your hand with the officers, which didn't help our position.'

K-Bar grinned.

'There was never a deal to be made. I just wanted to confirm something.'

'What could you have possibly confirmed from that interaction?' The solicitor frowned. K-Bar's grin only widened.

'We don't have long, but I need you to pass on a message for me.'

CHAPTER TWO

TUESDAY 7 APRIL, 2015

DELROY AWOKE with his usual stiffness. After staring at the ceiling for a few minutes, he clambered from the bed. Once ready, he checked his messages, but they were all business. No one had contacted him that he wanted to speak to, and he felt his chest tighten.

Traipsing downstairs, he made himself his usual breakfast of plain porridge. He wasn't supposed to drink coffee anymore—doctor's orders. Like many things in his life, he ignored them. He was an old man, and he had earned the right to live his life exactly how he wanted.

His kitchen, like everything in the house, had been designed by his wife, Elaine. She had taken control of all the decorations, so now he had a modern, ghastly, chrome nightmare. It took months to learn how all the various devices worked, but he had to admit, once he had, that they made things easier. He wondered what she was doing. He hadn't spoken to her since shortly after Eddie died. She was still using his money. The credit card bills were proof, but something was broken between them. There was no fixing it. As far as she was concerned, she had lost two children because of him. Because he was a criminal.

He couldn't make her understand.

Delroy had come from Grenada with a vicious reputation and

boundless ambition. He had looked at the gangs that were established in Chapeltown and, even early on, had seen the potential in selling hard drugs. That kicked off a series of wars, and he was simply more vicious than the rest. By the time crack, coke and heroin were established, he controlled most of the flow in the Hood. Not wanting all the attention, he allowed little gangs to run wild, figuring they would keep themselves distracted and away from him. This action led to more police attention, as they couldn't ignore the rising drug trade in Chapeltown forever.

Things settled down after that, and Delroy consolidated his power, growing richer and more influential. Things changed a few years ago, but no one was a bigger example of that than Lennox Thompson.

Lennox had grown up around the Hood and was committing robberies from a young age. Charisma set him apart from the rest. He was a natural leader who planned tasks with absolute precision. Only his temper held him back, leading to him serving serious time in prison. Like others, he used his time behind bars to cultivate criminal connections. Unlike most, Lennox didn't go the drug route. It was making everyone rich, but he didn't seem interested. Instead, he focused on extortion and robberies, working with other thugs like Marcus Daniels and Ricky Reagan.

Delroy had paid attention to him as he did all the interesting criminals, but Lennox wasn't a concern. He wasn't selling drugs, nor did he seem interested in anyone who was. Delroy put him to one side.

Until the attacks started.

No one picked up on the patterns at first. A dealer jumped in Bankside. Another in the Mexborough's. A few spots in the Hood robbed with no casualties. He increased security, but the problem only grew, leading to one of his top distributors getting shot twice outside his home. He survived, but it was a true sign someone was out there.

Delroy mobilised his son and right-hand man, Winston, to sniff out who was behind it. A great son, he took any opportunity to prove himself, and was a born negotiator. He quickly learned that Lennox Thompson was the man leading the charge, shocking everyone.

There had been no lead-up. No slights or crew issues. He'd started attacking with no reason, and they had to respond in kind. No one imagined it would be difficult. Even in decline, Delroy's team was still the biggest in Leeds. They hunted Lennox's people, but they were well hidden. They picked off some smaller fruit, but they couldn't get anywhere near Lennox or his inner circle. Winston grew desperate and began sending men to infiltrate the crew. This backfired and led to Lennox tracking him. Winston and his bodyguard had been cut down with ease, the rumour being that Lennox had executed him personally.

The murder of his son devastated Delroy. His wife had been inconsolable, and his second son, Eddie, had gone off the reservation, swearing revenge against Lennox Thompson and his crew.

Delroy reached out to Lamont Jones, wanting him to assume control and take the fight to Lennox. Lamont refused, and Delroy had reluctantly taken control of the troops, restructuring the crew and setting up several teams focused purely on tracking Lennox. They hadn't come close to finding him, and with the increased police pressure and the surgical attacks by Lennox's people, Delroy was close to losing, and he knew it.

Then Shorty became involved.

Delroy and Shorty had never got along. Delroy respected Lamont, but not the people he kept around him. Shorty was too bloodthirsty. He had no respect for his power and constantly clashed with Delroy's men. Lennox's people took a shot at him, and hit his young daughter instead. She survived, but Shorty took the war to Lennox, killing several of his men. Lamont backed his friend, and this cost him, when his girlfriend was murdered by Lennox's forces.

Lamont and Delroy had teamed up after this, with Delroy helping him to spring a trap against the powerful warlord, Akhan, making off with his load of drugs. Lennox quietened for a while, but had recently struck again, killing Trinidad Tommy along with one of Lamont's bodyguards.

The only way to get rid of Lennox for good was to kill him, and that was still Delroy's goal. He considered speaking with Lamont directly to devise a plan, but no one had heard from him lately, and he needed to do this. He hadn't earned his power by accident. He had fought for it every step of the way. Sacrificed for it.

If he couldn't defeat some upstart like Lennox Thompson, then what was the point of having it?

An hour later, he was being driven along Chapeltown Road, then down Newton Grove, a long, winding road with several semi-detached spots. Arriving at his destination, Delroy put his earlier thoughts to one side. He climbed from the car, surrounded by his men. They scoured the street, looking for anything out of the ordinary. Three youths stood outside the spot — a pale bricked house with a rusted black gate and a grey Mercedes that had seen better days parked outside. They straightened when they recognised Delroy, their eyes full of adoration and respect. He nodded at them, then made his way inside.

Mack sat in the living room, smoking a cigarette and holding a phone to his ear. He wore a creased grey shirt and black trousers with a visible brown belt. When he noticed Delroy in the doorway, he stubbed out his cigarette and told the person on the phone he would call them back.

'Boss,' he said, his tone neutral. Delroy's men secured the spot, leaving him alone with Mack. Neither spoke immediately. They had a long working relationship stretching back over twenty years. Mack had been instrumental to Delroy's takeover, using his viciousness to bring people around to the new regime.

Over time, he grew more bitter, less pleased with the newer, upcoming gangs, in particular Lamont's. He had hated Lamont immediately and disliked the fact Delroy was fond of him. For his own reasons, he publicly threatened him a few years ago, and the swift retaliation had kicked off a small conflict. Mack had been badly beaten by Shorty and Marcus Daniels, suffering a fractured skull amongst other injuries. He had spent time in hospital recovering and, in his own words, hadn't been right since.

The living room was cramped, a TV that was far too big taking up lots of space, along with two ghastly purple sofas that had been jammed into the room, regardless of how it would look. There were generic paintings on the wall, along with DVDs, empty bottles of liquor, and two ashtrays plonked on the coffee table.

'Do you want something to drink?' Mack finally asked.

TARGET PART III

'No. What do you have for me?'

'Nothing you're gonna like. Lennox and his people are still underground. We can't even get at the little ones right now. Won't last forever, but for now, we're shooting at shadows.'

'Someone has to know something. What are the streets saying?'

'Everyone is talking about Teflon getting punked. Way I heard it, Lennox's shooter was right there in front of him, and he crapped himself like he always does. Lennox could have finished him right there.'

Delroy ignored most of Mack's bitter re-telling of the story. People got word to him as soon as it went down, and most said Lamont had tried to save his bodyguard, and had been whisked away before the police could show. It made Delroy wonder about Lennox's end game. Lamont was exposed and vulnerable, and Lennox hadn't taken the shot. He had ruthlessly cut through Lennox's sons, along with attacking Shorty's daughter and Lamont's woman. He was ruthless and not afraid to kill, so it made even less sense to leave such a powerful enemy alive. Delroy pushed the thoughts away for now.

'No one is saying anything specifically about Lennox then?'

Mack shook his head.

'People are scared. He looks like the winning side right now.'

Delroy glared at Mack, but didn't refute his words.

'What about sales?'

'They're down. Police are still everywhere, and even though that *OurHood* crap is quiet, they're still out there, shutting down spots and targeting runners. Might be worth stretching further out if we want to sell. I've got people in Wakefield and Bradford crying out for more product. Just say the word.'

'Wakefield might be an idea,' said Delroy. He had high-placed contacts in Bradford that wouldn't want him stepping on their toes. The last thing he needed was more people trying to kill him.

'I'll send a couple' men out there to see how things are. You decided what you're gonna do about those drugs yet?'

Delroy scratched his head. He was torn between sitting on the drugs they had stolen and waiting for the war to end, and moving them out of town. He had money tied up everywhere, but there were places he could move it to in a pinch.

'That's a conversation to have with Teflon.'

Mack scowled and lit another cigarette.

'We should fuck him off and keep them all. What's he gonna do?'

'That would be silly. Teflon is a powerful ally.'

'He's a prick, and he's always been a prick, Del. You indulged him for far too long, and we lost face because of it.'

Delroy's face hardened.

'We lost face because you stupidly challenged Lamont in public, involving yourself in a situation you didn't need to. We lost face because you and Reagan could not see the big picture. You got your head cracked open, and for what? What did it gain you?'

Mack's eyes flashed with rage, but he held his tongue. Delroy rose to his feet, furious at his subordinate for his stupidity.

'Make sure everyone knows what they're doing. Keep juggling the spots as often as you can and make sure I'm made aware of the new locations.'

'Fine.'

Delroy gave him one last look, then left.

———

'We were lucky, Lamont.'

Lamont was on his way back to Levine's office. The police interview hadn't taken long. He'd *no-commented* their questions, and the police had multiple witnesses who saw Akeem's shooting. They weren't pleased, but couldn't push it any further.

'I had nothing to do with what happened,' said Lamont.

'That's not my concern. You pay me to keep you out of prison. Whether or not you're involved, I don't care. It was your business that was blown up. You were right next to this other man when he was shot.'

'Are you ever going to get to the point?'

Levine shook his head. 'Just be careful. Don't give the police any reason to focus their investigation on you. In the meantime, I will keep working behind the scenes to learn how things are progressing.'

'Fine.'

Levine glanced at Lamont, who stiffly stared ahead. He had been his solicitor for almost a decade and had never seen him look so fatigued.

'Are you sure everything is okay?'

'I'm done talking about this.' Lamont coldly cut off Levine, not wanting to discuss it any further. He was onto other things now. It was obvious the shooter had escaped. He could be hiding out anywhere. Lennox had likely planned well, and would have had an exit strategy for him. The shooter was extremely young, likely only a few years older than Lamont's nephew, Keyshawn. It was a sobering realisation.

Thoughts of Trinidad again hit him. It was a guilt that had slotted in next to his sorrow over Jenny's murder. Two innocent people he should have protected. Dead because of their association with him.

When Lamont left Levine, he drove back to his house, not feeling comfortable being out in the open. He called Maka whilst he was driving.

'L, is everything good?'

'It's fine. I want you to send someone to see Trinidad's family. Give them some money to help cover costs.'

'How much?'

'Five grand for now. Make it clear they only need to ask if they need more.'

'Are you sure you don't wanna do this yourself? I mean, you and Trinidad were close, fam. He loved you.'

Lamont closed his eyes for a moment, conscious he was still driving. Maka wasn't wrong. It should have been him speaking to them, but he couldn't face it. He had enough people in Chapeltown that hated him lately. He couldn't take seeing more angry faces right now.

'. . . make sure you send someone good. Get at me if there are any issues.'

'I'll send D. He's smashed it lately.'

Lamont hung up and dropped the phone on the passenger seat. He took another deep breath, focusing on making it home. Lennox had a lot to pay for, and he would make sure he did exactly that.

———

NICKY DERRIGAN WAS one of the few men that Lennox could claim to be intimidated by. He was brawny, beady-eyed, yet had surprisingly smooth features. His dirty blond hair was cut low, and he favoured simple crew neck sweaters and loose combat trousers. Lennox had known Derrigan for years and had used his services in the past. He didn't play sides and worked only with people who came recommended. Once you had his services, he was loyal until the job was done. The problem was that he was picky in the jobs he took.

When Lennox reached out, Derrigan had agreed to meet, providing he picked the location. It was risky for Lennox as he was in hiding. The only way to stay one step ahead was to control the surrounding people, and limit their access to him. Knowing Derrigan would play a vital role in his mission, he agreed.

They met at a lockup near Cross Gates. Lennox had fond memories of the area, and had laid a trap for Teflon's men here a few months back. He knew the area well, and had come alone, wanting to show Derrigan he was serious.

'Thanks for meeting me,' said Lennox, glancing around the empty lockup. It was damp and mouldy, and their voices carried around the empty place.

'We do jobs here,' said Derrigan. 'People keep their mouths shut. We bring people here and get what we need out of them.'

Lennox agreed. The locals kept to themselves and had allowed his men to operate in the area without involving the police. He didn't ask for details about the jobs. Derrigan liked to hurt people, but he was controlled, and that was the main factor. Lennox didn't need more idiots like Lutel lumbering around and making things worse. Lutel had been useful to a point, until he botched the hit on Shorty, instead shooting his daughter and uniting half the Hood against Lennox. It had taken some manoeuvring to regain the advantage.

'What's your schedule like right now?'

TARGET PART III

'Depends on the job.'

'It'll require your commitment for at least a few months. I want you on retainer.'

'You know the drill. I don't come cheap.'

'If you do what I want, there's half a mill in it for you. Fifty thousand up front.'

Lennox had him. Derrigan had a poker face, but he couldn't hide the gleam when he heard the fee.

'What's the job?' He asked, an evil grin flitting across his face.

'You know Delroy?'

'Williams?'

'That's your job.'

Derrigan leaned forward. 'You think you can get him?'

'How much do you know about what's going on in Chapeltown?'

'I'm in and out of town, but I hear things. Lot more shootings lately. Teflon's people are recruiting, but they never contacted me.' He grinned again. 'No idea why.'

Lennox understood why. Derrigan was brutal, and he was hard to control. Someone like Teflon wouldn't be able to use him effectively. He'd had enough trouble keeping a leash on Marcus and Shorty.

Lennox recalled the stories of Derrigan in his younger days. A skilled boxer, he was destined for good things, until a bout went awry, and he killed his opponent, continuing to hit him even after the referee had called off the fight.

'Don't worry about Teflon,' he said.

Derrigan frowned. 'You know he's gonna come for you. From what I heard, you've messed with people close to him. He's not the guy to shake that off.'

Lennox didn't want to discuss Teflon. He kept his eyes on Derrigan, letting the silence play out.

'Delroy is my target. Either you can help, or you can't.'

'Talk me through it.'

'There's a war going on. I've done well so far, but Delroy is finally getting off his arse and fighting back. I've lost a few key pieces lately, and I can't think of anyone better than you to restore the natural order.'

'He won't be easy to get to.'

'That's my problem to deal with. Are you in or not?'

The silence dragged on, but Lennox wasn't moved. He was skilled at playing this game, and no one had more willpower than him. Finally, Derrigan nodded.

'Tell me the plan.'

It was well after midnight. Lamont was on his sofa, staring into space.

The past few days had been draining, yet he'd attempted to sleep earlier, and it hadn't come. There were too many things in the air, too many threads that would need his work. He didn't know where to look for Lennox. People were making subtle enquiries on his behalf. He didn't know how long it would take, or whether they could sustain it. His organisation had taken some hits lately, and with Akeem's death, he felt more vulnerable than he had in months.

For a moment, everything had worked. He had struck against Lennox, removed the threat of Akhan, and ensured an alliance with Stefanos and Jakkar. Now he was dealing with an attack in the heart of the community he loved, and the deaths of a father figure, and a man who had protected him on more than one occasion. Both had given him wise counsel in the past, and now he was fighting through it alone.

No Akeem. No Trinidad. No Shorty. No Jenny.

Sighing, Lamont trudged to his kitchen, rooting around the cupboards until he found what he was looking for; a bottle of Wray & Nephew white rum. He hadn't had a drink since Jenny died, but right now, nothing was stopping him. Grabbing a glass, he filled it to the brim and drank it, wincing at the harsh taste. Without thinking, he poured another, and when that was finished, one more. When the room started spinning, he smiled for the first time in forever, desperate for the escape.

CHAPTER THREE
WEDNESDAY 8 APRIL, 2015

WHEN LAMONT AWOKE, he was dazed, and his head was aching. Gingerly shaking the cobwebs free, he checked the time, noting it was after midday. He had slept for over twelve hours. When he made it downstairs, he gulped down some water to get rid of his dry mouth, then made a coffee, needing the energy boost. He groaned as he checked his phone, noting the multitude of missed calls and text messages. Darren was his first port of call.

'Hey, L. You good?'

'I'm fine,' replied Lamont, feeling anything but. 'Maka said he gave you a job. Did you handle it?'

'Yeah. Dropped in on Trinidad's family. They wouldn't take the money.'

Lamont closed his eyes, staring out of his kitchen window for a long moment.

'L?'

'They just lost him. Can't expect them to be hugging and smiling.'

'It wasn't your fault. They need to recognise that.'

Lamont wanted to shout at his underling. He wanted to tell him it was his fault, and that Trinidad died because of his mistakes, but he didn't. Darren spoke again after a moment.

'What do you want me to do with the money?'

'Keep it.'

'Are you sure? We're talking five bags here.'

'Do something nice. Take your woman out.'

'Are you sure you're okay?'

'I already told you I'm fine.' Lamont's tone was icy now, and Darren recognised he'd pushed too far.

'Sorry, boss. I'll talk to you later then, if you don't need anything else.'

Lamont hung up, staring down at the phone. He'd made a mistake not going to see the family himself. He was so worried about facing them, that he'd made things worse by staying away. Maybe it was for the best, he reasoned. He wasn't at all liked in Chapeltown right now. Staying away was likely the best move.

Washing up his dirty cup and glass, he forwent breakfast and traipsed upstairs to take a scalding shower. When he was fresher and dressed, he made a few calls, seeking information on Lennox Thompson and his people, promising to pay handsomely for good leads. Planning to speak with Maka later, his attention was taken by one of the people who had tried calling earlier. He hadn't paid attention to the call log, but his stomach jolted when he saw Stefanos's number.

Lamont's relationship with Jenny's father was a strange one. She'd died not knowing her father was more connected to the life of crime than Lamont or anyone he knew. They had first met at the funeral, and ever since, he'd opened multiple doors for Lamont, and helped him remove a powerful enemy in Akhan. He called him back.

'Lamont. Are you well?'

'Had a rough night. Is everything okay?'

'I would like to speak with you as soon as possible.'

'Where?'

'Come to my home, please. I trust you remember the way?'

'I'll see you soon.'

TARGET PART III

LAMONT LEFT HIS HOUSE, realising he still needed to arrange some proper protection. He would either speak with Manson and get him to sort someone, or he would hire a personal team to look after him. It would be expensive, but far better than the alternative.

The ride to Stefanos's was quiet. His paranoia was high after the recent shooting. It could have been him. The thought kept resonating in his mind. Lennox could have ended his life right there, and he wouldn't have seen it coming. The more he considered it, the more stupid he realised it had been to rush down there. There was nothing he could do to stop the fire. Going after Lennox without protecting Jenny had been stupid. As he settled into traffic, he wondered how many mistakes he could get away with, before he paid the ultimate price.

Stefanos's sprawling estate was a comforting sight. It was larger than Delroy's property, with large iron gates, an attached garage, and fields surrounding the perimeter. Lamont had only been a few times. He imagined Jenny spending time here, sitting out in the open, reading, or walking the grounds, taking in the scenery. He wondered if she had cultivated her love of flowers out here, then dismissed the thoughts as his heart clenched.

Stefanos waited for him, a wide smile on his face. He wore a navy jumper, well-pressed trousers and slippers. Lamont found it endearing the man was so comfortable in his own skin. They shook hands, and Stefanos led him inside.

As they headed to the study, Lamont noticed a photo of Jenny on the hallway wall. She was smiling at the camera, eyes sparkling. He paused. His heart wrenched in his chest. He couldn't take his eyes from her. Stefanos noticed Lamont stop, studying his reaction to the picture. It was one of a collection his wife had placed all around the house. The pain in the younger man's eyes was palpable. Putting his hand on Lamont's shoulder, Stefanos's eyes flitted back to the photo, and he smiled for a moment. After a few more seconds, he led him away and into the room.

The study remained as luxurious as ever. Stefanos had an oak desk, several comfortable-looking chairs, and an array of photos on the walls. Lamont tore his eyes from another picture of Jenny, only to find Stefanos already observing him.

'You look tired, Lamont.'

'Rough night, like I said.'

'You need to take care of yourself. You're still a young man. I'm sorry about Trinidad. He was a good man, and a pillar of your community.'

'How do you know the things you know?' Lamont asked. It was unnerving just how much influence Stefanos seemed to have. Stefanos shrugged, pouring himself a glass of whiskey after offering Lamont one.

'Information is always useful.'

It was a vague answer that only made Lamont more curious, which he supposed was the intention.

'I trust there's a reason you wanted to see me?'

'Jakkar asked me to speak with you.'

Lamont had expected this. Reclusive by nature, Jakkar represented a powerful council back in the Middle East. The same council that had subsidised Akhan when he moved to England to sell drugs. They had links everywhere, and he had stumbled into an alliance with them through Stefanos. They'd recently made him an offer, wanting him to take over Akhan's distribution ring in Yorkshire and the surrounding areas. It was a tremendous opportunity, and he had accepted.

'I see.'

'No one is pleased about the situation on the streets. Less money is being made, and there are more police in Chapeltown and Harehills. When Jakkar made his offer, he assumed you could deal with this.'

'The police presence was stifling long before Jakkar made his offer. I didn't start any of this.'

'That being said, he has high hopes for you, and expected you to deal with it. What happened on Chapeltown Road shouldn't have happened.'

'I agree. Trinidad was a good man.'

Stefanos shook his head. 'That isn't what I'm talking about. You were out in the open with only one guard, a guard who is now dead.

TARGET PART III

Add to that you travelled here today without a bodyguard, putting us both at risk.'

Lamont grew annoyed. He didn't like the way Stefanos was speaking to him.

'It might mean nothing to you, but Trinidad didn't deserve to die, and frankly, that's more important than what might have happened to me.'

'That's grief talking. You are a powerful man, Lamont, and you are destined for great things. Use this conflict to show everyone what you are made of.'

'Lennox was responsible for the death of your daughter, Stefanos. You helped me track Nikkolo and Akhan. Help me track Lennox, and I can finish this.'

'I've spoken with Jakkar, and we don't want to get more involved than necessary. He has resources you can use, but only in defence of your drug routes.'

Lamont's mouth slackened. Akhan had multiple teams of killers that he'd used when necessary, and Lamont had hoped to have use of them, along with their extensive information network.

'Your daughter died. What the hell does that have to do with Jakkar?'

'Focus on the tasks we have given you. Finish Lennox, or the promotion will vanish.'

The meeting was spiralling out of control, and Lamont found he didn't care.

'Lennox is dangerous for everyone. He's ambitious and ruthless, and he won't stop. Nikkolo gave us nothing major about him or his organisation, but I know he was behind the *OurHood* Initiative, and used them to discredit myself, amongst others. He should be stopped as soon as possible.'

'Stop him then. We have faith that you can do this.'

'Faith, but no genuine support. What the hell is it with you and Jakkar? How does a Greek entrepreneur get involved with a Middle Eastern drug ring?'

Stefanos gave a momentary smile. 'All the product in the world is useless if you can't move it. They use my shipping resources and tankers to move their product wherever they need it. It gives me a modicum of influence where they are concerned, and we make a lot of money together.'

'All while the people responsible for your daughter's murder walk around free. Excellent.'

Stefanos's smile vanished, and his eyes were like flint.

'Do you want me to judge you as responsible for my daughter's murder too, Lamont? After all, her involvement with you got her killed. I put that aside because it was right, but if I hadn't, you would be dead. Instead, I remember my daughter in the best light, and respect the choices she made. I helped you remove Akhan because of that. I suggest you keep your mouth shut where it pertains to myself and my daughter, and get back to work.'

There was nothing Lamont could say to this, nor did he try. They held all the cards, and nothing good would come from making enemies of them too.

'No problem.' He slid to his feet and held out his hand. Stefanos shook it, and he turned to leave.

'Lamont?'

He turned at the door and faced Stefanos. The man's face was unreadable.

'Good luck.'

THE TENSE CONVERSATION had given Lamont a lot to think about. He couldn't help noticing the shift in tone between the last meetings he'd had with Jenny's father. His attitude had changed, and he wondered what sort of pressure Jakkar and his people were putting on Stefanos. It was a complex world of politics and subtext that he didn't have the energy to sift through.

The bottom line was that he would receive no help from them with Lennox, and he would have to go at it alone.

TARGET PART III

DERRIGAN STOOD in a garden in St Martin's, smoking a cigarette and enjoying the soft night breeze. He'd been standing there for the better part of thirty minutes and didn't mind. Many in his line of work suffered from impatience; they liked to charge in and make things happen, whereas Derrigan had no problem waiting if needed.

Delroy's men were not lying down and taking their defeat. As of late, they were attacking with a vengeance, hunting down spots where Lennox could be hiding with ferocity. None was making a more significant dent than the man Derrigan waited on.

Solomon was skilled and well-liked. A few nights ago, he had tracked down two of Lennox's couriers, executing both. Lennox wanted Derrigan to make an example out of him, and with the money he was paying, he was happy to do so.

Finishing his cigarette, he heard a noise behind him and turned, but it was nothing. He'd worried the family whose garden he was hiding in might stir, but they hadn't. One of his guys was watching the street, sitting in a parked car. He would ring Derrigan if there were any hiccups. Other than that, he settled in to wait.

Another hour passed by before a black BMW pulled to a stop outside a house. Two men climbed out. One was gangly and slightly balding. The other — Solomon — was shorter, with a powerful build and fluid grace. Solomon and the other man stood in the street talking, then Solomon lit a spliff, the smoke from the joint wafting around him. Derrigan was itching to go after him, but there was no way to take Solomon without the other man getting the drop on him, and he didn't know how armed they were.

The pair stood outside for another twenty minutes, with Solomon answering two phone calls in that time. He didn't know why they weren't going in the house, but it wasn't worth speculating. The night was pleasant, and there was nothing strange about enjoying it. Quietly, he stretched, watching the pair for any signs of weakness. He sent his spotter a text message, telling them to follow the BMW if it pulled away with Solomon inside, but then he had a reprieve. The other man touched Solomon's fist, then climbed back in the car and drove away.

Derrigan grinned, waiting for the car to drive out of sight before he made his move. Reaching down, he grabbed the small length of pipe he'd brought, padding across the road. Solomon was almost at the door before he realised Derrigan was on him. He turned but wasn't quick enough, as Derrigan slammed the pipe against his ribs, then jabbed him in the stomach before he could scream. He toppled to the floor, Derrigan looming over him, smiling. He hit him twice more, hearing his right arm crack, then his kneecap. No words were necessary. He let the pipe fall to the floor, working him over with his gloved fists, hitting him with powerful, vicious blows to the face. When he grew tired, he grabbed the pipe again, bringing it down on Solomon's skull.

Derrigan breathed hard, pleased with the attack. It would send a message to Delroy and his men that they could be picked off. He stalked off, leaving the destroyed gunman in his wake.

CHAPTER FOUR
FRIDAY 10 APRIL, 2015

LAMONT, Maka, and Manson met at a safe house in Harehills. The spot wasn't one that was used regularly. It was stocked with food and emergency supplies, but had a musty odour. Two soldiers waited outside, with another sat in a car. They were the first line of defence in case of an attack, but still, Lamont remained wary. Being out and about was more of a calculated risk each time he did it, and he had yet to secure adequate protection. He'd given the matter some thought and would hire a personal bodyguard team. The last thing he wanted was to take resources from the crew when they were stretched thin as it was.

Maka and Manson weren't sure what to expect from the meeting. Neither had seen Lamont since Trinidad's shooting, but quickly noticed how tired and drawn he looked. The usual glint of power in his eyes was missing, and they appeared dull. The pair shared a look.

Despite the odour, the living room was comfortable. There was a plush brown sofa that Maka and Manson currently sat on, along with an old-fashioned armchair that Lamont used. Several glasses were on the coffee table, along with a bottle of Courvoisier. Lamont wasn't partaking, but Manson had poured himself a glass, sipping it as they waited.

'Has this spot been checked?' Lamont asked. Manson nodded.

'My people checked it earlier, and then I went over it afterwards. It's clean.'

'What do we know then?'

'I dunno which of Lennox's people got to Solomon, but they did a number on him. Beat the shit out of him outside his house.'

'Is he still alive?' Lamont knew Solomon by reputation, and he was good at what he did. Back when they'd had their scuffles with Ricky Reagan's crew, he'd hoped Delroy wouldn't involve Solomon, and thankfully, he hadn't. To hear of him being brutalised was another stark reminder that no one was safe in this conflict.

'For now. Doesn't look good. People are saying he's got internal bleeding, broken ribs, fractured skull. Whatever they hit him with split his skull wide open.'

'No one's claiming yet?' Lamont didn't want to think about Solomon with his skull split open. Manson shook his head.

'Lennox isn't gonna claim it. People know what he's doing, and that's enough.'

'Forget that for a minute.' Lamont focused on Maka. 'Are you sure you're well enough to be here? You got shot.'

'The bullet barely grazed me, L. I'm good. It's not like I'm running a marathon.'

'Make sure you take care of yourself, Maka. Bullet wounds are no joke.'

Maka nodded, signalling for him to continue.

'I've got feelers out about Lennox, but people seem reluctant to share information.' He stifled a yawn, his rough nights of late catching up with him. He shook it off and continued. 'I'm willing to pay for proper information, but it isn't moving people yet.'

'People fear Lennox, L,' said Maka. 'He wiped out Delroy's kids. Add to that the moves he's made against you and Shorty . . . fact is that the longer he's out there, the weaker we look as a unit.'

'How bad is it out there?'

Manson blew out a breath. Lamont noticed the pair were practically taking turns to speak, but shrugged it off.

'Money is low. So is morale. Police are everywhere, and even when they're not, people are running scared that they're gonna get shot. The Feds are making low-level arrests, in and out of our crew. Makes it harder to get runners out there and working.'

'That could be a job for Darren then. He's young enough to appeal to them, and we wanted him helping with recruitment, anyway. We need more runners, and we need more shooters. We're running low on both, so let's make it a priority.'

'What about Shorty and K-Bar?'

Lamont didn't immediately reply. Both men would have been fantastic to have around in the current situation. He hadn't spoken with Shorty since their fight, and he wasn't going near K-Bar while the police had him in custody.

'I don't know what Shorty's doing, nor do I know where he is. K-Bar's release is a job for my solicitor. I'm paying him a lot of money to facilitate it. The fact is, I want Lennox Thompson dead, no matter the cost.'

Maka and Manson nodded, and they sat in silence. Lamont was tempted to tell them about Stefanos's warnings, but held his tongue. It would only make things worse. There was enough pressure on them as it was. Finally, he clambered to his feet, wiping his eyes.

'Use whatever funds you need to hire people and make sure Darren is on board with the plan.' After saying his goodbyes, he left.

Maka and Manson sat in silence for a few more minutes. Without a word, Manson refilled his drink, and poured one for Maka.

'What the hell was that all about?'

'He looked wrecked. All this shit that's going on is taking its toll.'

'What does that mean for the rest of us?' Maka shook his head. 'He's our leader, and he looks like he's cracking up. Do you think he's scared?'

'Course he's scared. None of us have ever had a challenge like this. Aren't you scared?'

Manson didn't reply straight away. 'I'd feel better if we had a proper plan in place. You saw the way L was talking. Feels to me like he doesn't even believe we can win. If Delroy's struggling, can we?'

'We have a better organisation than Delroy's crew. Always have.'

'Back in the day, maybe. Those people are gone. Dunno where the fuck Shorty is, but Tall-Man's dead. So is Chink. Even Akeem. We don't have Victor, or Grimer or Rudy. K-Bar's looking at life in prison. We've lost a lot, Maka.'

'We don't have a choice. We need to make our moves, unless you wanna just roll over and let Lennox win?'

Manson's eyes darkened. 'I don't roll over for anyone. All I'm saying is that L clearly isn't with it. That means we need to be.'

Maka met his friend's eyes. He went back the furthest with Manson, and they'd always had each other's backs. They were closer than brothers. He finished his drink and patted him on the shoulder.

'Tell me what you're thinking.'

FRIDAY 17 APRIL 2015

When the day of Trinidad's funeral arrived, Lamont hoped he was ready. He'd shaved and spent a lot of time examining himself in the mirror, unhappy with the man looking back at him. He looked haggard, with prominent circles under his eyes. It was hard sleeping at night without liquor, yet he didn't want to become dependent. Sitting in the kitchen in his expensive suit, he had some coffee to sharpen up, then finished getting ready.

After his conversation with Maka and Manson, he knew how people perceived Lennox, but the spread of the word still shocked him. People spoke of Lennox with reverence, and it was even harder for Lamont's contacts to get back to him. As far as the streets were concerned, Lennox was winning. When Solomon's death was confirmed, it sent things into overdrive. The fact someone could brutalise him on his doorstep made everyone wary, Lamont included. He'd spent a small fortune securing a bodyguard team. Several would guard his house, and the others would shadow him wherever he went. As he drove to the funeral, he had two with him.

As they arrived at the church, Lamont slipped inside, having timed his arrival so he would almost be late. Before he took his seat in the back row, he glanced at the coffin, and felt a wave of fury. It was a shabby excuse for a coffin; cheap, light brown, and as basic as could be. It didn't stand out, and Trinidad deserved better. He'd offered them the money to pay for a luxury service, and the family had turned it down. Apparently, they would rather snub him than ensure Trinidad got a good send-off.

The people on the row glanced at him, taking in his expensive clothes and demeanour. He didn't recognise them, but they seemed to have some idea who he was. Ignoring them, he stared ahead, singing along tunelessly when called for, and silently listening to people tell stories about Trinidad. He wanted to do the same, but knew it wouldn't be welcomed.

At the cemetery, he again hung near the back. His suit ruffled in the wind, but other than the breeze, the weather was calm. He could see people shooting him looks, but continued to ignore them. The funeral was almost over, and then he could go back home and wallow in peace. He already had the liquor ready.

'Lamont.'

He turned before he even recognised the voice, his bodyguards reacting instantly, positioning themselves around him in case of attack. He told them to stand down, moving forward to address Shorty. The pair stared one another down for a long moment. He wore a black jacket over a shirt and black jeans. Lamont had seen him get dressed up for funerals before, and wondered why he hadn't for this one. He'd also shaved, however, and his hair was neatly shaped up. He seemed more like his old self.

Shorty was his oldest friend, and Lamont regretted the fact they had come to blows. At the time, the grief over Jenny's death had been too much for him to take. He missed Shorty and wanted his friend back in his life. The way Shorty glared, he had a sneaking suspicion that wouldn't happen.

'Have you seen the light yet?' he asked.

'I came to pay my respects, not to get caught up with you.'

Lamont could have pointed out that Shorty had sought him out to speak, but didn't. Shorty never enjoyed being corrected in the past, and he suspected that to do it now would only make things worse.

'How's Grace?' Seeing Shorty was a reminder he hadn't spoken with Amy in a while. He hoped she was coping with everything that had happened, and that Grace's condition was improving. Shorty scowled.

'Keep my daughter's name out of your mouth,' he said. Glancing past Lamont, he looked at the people surrounding Trinidad's grave. 'Another one died around you. When does it stop?'

Lamont's stomach lurched as Shorty's words hit him. The night they fought, he had said in his rage that everyone around Lamont died, and this was a fresh reminder that Shorty's words had some truth to them. Trinidad died over his stupidity, and there wasn't a chance he would get over that.

'Shorty . . .'

'Save it. I'm done here.' Giving them one last glowering look, Shorty stalked away. Lamont watched, the ripples of guilt in his stomach growing. Nearby murmurs grew louder. Evidently, people had watched the exchange between the pair. The funeral was the last place he wanted to be, and he hated the idea of being the subject of gossip and entertainment.

'Let's go,' he said to his bodyguards. They were returning to the car when another voice stopped them.

'L.'

It was Ken, one of the old crowd who would frequent Trinidad's shop. Lamont had known him since he was a child. Ken would look out for him, giving him money to go to the shop. He was a bald-headed man in his sixties who looked good for his age. His dark eyes met Lamont's, concern clear.

'Hey, Uncle Ken.'

'How are you doing? I know this can't be easy.'

'Do you really care? You're part of *OurHood*, and I know what that group has been saying about me.'

'I care about my community, L. I want what's best for our people. Whether I agree with *OurHood* or not, we go way back, and I know how you felt about Trinidad.'

'If community is so important, why the hell was Trinidad buried in that matchstick box? He deserved something special. He was the heart of the community, but you buried him in that shitty coffin. How do you justify that?'

'It was the family's choice, and they don't have much money.'

'That's bullshit,' snapped Lamont. 'Trinidad always provided.'

Ken chuckled despite the tension. 'I knew Trinidad all of my life. He wasn't a saver; more of the *can't-take-it-with-you* variety. He put his kids through university and sent money back home, but after that, they were on their own.'

Lamont shook his head. 'The community should have banded together to give him something special.'

'It's not that simple, L. You know that. Regardless, Trinidad was loved. It's not all about money.'

'It's about respect. Plain and simple.' Lamont dismissed Ken's words with vitriol. The older man surveyed him.

'You look tired, L. Noticeably so. That might be making you irritable.'

'I'm not a child, Unc. I don't need a nap. All I wanted was to make things right. I offered them the money for the service, and they turned me down.'

'If you want to make things right, speak with them.'

Lamont glanced past Ken. He could just about make out several of Trinidad's family standing near the coffin. After a moment, he shook his head, the guilt too much.

'There's nothing I can say to them.'

Ken let this go.

'What happens next, L?'

'What do you mean?' Lamont frowned.

'I mean, what do you want from life?'

'That's a pointless question,' Lamont scoffed. 'It means nothing.'

'It meant something to Trinidad. He respected you. Loved you like a son. He wanted you to be happy, and he wanted you to be free.'

The words hit Lamont for six. He recalled his argument with Trinidad a few months back, where Trinidad had been furious about his lack of role in Chapeltown, and his refusal to get involved with community conflicts. He felt emotional at the thought of the old man that wanted nothing but the best for him, and that emotion made him think of Jenny. She had also wanted the best for him. She too wanted him to be free of the streets and happy, and now she was dead. They both were. He wiped his eyes and lowered his head, not wanting Ken to see him so weak.

'I'll see you around, Ken.'

'Are you free, L? Happy?'

Something in Lamont's chest hitched, and he glanced back at Trinidad's family, making their way out of the cemetery. He hesitated, overcome by guilt and frustration. Their lack of respect for Trinidad galled him the longer he stood there.

'Go on, L. Speak to them. It's the right thing to do.'

Lamont made his way toward them, with Ken following and his bodyguards maintaining a respectable distance. He recognised Gloria, Trinidad's ex-wife and the mother of his two children, Graham, and Marie, both of whom were there, alongside a retinue of older women. Lamont found he couldn't look at the women for too long. Their grief turned his stomach and made him feel worse, if that was possible.

'I'm sorry for your loss,' he said, thankful his words were clearer than he'd expected. 'Trinidad was a great man, and if there is anything I can do, don't hesitate to ask.'

Before they could reply, Trinidad's son Graham stepped closer, disdain visible on his face.

'Not sending your thugs to speak to us again, then?'

Lamont forced himself to meet Graham's eyes. He was an inch taller than Lamont, though his suit hung far looser on his gangly frame than Lamont's tailored masterpiece. He had a look of his father, with hard eyes, pronounced cheekbones, and a solid jawline. They had always got along, but those days were over. The resentment was palpable.

'I just wanted to help. Judging by what you ended up burying your father in, you should have taken the money.'

'We're fine with what we had.' Graham's family nodded their agreement. Lamont felt Ken's eyes burning into him, but he didn't stop.

'Trinidad deserved more.'

Graham took another step forward, disdain replaced by clear anger.

TARGET PART III

Lamont wondered if he was going to hit him, and whether he would stop him. Others inched closer, acting like they weren't listening.

'You wanna talk about what he deserved? He deserved not to die just because he was involved with some gangster who can't fight his own battles. If you truly respected him, Lamont, it wouldn't matter what his family buried him in.'

Lamont ignored the *gangster* jibes, and the muttering that followed from the crowd.

'Whatever I am, I never wanted to bring harm to your father.'

'You did a magnificent job of stopping that,' replied Graham, the sarcasm in his tone venomous. With a last look of disgust, he stormed off, his family following. Ken stood with Lamont as the crowd dispersed, not one person stopping to speak to him.

'That didn't go how I expected,' said Ken, breaking the tense silence.

'It went exactly as I expected. He should have taken the money. I stand by what I said.'

Lamont turned away before Ken could say anything. As he walked to the car, Trinidad, Jenny, Marcus, and all the others that had died around him resonated in his mind, and he knew Shorty was right about his effect.

He was bad for people, and there was no getting away from this.

CHAPTER FIVE

TUESDAY 21 APRIL, 2015

SHORTY RAISED the cup to his lips and took a deep sip. He wasn't a fan of tea at the best of times, but Amy offered, and he couldn't refuse.

Since his fallout with Lamont, it had been a turbulent few weeks. He had left Lamont's on a suicide mission, determined to go out in a blaze of glory by taking Lennox and as many of his goons as he could with him. He spent the next few days getting his money together, ready to leave it to his children. It was when he'd gone to see Amy that the problems had begun.

AMY HUNCHED over her kitchen table, pale and drawn. She looked up and immediately stifled a gasp.

Shorty stood over her, his face tense. He wore a black warm-up tracksuit with trainers. A woolly hat was pulled low, almost obscuring his eyes. On his hands, he wore a pair of black leather gloves.

'Shorty? What the hell are you doing here?'

He didn't reply, staring Amy down.

'Are you listening? You can't be here. What if the pol—'

Shorty left the kitchen and came back in with a black hold-all. He dropped it on the table in front of Amy. She opened it, her expression quizzical. The bag was full of money. Notes of various denominations were stuffed to burst. Even as she opened it, several ten-pound notes fluttered to the floor, resting at her feet.

'What's this for?'

'That's it,' Shorty replied.

'That's what?'

'That's all the money I have left. After everything. All the shit I did. That's all I've got,' he explained. 'I want you to split it with Stacey. L's got her address. He'll—'

'Why are you talking like this?'

'Did you hear what I said?'

'Did you hear what I said?' Amy retorted. He glared.

'You're smart. I breeded you for a reason. I wanted my daughter to be smart too.'

'What does my being smart have to do with anything?'

Shorty slid into the spindly chair opposite Amy and faced her. He took his hood down and peeled the woolly hat from his head, exposing unkempt, picky hair.

'You're smart enough to know why I've given you all my money.'

'Shorty, Grace is still alive. Whatever stupid thing you're planning, please don't do it,' Amy gestured toward the money. 'I know you think this is more important, but it isn't.'

'I've always provided for Grace. I always made sure you had money when you needed it. Don't tell me that isn't important.'

'As important as having you? Do you really think the money mattered to Grace when she cried herself to sleep night after night, wondering where her daddy was? Do you think it mattered when she sat in the room with her headphones on because I didn't want her to hear the police badmouthing you as they searched the house? The money doesn't matter.'

'Don't tell me it doesn't fucking matter!' Shorty slammed his fist on the sturdy table, shaking it. 'You don't get it. The money is all I have. It opens doors for Grace. Means her having all the opportunities I didn't. Do you know the things I've gone through on these streets? To survive?'

'Don't kid yourself that it was all for Grace, because that's not the truth. You love this. The life was more important to you than anything. Even me.'

'Once, maybe, but Grace changed everything. Believe that or not.'

'It doesn't matter now.'

'I know.'

They were both silent now, breathing hard. Amy's eyes widened, a sudden wave of horror cascading throughout her body.

'You're not coming back, are you?'

Shorty was shocked to see tears in her eyes. He wouldn't let it slow him.

'There is no coming back from this. I'm going after anyone who had a hand in the shooting.'

'What will that achieve? They already shot our daughter. You going after them will only make things worse.'

'They nearly took the thing I care most about on the planet. They don't get away with that.'

Amy shook her head. 'You'd murder half of Leeds just to settle a grudge?'

'I would murder all of Leeds if it righted the wrong.'

'What happened to you?' She gasped. Shorty frowned.

'What are you talking about?'

'How can you justify it? How can you make out that what you're doing is right? You kill—'

'So what!' Shorty thundered. 'You think I care? You think I lose any sleep over those fuckers who tried ending my life?' He glared at Amy. 'What would you rather have? Them alive, or me?'

Amy stared back at him, unable to reply. He wiped his eyes.

'This is what I am. I accept it. I'll do what I need to do.'

Amy gawped at him. He wasn't sure what he expected to hear next, but he was still shocked.

'Is it over three?'

'Is what over three?'

'Have you killed over three people?'

'Yes.' Shorty didn't hesitate.

'I don't know what to say,' Amy said, minutes later.

'I never said I was Mother Teresa.'

'And you're sure you can kill these people?'

'I don't have a choice.'

'How can you be so sure you'll find them?' Amy ran a hand through her bedraggled hair.

TARGET PART III

'Because, I already know who gave the order.'

'How?'

Shorty again looked at her. Pale and drawn with worry, he still found her achingly beautiful. In another life, they could have made it work, but in this one, he was just a killer.

'You really wanna know?' He locked eyes with his baby mother.

'Yes.' He saw her lean forward, ready for his words.

'I tracked down the shooter. He told me who hired him.'

'He told you just like that?' Amy's eyebrows rose.

'Course not. I got it out of him.'

'How?'

Shorty glanced at Amy again. She was clutching the table for support, but her eyes were lucid.

'You really wanna know?' He repeated.

'Yes.'

'I held a hot knife to his skin in his kitchen, then kept pouring salt on him until he cracked.' Shorty's words were utterly monotonous.

'And this man, the one who shot Gracey . . . Is he dead?'

After a long moment, Shorty nodded.

The pair sat in the kitchen with a bag of dirty money resting between them. It was the most peaceful moment the grieving parents had ever shared in their turbulent relationship.

'I SPOKE with Grace's doctors. They say she's doing a lot better. It'll take time and a lot of support, but it's not as bleak as it seemed even a few weeks ago.'

Relief washed over Shorty. Every day since his daughter's shooting, he expected to hear that she hadn't made it. She had taken two bullets to the chest, and as a young child, he didn't think she could survive, but she had proved him wrong.

'That's fucking brilliant.' He hung his head a moment, overcome with a wave of emotion. Amy waited for him to look at her before she spoke again.

'Is it enough?'

'What do you mean?'

'Grace is alive. With time, she will get better. Can you leave this vendetta of yours alone and not retaliate?'

'It's not that simple,' said Shorty, his eyes hardening. They had been over this.

'Have you forgotten our conversation last time, Shorty? I want Grace to have a dad. That is more important than what you feel you need to do.'

Shorty shook his head. 'You can't say that. This is something I *have* to do.'

'No, it isn't,' Amy's voice rose. 'You love Grace, Shorty. I had my doubts when I got pregnant, but you've proved me wrong every time, and she loves you because she knows how much you love her, and that you would do anything for her. You don't need to prove it to her, or to me. Why can't you just walk away?'

'Because this is my life. This is the man you met. I'm a gangster, Ames. Always have been, always will be. The fact of the matter is that you can't shoot at someone I love and get away with it. Walking away isn't an option. We're talking about dangerous people here. They killed L's missus, for fuck's sake.'

Amy paled. 'What?'

Shorty took a deep breath, regretting blurting it out like that.

'Jenny was killed on the orders of these people. As revenge against L.'

'How . . . Who the hell are you involved with?'

Shorty hesitated. Amy already knew far more about his world than he was comfortable with, but he trusted her. They had a child together, and she had never shown any sign of betraying him.

'Someone had a problem with me. We had a fight. I kicked his ass, and he tried to get back at me by shooting me, but missed and hit Grace.'

Amy didn't reply. Her eyes were wide, and her face even paler than before.

'And this is the man you told me about?'

Shorty nodded. 'It's his boss that's the problem. He's the one going after everyone, and it's kill or be killed with this guy.' He saw how terrified Amy looked, and his face softened. 'I'm sorry, Ames. I'd have never asked to spend time with Grace if I'd known they would come back like that. I'd never let any harm come to her.'

'I know that,' replied Amy, her voice softer. 'I know you love her. It was rocky after you got out of prison, but I was hoping your relationship with her would improve and be like it used to.'

'You and me both.'

Both parents sat in silence for a while. Shorty finished the rest of his tea, holding onto the cup just to have something to do.

'L must be devastated about Jenny's death.'

Shorty didn't respond.

'He came to see me at the hospital a while back. He was asking about you.'

'Right.' Shorty couldn't even muster any enthusiasm. He'd said his piece to Lamont at Trinidad's funeral, and as far as he was concerned, there was no further business between them.

'What's going on with you two?'

'Nothing.'

'Why would he ask me how you were then? That doesn't make sense.'

'Ask him.'

'Shorty.'

He looked up, meeting Amy's misty green eyes.

'What?'

'Talk to me, please. What's going on with you two?'

'We're no longer friends.' He gave it to her straight, hoping it would shut her up.

'You two are like brothers. How could you have fallen out?'

'It's not important.'

It was Amy's turn to shake her head. She looked at him with folded arms and raised eyebrows.

'Our daughter was shot, and L's girlfriend was murdered, and you don't think it's important that you've fallen out with your best friend?'

'Just leave it alone. I don't want to discuss it.'

'But—'

'What the fuck did I say!' Shorty snapped, making Amy jump. Shooting to his feet, he stormed from the house, slamming the door behind him. Amy remained seated, shaking with fear. Sometimes it was easy to forget how dangerous Shorty was, and how much his temper remained at the surface. Realising after a few moments he wasn't coming back, she went to lock the door.

Several days after Trinidad's funeral, Lamont was called by Stefanos, who told him to be at a warehouse on Elder Road at ten o'clock the following day. He gave him the address, wished him well, then hung up.

The next morning, Lamont and two of his new bodyguards drove to the spot. From the outside, it was unimpressive. A rusting metal blue fence surrounded it, and the entire building had a bleak, greying colour scheme. A man stood outside, smoking a cigarette. He was stocky, with thinning black hair and a pointed nose. When he saw Lamont, he nodded, taking one last drag of the cigarette and flicking it away.

'You must be Mr Jones.'

'Call me L.'

'Very well, L. call me Mustafa. We were told to expect you. I trust you found us without issue?'

'The instructions were excellent.'

'Fantastic. Ahmed is waiting inside for us. Your men can wait out here, or they can come with you.'

'Wait here,' Lamont said to his men. He followed Mustafa into the warehouse. Inside were several nondescript white vans, with men milled around each. They all wore grey overalls and looked up when they saw Lamont, sizing him up. He met the eyes of each man, then trailed Mustafa into an office at the far side of the room. The interior was cramped yet organised, and reminded him of his old office at Trinidad's. A man sat there, talking on the phone, his expression set in a frown. He had straight black hair, a flabby face, and dark eyes. He glanced up when they entered, his eyes lingering on Lamont. Curtly telling the person on the other end to call back, he hung up.

'Teflon, I presume?'

TARGET PART III

Lamont immediately noticed that Ahmed didn't get up to greet him, and took it as a slight. Whatever camaraderie Mustafa had shown would not be replicated by this man.

'I guess you must be Ahmed.'

'Our friends have explained the situation and decreed that you are to run the operation. It is our job to assist you and help with the transition.'

It was clear Ahmed wasn't pleased with the arrangement. His demeanour was unfriendly, and he viewed him with suspicion. Lamont skipped past all the posturing.

'I take it you worked for Akhan?'

Ahmed's jaw tightened. 'He was a great man. A great man and an even better boss.'

There it was. This was the reason Ahmed had a problem. He had obviously learned through the grapevine that Lamont was responsible for the death of his beloved boss, and he could not do anything about it. It was a bitter pill to swallow, but it also wasn't Lamont's problem.

'I trust you understand why he is no longer your boss?' He wasn't in the mood for playing around. Ahmed's brow furrowed.

'I'm going for a smoke. You can explain to him how things work,' he said to Mustafa, who rubbed the back of his neck.

'Sorry about that,' he said when Ahmed left.

'Don't worry about it,' said Lamont. 'It'll take a while for us to get to know one another.'

'Still, Ahmed showed poor judgement. Whether we agree with a situation, proper respect should always be shown.'

'Sounds like you've known him a long time.'

'Ten years and counting. We both began working for Akhan and Saj at the same time.'

Lamont hadn't thought about Saj in a while. Saj had loyally served Akhan, including his attempts to serve up Lamont's crew to his master after the robbery of their drugs hub. He had been executed, along with every loyalist Akhan had working for him. Based on Ahmed's attitude, they had missed one. Lamont had liked Saj, but he allied himself with Akhan, and was determined to bring down their crew. He needed to understand if Mustafa shared the same views as Ahmed.

'What happened to Akhan . . . how does that sit with you?'

'I don't want to get involved in anything.' Mustafa looked away.

'We're just talking. If we're going to work together, it's important we understand one another.'

Mustafa sighed. It was clear he didn't want to have the conversation, but to his credit, he didn't back away.

'Akhan was a good boss. He rewarded loyalty, and he always made it clear what he wanted. At the same time, he didn't play by the rules, and he knew what that could lead to.'

Lamont digested what Mustafa said. It seemed he was on the fence about trusting him, but he suspected he would have no problem accepting orders. Ahmed was another story, but he would deal with him when the time came.

'Tell me about the play.'

'I'm sure you know most of it. We supply multiple crews. Product isn't a concern, nor is the amount. We have people throughout Yorkshire and the surrounding areas, and we tend to over-order, ensuring there is a healthy surplus of product in case any of our people need it.'

'Do we work with minimum orders?'

'Nothing under five boxes a month. We cater toward the larger spectrum, your crew included.'

Despite everything, Lamont still enjoyed the fact his crew was one of the biggest. Mustafa carried on talking, and it was easy for him to follow along. He remembered his initial meeting with Akhan, and how open everything seemed. By working with Jakkar and his ilk, he hoped he had made the right decision, but was determined to see it through.

'What about the *accessories*?' he asked. Mustafa gave him a blank look.

'Accessories?'

'Security. What if things go wrong?'

'We have specialist teams available to handle any issues. They are at your command, but if you abuse their use, someone above may have something to say.'

Lamont smiled. This was a good thing. He knew the killers that Akhan had controlled, and if it hadn't been for Jakkar and Stefanos, he might have lost his life to them.

TARGET PART III

'Akhan had a knack for finding information. I presume there is a network I can tap into?'

Mustafa shook his head. 'The network is off limits to all but Jakkar.' He said it in a casual tone, but Lamont knew better. This was something that had recently been added. He was sure of it.

'Is that a new ruling?'

Mustafa looked away before he replied, 'I know nothing about it.'

Lamont let it slide. It wasn't a situation he could do anything about for now, so he would focus on making money and using his own considerable resources to track down Lennox Thompson.

———

LAMONT LEFT the meeting with more questions than answers. He wasn't concerned with Ahmed's petty vendetta, but the fact Jakkar seemed determined to curtail his access was jarring. Lamont had long admired the information network Akhan had at his disposal and had wanted to use the same network to finish Lennox and his organisation. Instead, he would need to rely on his own, and it hadn't been well-manned since Chink's death two years ago. This meant many of the information sources they had set up were obsolete.

Lamont was out of touch with the lower levels of the street. He could get hold of the big fish with a single phone call, but he didn't know who was running which crews on a local level, and that kind of information left him vulnerable. He didn't know if anyone had allied with Lennox, or how the crews felt about him, and he needed to. Lamont was at war, and information was vital. He would need to know everything in order to destroy Lennox.

Wiping his eyes, he stifled a yawn and shuffled to his feet to make more coffee. He was taking his first sip when his phone rang.

'Yes?'

'L, it's me.' It was Delroy.

'Nice to hear from you. How are things?'

'I think you know. I need to speak to you. It's important. Can you come to my house?'

Lamont's street instincts kicked in, but he forced them away. He trusted Delroy and didn't think he would have him killed in his own home.

'Can't give you a time, but I'll ring before I come.'

'Speak to you then.' Delroy hung up.

Lamont stood at the counter, staring at the dark liquid in the cup. They'd formed a loose alliance when they had worked together to take out Akhan, but it had stretched little further than this. Scalding his lips with a sip of coffee, he let his brain concoct theories and scenarios while he stared into space.

CHAPTER SIX

WEDNESDAY 22 APRIL, 2015

'DO you know what the meeting is about?'

Rigby busied himself, making sure his shirt was tucked in before he answered Murphy. Meeting with the bosses was never good, and he ignored them as often as he could get away with.

'No idea, mate. Let's get in there before she moans about us being late.'

Quickening their steps, they hurried into the meeting room on the station's second floor. It was a classroom-sized space, with several hard-backed chairs and a whiteboard in the room's corner. Detective Chief Inspector Lisa Reid was already there, sipping a cup of coffee, a selection of files in front of her.

'Rig, Murphy. Thanks for coming.' She signalled to the seats in front of her. They sat down.

'I don't mind waiting if you both want to get a drink.'

'We're okay,' said Rigby. Murphy nodded in agreement.

DCI Reid had been transferred to their building six months ago. She was middle-aged, with light brown hair, glasses and a steely determination that had won her the respect of most of the station. Rigby was reserving judgement. He'd dealt with far too many manager types to be on board with her immediately.

'Good. We can get started then. You'll notice a distinct lack of supervisors. There have been some recent reshuffles, and suffice it to say, I will be running the criminal teams for the foreseeable future. Now, Keiron Barrett . . . Also known as *K-Bar*. I understand he requested to speak to us recently after being on remand for some time.'

It was clear that Murphy would not talk unless specifically addressed, so Rigby spoke.

'Seemed like he was just messing around, Ma'am.'

Reid's eyebrow rose. 'Messing around?'

'We have K-Bar on a laundry list of charges. He arranged the meeting to see what he could get from us.'

'From what I've read, our paperwork is a little shaky. We have a witness who claims she knew about the setup of some gangland hits, but we have no weapons or tangible evidence. I'm surprised this made it through CPS.'

'K-Bar is a shooter for Teflon. He's the second major arrest we've made, the first being Franklin Turner, also known as *Shorty*.'

'It's my understanding that Turner was released. Something to do with a lack of evidence?'

Rigby felt his temper rising, but kept his voice steady.

'These people have been operating a long time, and they're savvy when it comes to the law, hence the pressure.'

'What do Teflon, or K-Bar, or Turner, have to do with the shootings ravaging Chapeltown? We are putting more resource into the area, which is doing nothing to improve relations with the locals. We're the enemy, and we need to change that perception.'

'Maybe we should sack the officers that smacked around the kid then,' Murphy snarkily said. Reid shot him a look, then surprised them by smiling.

'I know that I'm fairly new to the case, but I've dealt with similar cases in other areas, and we need the locals to believe we're the good guys. That means stopping this gang war and involving ourselves with the local organisations and people. If Teflon isn't involved, we can't prioritise K-Bar. We'll take our chances with him in court, but I want you guys all over the conflict. Find out who the major players are and then plug it.'

TARGET PART III

'Look, Ma'am, I understand the pressures involved, but Teflon is a problem, and if we don't strike now, he will continue to grow more powerful. He is connected to everything going on. K-Bar is highly placed, and he is our best bet at winning.'

'Teflon isn't involved in the gang war, Detective.'

'His girlfriend was stabbed a few weeks back. That was not an accident.'

'When you questioned him afterwards, what did he have to say?'

'He refused to answer. He was involved in a shooting in Chapeltown recently, however.'

'He was the shooter?' Reid's stare was unblinking.

'No. His bodyguard was shot, and there was a fire in a building he was linked to. He's involved, Ma'am. I know it.'

'Maybe so. And during your investigation, if you can piece him in, then go for it. For now, this is your priority.' Reid rose to her feet and headed for the door. 'Keep me updated.'

'How are we solving this gang war then?'

Rigby wanted to sulk after his meeting with Reid. He was tired of dealing with bureaucrats who only cared about stats and not quality policing. Rigby saw Teflon and his organisation as the biggest threat in Leeds. Delroy's crew was a bigger outfit, but there was something about the running of Teflon's crew that worried him. He didn't want to see a man with so much power; they needed to do something about it. K-Bar was the best chance to do that, but he couldn't get Reid to see it. She either didn't know how, or didn't care.

Rigby and Murphy had spoken to Peterson, who had been assigned to make inroads into the gang war. To say he'd had nothing would be a gross understatement. He didn't know the major players, what they were warring over, or any major victims. It was no surprise Reid was getting antsy.

'We'll see what Worthy has to say, then shop around our other squirrels. It involves Teflon. I can feel it.'

'Are you sure you don't just want him to be involved so you can stick it to Reid?'

'She doesn't have a clue, and she won't last long in the job if she doesn't pull her finger out.'

'Fuck her, mate. We crack this war, we jog onto the next case. Don't worry about Teflon.'

Rigby didn't bother replying. No matter what Murphy or Reid thought, he felt in his bones that Teflon was connected to the conflict.

SHORTY TOOK a deep breath and squared his shoulders. Knocking on the door, he waited for Amy to answer. She gave him a small smile when she opened the door. He regretted storming off the way he had. Amy had just been trying to talk to him, and he had overreacted and flown off the handle. Hopefully, it wasn't too late.

'Hey, Shorty.'

'Ames. Can I come in?'

They headed for the kitchen. She pottered with the kettle as Shorty slid into a chair at the kitchen table.

'Can I get you something to drink?'

Shorty shook his head.

'Is everything okay?' She continued.

'I wanted to say sorry for the other day. You were just trying to help, and I was being a dickhead.'

Amy smiled again, shaking her head.

'I've known you a long time, Shorty. I know what to expect from you.'

Shorty didn't want that. He didn't want Amy to associate him with losing his temper when he didn't get his own way. Not anymore.

'That's not me,' he said after a moment. Amy raised an eyebrow, and he hurried on. 'I don't want to be flying off the handle for no reason. Especially not with you.' When he looked up, it was Amy's turn to look at the floor, unable to meet his eyes. The reaction puzzled him, but he put it out of his mind and continued. 'You deserve to know what's going on. I want you to know.'

Amy sat down and waited for him to continue.

TARGET PART III

'Me and L fell out. Big time.'

Amy didn't even react. 'You've had arguments before. What's different?'

'We got into a fistfight, and we both said some things. We're not cool anymore.'

Amy's hand went to her mouth, her eyes widening.

'Are you serious?'

He nodded.

'What caused that?'

Shorty told her about the fight after Jenny's murder, and the things they hurled at each other. Amy paled, but didn't speak until he had finished.

'I can't believe it. He'll need you, though, Shorty. Now more than ever. You know that.'

'He made out like it was my fault his missus got killed. Even mentioned Gracey's name and said it was my fault.'

'You told him everyone around him died, Shorty. Is that any better?'

'Wait, so you're taking his side?' Shorty snapped. Amy held up her hand.

'Slow down, before you get annoyed and have to apologise again. Him using Grace against you like that is deplorable, and he definitely knows better. All I'm saying is that he was hurting over Jenny. You told me yourself it was serious. How many women have you known L get that deep with?'

Shorty folded his arms, his nostrils flaring.

'Exactly. There's all this stuff going on at the moment, and you two need one another. I'm not saying it'll be overnight, but you need to fix this.'

'It's not that simple.'

'Shorty . . .' Amy trailed off. He noticed.

'What?'

'It doesn't matter. It was silly.' Her face reddened, which intrigued him further.

'No, say it.'

'Were you sleeping with Jenny?'

'Are you serious? Where the hell did that come from?'

'I'm just asking. I won't be mad either way. Can't be, really. We're not involved like that. I'm asking because you two fought, which suggests it was really serious. What was going on you with you and Jenny?'

Shorty frowned, gathering his words.

'Remember a few years back, when I got mad about you and L spending time together?'

Amy nodded, understanding.

'After I got out, I stayed with them for a bit. I could see Jenny breaking down, and I saw something was wrong between them. I just couldn't put my finger on it. I considered her a friend; she was someone I could speak to. About Grace. Even about Dionte.'

'L found out?'

'We weren't hiding it. It wasn't like that. We just all had our shit, and I wasn't clicking with L.' Shorty remembered those first few days of being out of prison. Going to see Lamont. Getting a stack of cash he'd saved for his return. Watching him return to his office with a bottle instead of going upstairs with Jenny. His vague explanation about why he was still in the game. All of it contributed to the disruption of their friendship.

'Because you got locked up?'

Shorty rubbed his eyes. Talking about this was giving him a headache, but if there was anyone he wanted to confide in, it was Amy.

'L tried walking away before he got shot, and I thought he was doing it for Jenny. Then, Marcus died. People tried to kill us. We just never really found our way back.'

'Maybe now is the perfect time to do that. You're both hurting. You need each other.'

'I don't need him.' Shorty's breathing intensified. He didn't know why he was so angry. There was something deep between him and Lamont, but he couldn't put his finger on it. Women had added to the issue, but it was more than that. 'He got shot while I was on the run, and I dunno . . .'

Amy saw where he was going. '. . . You feel guilty that you weren't there?'

Shorty shrugged, but they both knew that was the case.

'Shorty . . . Grace is alive. She will get better. Surely that, more than anything, is a sign you and your best friend should bury the hatchet?'

Taking a deep breath, Shorty changed the subject. Amy smiled, knowing him well enough to know he was done sharing. She had given him food for thought, just as she intended.

AS ALWAYS, Lamont was impressed when Delroy's mansion loomed in front of him. It was a sign of his kingpin status. It had a long drive that led up to the property, with well-tended gardens and multiple luxury vehicles parked outside.

'Wait here,' Lamont said to his security, climbing from the car. One of Delroy's people approached, nodding when he recognised Lamont, leading him to a room where Delroy waited, slumped behind his desk.

'Drink?' he motioned to several bottles of liquor on the desk in front of him.

'Brandy, please,' replied Lamont. He wasn't driving and had no reason to hold back. Delroy shuffled to his feet to fetch glasses, moving even slower than he had the last time Lamont saw him. He seemed thinner and more drawn, and Lamont felt a pang of hurt that he was showing his age. Despite his stature, he wore his usual shirt and trousers combo, the shirt loose around the stomach. Delroy's eyes were full of a tired vitality that only the old could pull off.

'How are you?' Delroy asked when Lamont was seated opposite him, holding his drink.

'I'm fine.'

'You don't look fine. I'm not the only one who can see that either.'

'You pay more attention to what others think than me.'

'Depends on the person.' Delroy's features softened. 'I knew Trinidad for a long time. He was a good man. Loved you, spoke highly of you . . . when you invested in the shop, you changed his life. He might have gone out of business like a few other local businesses did around that time.'

'How come you never backed him?'

'Maybe I would have, if he'd come to me.'

Lamont accepted this, mulling over his words. They seemed familiar.

'Ken said something similar about Trinidad. Said he cared about me a lot.'

'Course he did. Ken's been around a long time too. Sees everything, even if he doesn't speak on it.'

'Did you invite me to speak about Ken and Trinidad?'

Delroy took a sip of his drink. 'Partly.'

'Why?'

'Trinidad's death wasn't your fault. It was Lennox's fault.'

'Did Ken tell you to say that?' Lamont tried for a smirk, but couldn't pull it off. He hated the idea that people were telling tales, and he definitely hated the idea they thought he was weak.

'He's worried about you.'

'Respectfully, he doesn't need to worry about me. Neither of you do. Lennox went for Trinidad because of me, and I should have protected him.'

'How?'

'I should have told him Lennox was a threat and made him hide.'

'Wouldn't have worked. Trinidad lived for his business and his family. He wouldn't back down from what he saw as a threat. Too much pride.'

Lamont didn't reply, so Delroy continued.

'Power, L. Power ain't easy. You're at a level few people get to in our game, and you need to let things go if you want to survive. Blaming yourself for everything in the world will only make it harder in the long run.'

Lamont couldn't believe what he was hearing from Delroy. It was a far cry from the previous conversations the pair had shared. The earliest tenure of their relationship was Delroy subtly bullying Lamont into working for him. When that didn't work, he was forced to accept

TARGET PART III

his supply in order to get a line on a dangerous criminal moving against him. The thought made him smile for a moment. Sixteen years later, he was still getting caught up in ridiculous drama.

'You've never let a grudge go in your life,' he finally said.

'I let it go when we had our problems a few years back. Things could have easily gone another way. You remember what I told you? When we met in the restaurant after Mack's beating?'

Lamont did, but rather than respond, he took a sip of the expensive brandy.

'I said war isn't a picnic. I stick to that. No matter how high we rise, we're not invincible. Someone else always comes along.'

'Is Lennox that someone?'

Delroy downed his drink and topped it up. He offered the bottle to Lamont, but he shook his head.

'I don't know what's gonna happen with him, if I'm honest. He's crafty, and he doesn't poke his head out often. My people are out there, and we've had a few wins, but nothing major. He took out Solomon, and that shook up a few of the people I had working for me. Solomon was good. Not in the league of Reagan, or Shorty, or Marcus, but he was well on his way.'

This was the conversation Lamont had been waiting for.

'Let me in, Del. Point my people in Lennox's direction, and we can work together.'

'No.'

Lamont's eyes widened. Of all the things he'd expected Delroy to say, a blunt refusal wasn't even on the list.

'I can help you. We can pool our teams and get him together, like we did with Akhan.'

Delroy shook his head.

'You're worth more than succumbing to revenge, L. Leave Lennox to me and my people.'

'What the hell are you talking about? You're acting like I'm some helpless little shit. You talk about revenge, but why are *you* warring with him? Is it not because he murdered Winnie and Eddie?'

'This is my life, L, don't you get that?' Delroy suddenly roared, catching Lamont off balance. 'This is it for me. My wife refuses to live with me. My daughter hates me. All I have is my money and my reputation. Lennox is the only thing keeping me here. When I've killed him, I'm heading out to Grenada. Already got my tickets booked.'

'Why Grenada?' Lamont didn't know everything about Delroy's history, but knew he'd fled his homeland when he was younger because of a legal situation that many speculated was murder. As long as he had known him, he'd never heard Delroy even mention the place he grew up.

'I can be free out there.' Delroy smiled. 'Never take freedom for granted, L.'

Lamont's eyes narrowed. He suspected there was a lot he was missing in the exchange, and he hated feeling outmanoeuvred when dealing with anyone. He was still irritated that Delroy was refusing his help with Lennox.

'What changed?' he finally asked. Delroy frowned, signalling for him to continue.

'A couple of months back, you were willing to pay me one million pounds to lead your crew for you while you warred with Lennox. What changed?'

'The entire situation changed. More than that, *you* changed.'

'I haven't changed.'

'You have, and if you don't see it, that's even worse. You're tired, L. I don't want you crumbling under the pressure of people's expectations. Put that shit behind you.'

'You can't say that, not after everything that has gone down. The fact is, I have as much reason to go after Lennox as you do. He took people from me too.'

'This is bigger than that, and it only needs one of us.'

'I have my own resources. Whether you work with me, I'll go after him, regardless.'

'Drink your drink,' replied Delroy. It was the last thing Lamont expected him to say, but he complied, downing the drink and placing the empty glass on the table. It would help him sleep tonight.

'Del—'

'Let me just quietly enjoy your company, L,' said Delroy, his tone softer than it had been all night. 'No more talk about Lennox or revenge.'

Lamont blew out a breath. None of this conversation had gone how he expected, and he wondered, not for the first time, if he was truly losing his edge.

'So . . . Grenada then?'

Delroy nodded. Something he'd said earlier finally resonated with Lamont.

'Wait a second? *Tickets* . . . plural?'

'Two tickets. One for me and one for Elaine,' replied Delroy, as if it was obvious.

Lamont was surprised, remembering Delroy's earlier words about his wife.

'I thought you weren't on the best of terms?' He said slowly, trying to be delicate. Delroy's eyes softened for just a second.

'Guess I'm living in hope that she'll come back to me.'

Another silence descended. Lamont broke it after a minute.

'They offered me Akhan's role,' he said. 'The people backing him. After Akhan was killed, they asked me to step up.'

'I take it you did?'

Lamont nodded.

'It's an impressive role. Do you trust the people you're working with? You rushed to work with Akhan to spite me, and look how that turned out for you.'

'Akhan is gone. It's irrelevant.'

'You're right. He is.' Delroy gave Lamont a knowing look. He didn't react, pressing on with his point.

'I trust they want to do business. Seems dangerous to go beyond that.'

Delroy grinned, showing worn teeth. 'Maybe you *are* learning something, after all, L.'

'I have access to as much product as I need. All the best quality. If you switch your supply, I'll cut you one hell of a deal.'

Delroy's smile didn't fade. 'Maybe in the future. Not right now, though. I want things to remain as they are.'

Lamont didn't argue. They would revisit it at a later time. He allowed Delroy to top up his glass now, stifling a yawn. The old man had given him a lot to think about, but he couldn't give weight to most of what he said. He had messed up, and his mistakes had led to multiple deaths. No matter what Delroy said, he'd got himself into this mess, and no matter the cost, he would get himself out of it.

CHAPTER SEVEN
FRIDAY 24 APRIL, 2015

'WHAT DO you have for me then?'

Lamont had spent his morning working out. He'd taken to it after recovering from his shooting, and kept up with it. Sharma sipped a Lucozade, his appearance much improved since Lamont last saw him. He'd worked for Marcus, and other than doing the odd job for Lamont, they had never hung out. Sharma had been loyal to Marcus, and competent. He'd done a lot of work with Victor, another henchman of Marcus's who was currently serving a sentence for murder.

Lamont still felt bad that he had forgotten about him in the aftermath of Marcus's death, but consoled himself with the fact he'd been shot, and his recovery had taken almost a year. Sharma had gone under the radar until he'd gone looking for him, but he had kept him employed ever since.

'Thompson's people have completely removed themselves from the day-to-day, even the little fish. People think they're on the back foot. Delroy's people have come back strong lately.'

Lamont thought back to his conversation with Delroy, and the resolve he'd seen in the man's eyes. He had nothing to lose. Lennox had pushed him to the limit. His back was to the wall, and he was coming out swinging.

'There's a reason he's been on top for so long. Len's mainly into what, though? Protection? Loans? Guns? You can't hold down that racket without a street presence.'

'Why does that matter?' Sharma looked nonplussed.

'Lennox has fought a continuous battle for months. He has shooters. Safehouses . . . it's a lot. Unless he has a sugar daddy sponsoring him, I don't see where it's all coming from.'

'Len's been around longer than you, L. He was never one for spunking money in the club or buying new cars.'

Lamont stifled a yawn. The late nights were catching up with him.

'One thing I've learned about this lifestyle is that it's possible to make a lot of money, but the lifestyle costs.'

'Even when he was banged up, he had people running his rackets. Fact is, I remember Thompson when he was knocking around with Marcus, and he always had money.'

Lamont didn't reply, but Sharma was missing the point. Lennox had seemingly limitless funds in this battle, and unless he'd saved every penny he'd earned, it didn't seem workable. Drugs were still the principal source of income for criminals in the hood, and he had been staunchly against them from the beginning. There was something Lamont wasn't seeing, and he was determined to do so.

He thought about *OurHood*, and Lennox's influence in that organisation. He'd used Malcolm Powell as his mouthpiece and had apparently funnelled money through the company. It was possible he was laundering money for other criminals and taking a cut, but even that was a reach. *OurHood* was a grassroots organisation, and there was only so much money they could hide before the authorities cottoned on.

'What do you want me to do now, boss?'

'Keep looking for his people. I want to know more about his money. Find me clients that he lent to. Punters that have dealt with him. Keep the info coming.'

Sharma nodded and left. Lamont closed his eyes and sat back. Having a nap now would only mess him up later, but he couldn't stop the sleep from creeping over him.

TARGET PART III

'Thanks for meeting me.'

Shorty nodded at Maka.

'Course I was gonna meet you. You said it was important.'

'It is. C'mon, let's get some drinks.'

The pair were in a club in the city centre. It was a large, flashy place, with small black booths dotted all around, and a VIP section overlooking the dance floor. Maka had called him and invited him out. Shorty's social life hadn't exactly been rocking lately, and he agreed to come. The club was on Albion Street and mainly catered to a younger crowd. It was just after nine pm, and most of them didn't come out before midnight. Shorty remembered the days of being young, drinking and taking drugs all night. It exhausted him just thinking about it.

After ordering their drinks, they found a booth to sit in.

'What did you want to talk about then?'

'You,' replied Maka. Shorty's brow furrowed.

'What about me?'

'What's your plan now? What are you doing?'

'I need to get at Lennox, but he's not an easy guy to track down. Other than that, I'm focusing on Grace.'

Maka's eyes softened. 'How is she doing?'

'She's not on death's door anymore. The doctors say she's getting better, but I don't even know what they're talking about half the time.'

'I'm glad she's doing well, Shorty. What happened to her shouldn't have happened.'

'I know, fam. She's gonna get better, though. Let's talk business.'

Maka blew out a breath. 'Where did it all go wrong with our crew?'

Shorty couldn't put his finger on it. The crew had run without issue for years. Even when conflict erupted, they had all the pieces in place to beat down any challenges. Somewhere down the line, that all changed, and everything became a lot more political. A gulf sprang between Lamont and Shorty, and people in the crew began going in their own directions.

'Guess we just all stopped communicating. We started beefing with

Delroy and his people, and L wanted out. Marcus died. Chink snaked us, and we've been trying to catch up ever since.'

Maka drained his drink. Shorty hadn't touched his yet.

'Brings me onto my next point. What's going on with you and L?'

Shorty shrugged.

'Nothing.'

'Don't give me that, Shorty. I'm right here with y'all. We're all trying to keep our heads above water, but I need to understand the situation. People are saying some wild shit. They're saying you were nearly fighting at Trinidad's funeral.'

Shorty scowled. 'We had words and kept it moving. People need to keep out of my business, or I'll make them.'

'Fine. I'm not gonna push you if you don't wanna talk to me about it. We need you to be down with the crew.'

'What does L think about that?'

Maka scratched his head.

'L's not around to ask. We're running the show at the moment. You know how he is right now.'

Shorty knew little bits. He'd noticed how destroyed Lamont looked at the funeral, but didn't know what was going on in his world. He still didn't understand why Lamont was still in the game. Maka had presented an intriguing offer. He had helped Lamont build the crew. They had accepted Lamont as the leader, but if he wasn't stepping up, maybe Shorty needed to.

'L's gunning for Lennox. We need you back. Manson feels the same. Things haven't been clicking right for a while.'

'I thought everything was good?' Shorty recalled the stack of money Lamont had given him when he touched down after prison.

'K-Bar did his best, but he wasn't a leader. He's a street goon, not the guy who should make business decisions. He put off a lot of people with his way of doing things, and the money dropped.'

Shorty understood. He'd known K-Bar longer than any of them, and he had his strengths. Leadership wasn't one. It was one reason he had always deferred to Shorty and Lamont.

'L retook the reins, as you know. Things got better. He had people collecting debts. He sent K-Bar to do that job on Big-Kev to send a

TARGET PART III

message. Then all that stuff happened with Lennox, and then Akeem. Now, he's missing again, and we look weak. Spots are getting raided. A few smaller crews are getting brave and casing our spots. One of our runners got jumped the other night. We need to get back on track, and we need you for that, fam.'

Shorty shook his head.

'I feel you, but with the way things are with me and L, stepping back into the crew wouldn't be right.'

'I don't know what the things are with you and L. What I do know is that we need you, and you need us too. You can't take on all of Leeds by yourself. You've got skills, but you're not that good. I was there when we got ambushed, remember? I took a bullet.'

Before Shorty could reply, a third man approached the pair, beaming widely. He wore a salmon shirt with a navy waistcoat and matching trousers. His ostentatious jewellery caught the light, and Shorty glanced at the chunky Rolex around his wrist. Back in the day, he'd had a similar one. He didn't know what had happened to it, which made him realise how pointless buying one had been.

'Nice to see you both tonight. I thought you were coming tomorrow?' he said warmly. Maka shook his hand, and Shorty followed suit. Naveed was one of Chink's old disciples. With Chink making a foray into the Leeds club scene years back, he'd cultivated people to do his running around. Naveed had been a significant find. He understood money, was charismatic and knew absolutely everyone, making him perfectly placed to step up after Chink's murder. Shorty hadn't seen him in years, but he still looked exactly the same. He had a similar coiffed look to Chink, and it annoyed him. It wasn't the time for old grudges, though.

'It was a last-minute thing.' Maka glanced around. 'Mind if we use your office to finish our chat?'

Naveed shook his head. 'Of course not. Come on, let's go.'

The trio headed to the office. It was on the second floor next to the VIP section and overlooked the club. It had a comfy-looking leather sofa, along with a small dark brown desk and a few spindly chairs. Naveed began smoothing the papers on the desk, apologising profusely as he did so. Finally, he took a seat facing them and invited them to sit. Maka did, but Shorty remained standing.

'Give him that thing,' said Maka. Naveed nodded, unlocking his desk drawer and handing him a thick envelope. He opened it, thumbing through the bands of money inside.

'What's this for?'

'That's your cut.'

'There's about twenty grand here.'

'So?'

'Why is L still paying me?'

'If he wanted your cut to be stopped, he'd have said something. Like I said, his head ain't with it at the moment. He's like the invisible man lately.'

Shorty gave Maka a searching look. 'You think you can bribe me to work?'

'The money is yours. It's your cut. I've told you why the crew needs you, but I've known you a long time. If you don't wanna do it, you won't.'

Shorty wanted to say no again, but Maka had made good points. If he was ever to get a shot at Lennox, he would need the crew's resources. The money was excellent too, and if he could get the crew clicking again, he would make even more. His kids would get all the money they needed, and he could stay busy. Lamont was the only reason to say no; if he wasn't around, he wouldn't need to see him.

'Fine. I'll do it.'

Maka grinned, showing all his teeth.

'We're gonna kill this shit, just like we used to.'

Shorty ignored him, glancing at Naveed. He was still watching the pair with a wide smile that Shorty found weird.

'Give us a minute,' he said. 'Need to talk with Maka about some sensitive shit.'

Naveed's smile dimmed.

'This is my office,' he reminded him. Shorty shot him a hard look, and he jumped to his feet.

'I need to go check things are running properly, anyway. Take your time,' he sputtered.

'Bring more drinks on your way back,' said Maka. Shorty had left his untouched drink at their table, but Maka didn't seem to care. 'What's up?'

'K-Bar got a message to me from inside.'

'How? He got a phone in his cell?'

'He got word through his solicitor. About the witness.'

Maka straightened in his seat on the sofa, ready to listen.

'Who is it?'

'Some little party girl called Adele. She was best friends with that Naomi bitch that got dropped. The one Chink was banging.'

'I know which one you mean. Think her surname's *Chapman*. She was joined at the hip with Naomi when she was grinding Reagan. Are we taking her out?'

'I'm not sure,' admitted Shorty. It had been on his mind since the solicitor had contacted him. He wanted K-Bar out of prison, but he wasn't sure killing a potential witness was the right step.

'We drop her, K-Bar's out. Seems pretty simple.' Maka tapped his fingers on Naveed's desk.

'More murders will only make things harder. We need to get Lennox, and that's the only time we need to drop bodies. With the Feds sniffing around Leeds, and all the *OurHood* snitches, we need to play this one differently.'

Maka nodded. This was why he wanted Shorty helping them. He was a hothead, but he was also a street general who was extremely tactical when needed.

'What are you thinking then?'

'If it's the Adele I'm thinking of, I banged her sister years back. *Shanice*. I'm gonna get in contact, see if I can learn anything.'

Maka grinned. 'Okay, fam. We'll meet with Manson and let him know the play with the crew. For now, let's get some more drinks and make a night of it. You down?'

Shorty was. He needed a night to cut loose and forget about the world for a while.

'Yeah, I'm down. Bet we can scare Naveed into giving us some champagne.'

CHAPTER EIGHT

THURSDAY 30 APRIL, 2015

SHANICE CHAPMAN DIDN'T KNOW what to expect. She had been traipsing through social media one evening when she saw a friend request from a blast from the past. Before accepting, she perused Shorty's profile, smiling at several photos. When they'd hung out back in the day, he was a player. He was good-looking and connected. He'd walk into clubs and buy out the bar, ensuring everyone had a good time.

She was under no illusions. She refused to fall for a hustler, and soon they fizzled out. Looking at him now, she was curious. His Facebook wasn't bursting with information about his life, but there was a photo someone had taken of him in a club back in January, with the caption 'fresh out'. Shorty was posing along with K-Bar and Maka. He looked older in the photo than he had when their paths last crossed, but he still had the look, especially in the eyes. It didn't take her long to accept the friend request.

Shorty immediately turned on the charm, telling Shanice how good she looked. She liked the compliments. Life had grown boring lately. She had two kids, a baby father uninterested in either of them, and a dull office job in town. Despite knowing it couldn't go anywhere, flirting with a thug from the Hood was appealing. She knew he had

TARGET PART III

been through the wars, but she was sucked into the conversation, and when Shorty suggested meeting, she was ready.

SHORTY AWOKE IN A GOOD MOOD. He was taking Shanice to dinner tonight. His day was open, and he planned on using the time to sort out the crew and get things back in line. After some press-ups and sit-ups, he showered, ate breakfast, and left the house after eleven. He had a message from Amy that he hadn't responded to. She didn't know about his plans to help K-Bar, and he wasn't telling her. Whatever was going on with them was separate from this situation.

It had never crossed Shorty's mind that K-Bar would snitch. He wasn't built that way, just like Shorty. When he'd turned himself in, the police tried everything to get him to *cooperate*, but he'd stood tall, and when he got out, he had been well compensated. The same would happen with K-Bar, but it made getting things back in line even more of a necessity.

The crew had been going for almost twenty years, and they had amassed a lot of money, but there was a tremendous amount of overhead. There were wages to pay, supply reloads, along with special considerations such as the *hazard pay* for the people behind bars. Their loyalty was bought and paid for, but if those funds stopped, it would make the situation much harder. It was vital the crew continued to profit, and he would ensure it did so.

SHORTY WENT TO SEE DARREN. The young man had come a long way, even in the last few months alone. He was one of Teflon's favourites, according to Maka, and one of the last moves Lamont made was to involve Darren in recruitment, recognising the need to replenish the crew and attract the best people. Shorty's only concern was that Darren was a little inexperienced for the role, but he had recently stepped up while Maka was recovering, and was a definite asset for the future.

He was holding court outside a house on Markham Avenue with a few of his boys, when Shorty pulled up. Darren nodded when he saw him and said something to his crew, who all dispersed when he climbed from the ride. Shorty approved of the gesture and the youngster's instincts.

Maybe what everyone said about him was true.

Shorty knew Darren's older brother, Lucas, and he was an attention-seeking idiot who couldn't stay out of prison. It seemed Darren was cut from a different cloth. He touched his fist.

'Everything good?' he asked.

'No surprises so far. Delroy's people are active. They've been driving up and down, looking for any of Lennox's people.'

'How's that working for them?'

Darren shrugged.

'Heard they caught a few people the other night, but no one special. Lennox made a big move getting to Solomon, though. No one saw that coming. We thought he had eyes in the back of his head.'

Shorty privately agreed. Solomon deserved his reputation. Shorty would have tried bringing him into the fold if he hadn't been so loyal to Delroy. They had sparred together a few years ago, and he still remembered being rocked by Solomon's killer left hook. It seemed that more of the old guard were dying every day, and he often wondered if that was a sign he should do something else.

As always, he dismissed the thoughts. He had nothing else. He'd worked his whole life for the reputation he had now, and he saw nothing beyond that. Amy flitted into his mind then, but he forced the thoughts away. He needed to focus.

'Solomon was good. Someone will get Lennox, though. If Del doesn't, we will.'

'What he did to your daughter was fucked,' said Darren. Shorty's stomach lurched. He didn't want to think about that fateful day again.

'He'll get his. Don't worry about that. I need to talk business with you.'

Darren nodded, instantly straightening, his face serious.

'What do you need?'

His attitude impressed Shorty. He'd sent his friends away, knowing Shorty wouldn't want to speak around them, and he had immediately

TARGET PART III

switched on when Shorty said he wanted to talk. He filed away these facts for future consideration.

'I heard you were looking to bring new people into the crew. I wanted to see who you were considering.'

Darren grinned.

'People are keeping low until the streets cool down. They don't want to be mistaken for one of Delroy's or Lennox's people and end up dead. Maka put me onto some old-timers. He's meant to be setting up the meets, so you'll need to talk to him about them.'

'Who've you seen closer to your age?' Shorty asked. They needed young blood in the crew. If they could get more people with Darren's mindset, they would come out of this situation even stronger.

'Roman and Keith. You know them?'

Shorty thought the name *Roman* sounded familiar, but he couldn't place him.

'I think so. Tell me what you know about them.'

'They're independent. They don't rock with any of the big crews, but they've carved out a nice base and clientele. Nothing on our level, but they're making decent money.'

'If they're doing well alone, why would they want to join up with us?'

'I've heard through the grapevine they're having problems with other gangs. I figure we can help one another, and calm the streets at the same time.'

'Do you know the other gangs they're beefing with?'

'I've heard the name *Aaron*, but I know a few. There's one I'm leaning towards.'

'I do too,' said Shorty. 'Set up a meeting with Roman and Keith. I'll go with you to check them out.'

'They're squirrelly. They might think it's a trap. I'm thinking we should just roll up on them.'

'Don't you think they might think *that's* a trap?' asked Shorty. In his experience, randomly pulling up on a crew was more threatening than calling to arrange a meeting on neutral ground.

'I think we'll be alright. They're not gonna pull anything with me. I know a few people in their crew.'

'What about me?' asked Shorty, smirking. Darren grinned.
'Everyone knows your rep, fam. Something tells me you'll be safe.'

They climbed in Shorty's ride. Darren made a call, trying to narrow down a location for Roman and Keith. Shorty tuned out, thinking about his meeting with Shanice and how to play it. He was considering telling her he just wanted sex, but hadn't been able to glean much about her situation when he had spoken to her. He would have to play it by ear.

Darren finished his call and stowed the phone.

'They're local. Someone saw them hanging on Hill Top Mount about an hour ago.'

'Do you have an address?'

Darren told him, and he drove over, knowing the area well. He pulled to a stop outside a red-bricked terraced house with a white door. They heard the thumping Drill music as they exited the car. There was a single person in the garden. He was rail-thin and wearing a vest and tracksuit bottoms, smoking a spliff with his eyes on his phone. He looked up as they approached, then straightened.

'Who are you lot?'

'Roman about?' Darren spoke first. Shorty was happy to let him do the talking.

'Who's asking?'

'Tell him Darren's out here.'

The man glanced at Shorty, obviously expecting him to introduce himself. When he didn't, the man shrugged and headed inside, giving one last look over his shoulder.

'Think we're gonna have any trouble with them?' Shorty asked. Darren shook his head.

'They're rowdy, but they know my name. We'll be fine. Worst comes to the worst, the people I left will spray up the spot if we're not back in an hour.'

'A lot can happen in an hour,' said Shorty, but before he could reply, the man was back, signalling for them to come in.

TARGET PART III

The house was stuffy, with a lingering scent of takeaways, cigarettes, and weed smoke. They followed the man through a hallway to the kitchen, where four people waited, none of whom Shorty recognised. Two of them — both lanky and hard-eyed — immediately left the room, eyeballing both Shorty and Darren as they did so. Not to be outdone, the pair stared right back.

'Been a while, D. Thought you got too big to be around little guys like us,' one of the seated youths said drily. Shorty guessed this was Roman. He was slender and light-skinned, wearing a black jacket and tracksuit bottoms. Something in his eyes reminded him of Darren. There was a confidence that set him apart as the leader of his little crew.

'Never, boss. You lot have done well.'

'Good of you to notice,' said the other youth. He was darker than Roman, with fathomless eyes and closely cropped hair. Broader than the others, he appeared to be the *muscle* of the team, and was eyeing Shorty in particular with dislike.

'You two, speak to Joey and the others. Make sure everything is humming. We can handle this,' said Roman. The two youths still standing hesitated a moment, then did as ordered.

'You're Shorty,' said Roman when they were alone.

'You're Roman. Your boy there must be Keith,' replied Shorty. Keith's glare only intensified. Shorty wondered if the kid would try him, silently vowing to knock him unconscious if he did. It would take more than a glare and some gym muscles to intimidate him.

'That's right. How come you're here?'

'We wanted to talk business,' Darren interjected himself into the conversation.

'Okay. We're listening.'

'We heard about the trouble you're having with Aaron and his people, and we want to help.'

'What makes you think we need help?' said Keith. Roman barely reacted, rubbing his knuckles, supremely unconcerned.

'If it's the one I'm thinking of, he's banded together with Morby's crew, and Prezzie's. You guys are good, but that's more than you can handle, and you know it.'

'I still don't see how it concerns you,' said Roman.

'We want to present a mutual arrangement. We back you against the other crews, and you become allied with us.'

'Allied with you how? We do our own thing. There's a reason we didn't go chasing after you lot or one of the other big crews. We handle our own business and stay off the radar. Throwing in with you lot puts us on the stage in a major way, and that brings problems.'

'Brings money too. A lot more money than what you're making now. Money and a responsible organisation that takes itself seriously. You have nothing to lose by signing up with us. Your enemies become our enemies, and we help you get what you want.'

'We don't want to become your lackeys. The only way powerhouses like you lot come looking for little people like us is because you think we're some kids to throw in front of your enemies. That ain't the case, and if it's what you want, I'd suggest you speak to Aaron and those lot, and get them to back you.'

Shorty respected the way Roman was responding, but he also liked Darren's negotiating. He'd maintained his composure the whole time, showing little reaction to Roman's comments. Keith alternated his glare between Darren and Shorty, but Darren wasn't fazed. He was focused on his words and on resolving the situation. Shorty also noticed he'd shown some knowledge of Aaron, despite being unsure earlier. He filed it away, not wanting to disrupt the flow.

'Our crew doesn't use people as lackeys or cannon fodder. Like you, we believe in being low-key where necessary, and in working with our partners to make sure everyone profits. You've gone further than anyone could have imagined with this team of yours. We're just trying to help you stay around longer. We have the best product. You'll make more money doing less work, and you won't have to take everything on your shoulders.'

Roman shot a look at Keith, who still looked sulky. He shrugged in response to his silent question, and Roman sighed.

'What are you proposing? Who are your enemies?'

'We suspect Aaron and his people recently attacked one of our spots, and jumped one of our runners.'

TARGET PART III

Roman again glanced at Keith, scowling at his partner's lack of effort in involving himself in the conversation.

'We'll work with you, but *we* control the people under us, and we get your supply and backup.'

'In exchange for?'

Roman mulled it over for a moment. 'Thirty percent of our profits.'

'Try sixty. We're bringing the supply, not to mention the protection,' said Darren.

'Fine. Sixty percent *our* way, forty percent yours.'

They negotiated for a few more minutes, with neither man backing down from the other. Finally, they agreed on a fifty-fifty split, which Shorty suspected both had wanted all along. He was impressed with how it had gone. Roman had savvy and street smarts. With him working alongside Darren and backed by the others, it would be the push their crew needed to rise back to their position at the top.

He tuned out of the rest of the discussion, thinking again about his night. Getting K-Bar out of prison would help tremendously in providing both depth and experience to the crew. There was a chance it would all blow up in his face with Shanice, but he would understand more when they were around one another.

'You did well,' he told Darren as they climbed back into the ride.

'He's a tricky one. He's got some serious steel.'

'Reminded me of someone,' said Shorty, as he drove them away. 'When do we get this Aaron kid then?'

'We're gonna give them a few soldiers, and they'll do the heavy work with Aaron and his crew. They'll be on board after that, and we'll get the streets back in line. Should take a day or so to track Aaron.'

Shorty grinned. 'Nicely handled. I thought you'd be louder about it, but you played it subtle. Keith seemed like he had a problem.'

'He's one of those guys that doesn't like anyone but Roman. He's tough, though, and he can handle himself. The whole crew can. Probably why they've been left alone.'

'Why would Aaron try it with them then?'

'He's dumb. Doesn't scare easily, thinks that the loudest is the roughest and the toughest. Guess that's how he bullied people into accepting him as a leader. Roman and his guys make money, and

Aaron wants a piece. From what I hear, he's part of why the streets are so hot.'

'There's a war, D. Lennox and Delroy are trying to kill each other.' Shorty gritted his teeth when he said Lennox's name. Things wouldn't be truly right for him until he had put a bullet or two into the man's head.

'I know that. Everyone does. Aaron isn't quiet, and there's a difference between people knowing not to be on the streets because two gangs are trying to kill each other, and a loose cannon running around those same streets, robbing and beating up everyone in sight.'

Shorty couldn't argue with that. Politics aside, it had been a productive meeting, and was one thing off his mind.

CHAPTER NINE
THURSDAY 30 APRIL, 2015

SHANICE WAITED by the door when Shorty pulled up in the evening. He'd left Darren and chilled for a few more hours before freshening up. Amy had finally got hold of him, and they'd spoken about Grace. Guilt had swirled in his stomach when he hung up. There was nothing between him and Amy, but he'd never stopped caring for her. There was no way he could tell her about what he was doing. While she had accepted his execution of Lutel, he didn't think she would be on board with what might happen to Adele.

'You look good,' said Shorty, when Shanice climbed into the ride. He wasn't exaggerating. She had a cute, round face and a curvaceous figure, having maintained most of the weight she gained after having children. She wore a tight cleavage-displaying blouse and tight grey jeans with a pair of heels.

'You look good too. Even after all these years, you've still got the look.' Her eyes flitted to the Rolex on his wrist. 'Business must be good.'

'I'm gonna get mine regardless,' said Shorty, winking and showing her his cocky side. Although he'd borrowed it from Maka, having misplaced his own, she didn't need to know that.

They made small talk as they drove into the city centre and parked, then walked to the restaurant. It was a fancy Italian spot on Greek Street, with immaculate dark brown floors, white beams, and small, intimate tables with sturdy black chairs. There were plants nearby, dotted with lights. They were shown to their tables and ordered glasses of wine while they waited for the menus.

'This is a nice spot,' admitted Shanice. 'I've never been here before.'

'Same. Came highly recommended, and the food is meant to be amazing.'

'Do you eat much Italian food?'

Shorty shook his head. 'I like my Hood food too much.'

Shanice grinned. 'Same. My kids love Spaghetti Bolognese, though.'

'How many kids do you have?'

'Two boys,' said Shanice, watching him closely to see how he would react. He already knew. Her Facebook page was full of photos of them.

'How old?'

'Eight and twelve.'

Shorty didn't ask their names, and she didn't give them. He didn't care, but knew talking about children would make it easier to keep the subject on family.

'How many do you have? I heard you had a girl?'

'One of each. Roughly the same ages as yours.'

Shanice again smiled. 'Must be fate. What have you been doing, anyway?'

Shorty wasn't sure how honest to be with Shanice. He didn't want to lie and have her already know what was going on in the streets.

'I've been keeping things quiet for a while. My daughter had an accident.'

Shanice's eyes softened. 'I heard. I'm sorry. If my kids were hurt like that, it would kill me.'

Shorty bowed his head, the emotions easy to replicate.

'I was right there, and I was powerless to stop it,' he admitted. The images of Grace's prone frame were seared into his brain. He didn't have to search far for them. Shanice put her hand on top of his, gently squeezing. Amy had done something similar recently, but there was none of the warmth he'd felt then.

'She's lucky to have you.'

Shorty nodded. They were quiet now, waiting for the food to arrive. The small talk soon started up again, and Shanice spoke about her baby father, and the issues she had with him and his inability to be there for his kids. It made Shorty wonder if Stacey or Amy ever said similar things about him. Whether they had, he reasoned, he was making up for it now. He and Dionte had spoken numerous times since their meeting, and though the conversations were still a little awkward, it was still progress, and he was thankful for it.

'Why did you really look me up?' Shanice asked a while later. The food was finished, and they were savouring wine and sitting in comfortable silence. Despite himself, he'd enjoyed the night. It had been a while since he had been on a date, and even if this was a mission, it was enjoyable. Shanice wasn't as annoying as he remembered, which he guessed was due to her being older and more mature. Shorty thought about how to answer. He didn't want her getting emotional if he said the wrong thing. Finally, he just went for it.

'Kinda felt like we had unfinished business. I was curious about you,' he said. Shanice blinked, surprised by his words.

'Really?'

'We had fun back in the day, and sometimes I remember those days and how free we all were. I had my people around me, and the entire world was just *there*, you know?'

Shanice was wide-eyed as she gawped, and he didn't know why. He'd spoken from the heart. He often thought back on those days and how alive and *whole* everyone was. Their crew controlled the streets, he did what he wanted, and made serious money. Lamont had his back, making sure they mostly stayed out of trouble. He'd been young, carefree and invincible. Now, he was older, guarded, barely surrounded by the remnants of that glorious era.

'I always had a thing for you,' she finally said. 'I know it was never serious, but being around you was something different. You had something about you that drew me in.' She paused. 'You still do.'

Shorty felt a wave of guilt at her words, and this one had nothing to do with Amy. He was deceiving a woman that had potentially never gotten over him. Steeling himself, he remembered why he was doing it. He would not let K-Bar rot behind bars.

'Wanna get out of here?'

———

Shorty sat up in the unfamiliar bed, still naked, covered in marks and scratches. Shanice had been an absolute wildcat in bed. Whether it was years of pent-up pining or if it had simply been a while for her, he couldn't say. After leaving the restaurant, the seduction was easy, and the sex had been fun. It struck him how little he had been laid since getting out, and that shocked him. Having sex had once upon a time been the be-all and end-all of his life. Sex and getting money.

Had he changed so much without realising?

Shorty's conversations lately had been tinged with more realism than he was ready for. He'd gotten Amy back on side by being honest with her, and the same thing had worked to a degree with Shanice. He hadn't spoken with her about Adele yet, but he would work it into conversation and take it from there. Scheming in the darkness, he wondered when things would grow easier. He was back in the crew's fold. Grace was steadily improving. He was bringing in serious money, and he had things to live for. It was strange for him to sit and wonder what would come later, and he quickly decided it didn't matter. For now, he would focus on K-Bar.

———

'That's him.'

A black Ford 4x4 idled at the end of Hillcrest View in the Hood. The occupants of the ride watched a group of men hanging outside a house. Five men were passing around a spliff, talking and laughing in loud tones.

'Which one?' said the driver.

'The guy in the grey hoody,' said Roman.

'Okay,' said Manson. 'We go for him. Sharma, make sure they back

TARGET PART III

off.'

'Got it.'

Accelerating sharply, Sharma gunned the ride forward, and they were on top of the group before they reacted. Aaron was the quickest and was already in motion as Manson, Sharma, Roman, and Keith jumped from the vehicle. The men froze. Sharma's gun was trained on the group, ready to cut them down if they moved. Aaron barely made it around the corner onto Shepherds Lane, when Roman tackled him to the ground, knocking him into a nearby green electrical box. The pair tussled, Aaron having the advantage, until Keith dragged him off and began kicking him. Roman joined in, his fist repeatedly crashing against Aaron's face.

'Hold out his arm!' shouted Keith. Roman complied, and Keith brought all his weight down on the appendage, causing Aaron to scream in pain.

Meanwhile, Aaron's crew were being robbed at gunpoint. They could hear the cries of his beating, but there was nothing they could do. Roman and Keith dragged him back to the group, dumping him on the floor. He clutched his arm, tears of pain in his eyes.

'You lot are fucking dead! Watch when I catch you.'

'This is the end, Aaron. You're out of business.' Manson turned to the crew. 'We'll make a deal with you lot. Work for Roman, or you can try to set yourselves up in another city.'

The four men looked from their beaten, snivelling leader, to the well-organised group that had ambushed them. It was a simple decision to make.

'We're in.'

'Roman and Keith will let you know how this works. Any problems, get them, and they'll handle it. Understand?'

The men nodded. Sharma and Manson zip-tied Aaron's hands behind his back and dumped him in the boot. Without a word, they climbed in and sped away. Roman and Keith turned back to the men, grinning.

'Where were we?'

Shorty sipped his brandy and coke, looking to Shanice by his side. They were watching a comedy special on *Netflix*, but she was paying more attention than he was. He had spent every night at Shanice's since their *date*. He'd expected to have to work to wrap her around his finger, but she was wide open and prime for manipulation.

'How's your family? I haven't seen your brother in years?'

'Trevor doesn't live in Leeds anymore. He got married a few years ago and moved to Wolverhampton. Adele is still around.'

'Yeah, I remember her. Party girl? Liked a drink?'

Shanice kissed her teeth. 'Sounds like her. Don't know if she's still like that anymore.'

'Did she get married too?'

'Nothing like that. I just haven't seen her in a while. She's still in Leeds, but she turned weird. Basically went into hiding and cut everyone out of her life.'

'You don't know where she is?'

Shanice sighed. 'I know. She rang me and told me about three weeks ago. She wouldn't tell me what was going on, and we argued. Mum misses her, but Adele won't speak to her.'

'Did you ask her what was going on?' Shorty hoped she said no.

'She wouldn't tell me. Mum is always asking where she is, and it's like she doesn't even care about her nephews.'

Shorty pulled Shanice close and gave her a quick kiss as she relaxed in his arms.

'Take the kids to see her.'

'You think?'

'Don't take family for granted. Cherish them while they're still here. I lost my cousin a few years back, and it sits with me every day. The last time we spoke, we argued, and I have to carry that the rest of my days.'

'I'm sorry, Shorty,' she murmured, snuggling closer and kissing his chest. 'You're right. I'll take them to see her at the weekend.'

Shorty hid his smile. He would follow her, learn where Adele was, and how many police officers were guarding her. From there, he would make his move, no matter the obstacles.

CHAPTER TEN

SUNDAY 3 MAY, 2015

SHORTY WAS PARKED down the street from Adele's place. He had followed Shanice to the spot, watching as she and her two boys were shown inside. Since then, he'd watched the spot for anything out of the ordinary. He had seen Adele leave a few times, returning with shopping bags. Even from a distance, he noticed the bags under her eyes. Clearly, the pressures of being a snitch were getting to her.

During his surveillance, he noticed one thing that had thrown him for a loop. There was no police presence. Shorty expected them to be well-hidden, but they were non-existent. When Shanice visited, no one had stopped her, or gone to the premises afterwards. He couldn't get his head around it. Adele was their star witness, but they had left her unattended.

The paranoid part of his brain wondered if it was a ploy to get him out in the open, but that made little sense. Surely it wasn't worth the risk. Jamal had taken an earlier watch, and reported nothing out of the ordinary. This was it. There would be no more waiting. Shorty was going in.

ADELE RARELY SLEPT well these days. She lived in fear of the world learning what she had done. Her friend Naomi had been murdered by gangsters a few years ago, and the police tracked Adele down and compelled her to testify. They promised to keep her safe, but it didn't stop her worrying. She had gone against some powerful gangsters and knew K-Bar had been arrested.

Removing herself from her world, she had avoided contact unless necessary, and had kept to herself. Her sister had visited recently, bringing her nephews along, and it was great catching up with them. It made her feel guilty for neglecting her family, and she'd promised Shanice she would keep in touch more, without going into the detail of why she had remained hidden. Shanice had spoken at length about a new man that had come into her life, though she was coy about giving his name, saying it was early days. Adele was happy for her, but also jealous that her life was so uncomplicated.

When her eyes fluttered open in the middle of the night, it was no big deal. The big deal was the man loomed over her. Before she could scream, his gloved hand covered her mouth.

'Stop fucking moving,' he hissed. 'Keep still, and don't make me use this.'

Even in the dark, Adele saw the pistol in his other hand and froze. Her blood ran cold as she realised who the man represented, and why he was there.

'You shouldn't have spoken to the Feds.' He moved his hand from her mouth.

'I di—'

'Don't lie. We know it was you that got K-Bar locked up. Dirty snitch. I should blow your head off right now. Send a message to anyone else thinking of trying it.'

Adele frenziedly shook her head, not daring to speak. There was no doubt in her mind that the man meant it. His voice was full of conviction, and he'd broken into her house with little effort.

'What should I do with you?' he asked. She gasped, tears spilling down her cheeks.

'I'm sorry. They made me do it.'

'Doesn't matter now. We know where you are and how to get you.

TARGET PART III

More than that, we know where your whole family stays, including your mouthy sister and her two kids. You want their blood on your hands?'

Adele shivered. 'No, please. I'm sorry. Please don't touch my family.'

The man paused, then flicked on her bedside lamp. His face was covered by a mask, and he wore all black. He pressed the gun to her head.

'Tomorrow, you're gonna contact the police and tell them you made up the story. You're gonna refuse to testify, and if you do that, you're gonna get ten bags. More than that, you're gonna get to keep your life.'

'Thank you. I'm sorry,' Adele cried, overcome with fear mingled with relief.

'If you don't, I'm gonna kill your mum and dad. Then I'm gonna kill every member of your family that I can find. Even if the police move you, it won't matter. I'll get to all of them, and it'll be your fault. Understand?'

'I'll do it. Please, just don't touch my family.'

'Tomorrow,' the man repeated. 'Ring them first thing in the morning. Don't make me come back. The Feds can't protect you from me and my people.'

With that, he left, leaving Adele sobbing, the terror growing. She couldn't stop shaking. Despite their assurances of protection, the police had left her completely vulnerable, and a man had held a gun to her head while she was in her bed. As her tears grew louder and more frequent, Adele cried for her family, and for her friend Naomi.

RIGBY MADE his way into work, pumped after three strong coffees. The last few days had been a medley of digging into the gang war and seeing what they could learn. He'd met with Terry, who had clued them in on the situation with Delroy and Lennox. Their other informants were parroting the same story. There had been deaths on both sides, including the murders of Winston and Eddie Williams. A man affiliated with *OurHood*, Malcolm Powell, had also been gunned down, though Rigby didn't understand the connection between an organisation like *OurHood*, and gangsters like the Williams family.

There was a lot remaining to unpack, and Rigby still didn't understand how any of the above connected to Teflon, but he was determined to find out.

Sitting at his desk after nodding at his colleagues, he'd barely turned on his computer when Piers approached. Piers worked in admin and did a multitude of tasks for Reid and other supervisors. He was in his mid-twenties, with pointed facial features and a grating, nasally voice. Rigby disliked him and knew the feeling was mutual.

'Before you get set up, the boss wants to see you straight away. It's urgent.'

Rigby locked his computer, not even looking at Piers.

'Where is she?'

'In her office. Just knock and go in.'

Rigby clambered to his feet and headed to Reid's office. He began collating all the facts in his head in case she asked for an update on the gang war. He hadn't updated his paperwork yet, but with the facts he knew, it would be enough to get her off his back for a short while. After knocking and walking in, he waited for Reid to notice him. He didn't know how long she'd been in the office, but she looked alert and ready. An empty mug of coffee was on her desk, along with a large water bottle, half-full, and a selection of paperwork that the very sight of gave him a headache.

'Good to see you, Rigby. Please have a seat.'

He sat opposite her. She met his eyes with her steely own, but he matched her stare, refusing to let her intimidate him.

'Have you learned anything more about K-Bar?'

'I've focused on the gang war like you asked,' replied Rigby, frowning at her question. She had ordered him to get stuck into the war in Chapeltown. He wondered if there was something he had missed.

Reid nodded, as if he'd confirmed something she already knew.

'The girl recanted her story.'

Rigby's mouth fell open, heart leaping into his chest.

'What?'

TARGET PART III

'She called in first thing this morning and said she made the whole thing up.'

'No, ma'am. That's utter shite. She's involved. She knew key details about the setup, and the fact her friend Naomi had helped set up Xiyu Manderson, aka *Chink*, back in 2013. Someone got to her. Who has been watching her place?'

'I took the men off her place. We were short-handed on another case, and they were needed.'

'Why the hell would you do that? I told you she was a high-priority witness. She should have been watched twenty-four seven.' Rigby raked a hand through his hair.

'The decision was made based on the fact the case wasn't moving. K-Bar wasn't cooperating, and I and several others believed that the case wasn't strong enough to win at trial.'

'You didn't give me a chance to pressure him. You took me off the case, then sabotaged it by removing Adele Chapman's protection. If you hadn't, we'd have a result.'

'Watch your tone, please, Detective Rigby. Remember, you are speaking to a superior officer.'

Rigby was disgusted. Reid's actions had led to the case collapsing, and she didn't even care.

'K-Bar will be released now, you realise that?'

Reid sighed, slowly nodding.

'His solicitor has been on the phone all morning, pushing for the charges to be dismissed. If there is no other evidence linking him to any crimes, we'll have to let him go.'

Rigby couldn't believe it. K-Bar was extremely dangerous. Him being back on the streets wouldn't help anyone, but there was nothing he could do.

'Do you have anything else you would like to add?' Reid asked. Rigby shook his head. There was nothing else they could link him to. Everything was all hearsay, with no strong evidence. He knew K-Bar was responsible for multiple murders, including Big-Kev's and Chink's, but there was no proof. He couldn't even bring himself to speak.

'I expect a report on the war by the end of the week. I have people breathing down my neck to know where we're at with it. I told them we had our best detective on it. Please don't prove me wrong.'

Rigby ignored the compliment and nodded, climbing to his feet and leaving the office. He wanted nothing more than to go outside and smoke a cigarette, but he wouldn't give Reid any reason to discipline him. Piers still stood there, watching him with a smug look. Ignoring him, he headed back to his desk, loading his computer. He'd cleared his emails and sorted his schedule for the day when Murphy approached. He had a face like thunder, and Rigby knew why.

'Nothing we can do, James,' he said. Murphy's eyes were blazing, his face almost puce. Rigby hoped he would stay calm and not fly off the handle. The last thing he needed was his partner being reprimanded, even if he agreed with his anger.

'They bloody took them off the house. It's like they wanted the case to get scuppered,' he hissed.

'We'll discuss it later. Her little parrot is watching. Let's get cracking on this case for now.'

Murphy didn't like it, but he took a deep breath and nodded, taking a seat at his own desk. Satisfied, Piers returned to his desk, and Rigby began typing up his reports. Now, more than ever, he needed to confirm the link between Teflon and the gang war.

With K-Bar's imminent release, there was a possibility that he would be involved, and that would allow Rigby the opportunity to catch him again. He would get Terry Worthy to keep his ear to the ground for any information regarding K-Bar and his activity.

CHAPTER ELEVEN
WEDNESDAY 6 MAY, 2015

RIGBY WAITED OUTSIDE as K-Bar was processed and released. It hadn't taken long for the motion to take place. Reid and the other bosses weren't bothered about setting a dangerous criminal free, and his solicitor was making a lot of noise.

Soon, K-Bar was all smiles as he left the station with his solicitor. His smile only widened when he noticed Rigby. Sending his solicitor on, he stopped in front of the officer.

'I guess you finally realised I was innocent, right Detective Rigby?' he said, his voice oozing smugness. Rigby's fists clenched, but he kept his cool. He would not lose his job scrapping with a criminal like K-Bar.

'We both know what you are, Barrett. I don't care what you think you've escaped from. I'll be here, watching. I caught you once, and I can catch you again.'

'If you say so, *boss*. Fact is, I told you I was innocent, and you didn't want to listen. Now, I'm free, so watch away.'

'When you slip up again, I'll be there. I want you to remember that, and I want your boss Teflon to know I am going to bring his entire operation crashing down around him.'

K-Bar nodded, unaffected by the declaration. 'Good luck, mate.

Stay in touch.' With another mocking grin, he slipped past Rigby and followed his solicitor. Rigby watched them go, growing angrier by the second. His superiors had fucked up on this one, and he felt utterly impotent. He'd tried speaking with Adele and convincing her to tell her story. He had all-but promised he would guard her twenty-four-seven, but it wasn't enough. Whoever warned Adele had done so thoroughly. There was no getting through to her.

Rigby watched him drive away, likely going to celebrate his release. He stared at the ground, closing his eyes for a moment. He needed to rise above this. There was still work to do, and if his hunch about this gang war was correct, he would be seeing K-Bar and the others soon enough. Confidence slightly restored, Rigby went back to work.

LAMONT'S TIME as a supplier had been plain sailing so far. Sales in Chapeltown were lower, but this had led to more traffic in other areas, meaning more profit being made, regardless. He met with few clients, letting Ahmed and Mustafa handle most of it. They had working relationships with many of the customers. He went to a meeting every once in a while, but it was rare, and he didn't have to talk much. It gave him more time to focus on Lennox and his people. He had a few names of some low-ranked soldiers and workers, but no one major.

It worried Lamont how little the people he got to, knew about the organisation. Nikkolo had been worked over by Akeem and others, and hadn't given up any information about Lennox's team. Lamont hoped that with Delroy turning the tide, it would make people open up and reveal more about the workings of the crew. He wondered if it was worth attempting to meet with Ken to learn more about *OurHood*. He was sure the group was crucial for unearthing Lennox's financial position, but hadn't ruled out the possibility someone could be funding him. All he had at the moment were half-baked theories. He needed more substance.

Lamont was driving from a meeting with his business partner, Martin, when his phone rang. It was Ahmed.

'How are things?' Lamont said by way of greeting. Ahmed hadn't warmed to him since the first meeting, and he'd done nothing to bridge the gap, remaining cordial. Mustafa was easier to get along with, meaning he focused more on him.

'Good enough that we will need to put in an order soon.'

'Can we last another forty-eight hours?'

'I believe so. A few people are buying in bulk, especially in Halton Moor and Middleton. There's a lot of traction outside of Leeds as well.'

'I'll make the call tomorrow. You'll have what you need the day after.'

'Thank you.'

There was a brief, uncomfortable silence, and Lamont sought to end it.

'Would you like to go to dinner?'

'Excuse me?'

'We're still not seeing eye-to-eye. If we're going to work well together, we need to try to get along.'

Lamont could almost hear Ahmed considering this.

'When?' He replied.

'Tonight.'

'I'm free.'

'Excellent. I'll text you some details. Speak to you later.' Lamont hung up, wondering if it was the right move. It wasn't essential to have Ahmed onside, but it would make things easier in the long run. Lamont was still annoyed at the fact he'd been denied access to the network. He had tried speaking with Mustafa again, but the man had nothing new to say.

Thankfully, his own attempts to build his personal network were coming along nicely. Several people had come forward, offering to look for information on Lennox and anyone else making waves on the streets. He hadn't heard from Maka or Manson lately, but that wasn't a concern. They had placed an order, and the money was still going to the people he had in place. The pair had impressed him, as had Darren Lyles. He would arrange for them to get a bonus for their hard work. Maybe giving Ahmed and Mustafa one would get them onside too. It was something else for him to consider.

THAT NIGHT, Lamont and Ahmed went for a curry in Bradford. Ahmed picked the spot, and though Lamont wasn't a fan of curry, he had agreed. The restaurant had spotless white floors, with black tables and white and brown chairs. It was packed, but Ahmed was known, and they had procured a nice table near the middle of the restaurant.

The beginning of the meal had been quiet. They ate their food, Lamont sipping his wine while Ahmed had water.

After a while, Lamont spoke.

'How am I doing?'

'Pardon?'

'With the organisation. The new role. You've been part of it far longer than me, so I'm curious to know your thoughts.'

'Why would you care?'

Lamont shrugged, forking a mouthful of food before replying once he'd chewed.

'I've been in the game a long time, and in my experience, things always run smoother when everyone is on the same wavelength.'

Ahmed seemed to accept this, but didn't hurry to respond. Lamont didn't mind. He was using the evening to gain the measure of the man, wanting to see if he could change his initial impression.

'You've done well. You've adapted quickly to the way we do things, and you haven't tried to micro-manage us.'

'Was that a concern of yours?'

Ahmed shrugged now.

'You and Mustafa both began working for the organisation at the same time.'

'Correct.'

'Before this, were you friends?'

'No. We both knew Saj, however. When Akhan was looking for reliable men, we were the first ones Saj brought into the fold.'

'I'm sorry about Saj.'

'Are you?' Ahmed's eyes were ice cold now.

'He was a good man. Unfortunately, he was loyal to someone who didn't have his best interests at heart.'

TARGET PART III

'That's not for you to say.'

'I think it is for me to say,' replied Lamont, slipping into his element. He had no headaches, aches, and pains or tiredness. Right now, he felt good, and was taking full advantage of this state of mind. 'Akhan and Saj tried to kill me, and they had no reason to do so.'

'You robbed them,' replied Ahmed. Lamont's eyebrow rose.

'Is it really a robbery, if your bosses ask for it to take place?'

Ahmed's eyes widened. He evidently hadn't expected him to say this. Lamont continued.

'Why else would I be here? Why would your bosses want Akhan removed? Do your organisation often promote black men to positions that have always been held by Asian men?'

'What are you trying to say?' Ahmed avoided the questions.

'Akhan brought a level of conflict to the surface that was deemed unacceptable, and that was the end of the road for him. Saj didn't have to go along with that. My question to you is, where do you stand in all of this?'

'Trying to kill me too?'

'I'm trying to get to know you, Ahmed. I want us to work together in harmony as we have done so far, but without the tension.'

Ahmed didn't respond, and they finished their food in silence. Both men ordered dessert, and Lamont asked for another glass of wine.

'I think we can work together,' Ahmed finally said. 'You're right about a lot of the things you said. Saj was unflinchingly loyal to Akhan, even when he was wrong. If you are wrong, I will tell you. I won't blindly go along with everything you say, nor will I allow Mustafa to either.'

Lamont nodded. 'I can accept that.'

The conversation became fast-paced, and they spent their time talking about football. Ahmed was a die-hard Manchester United fan, and Lamont had supported Leeds United his entire life. The tension slipped away the longer they spoke, and they were soon laughing like old friends. Lamont was under no illusions that everything was fixed, but over time, he would bring Ahmed around to his way of thinking. Mustafa would be pleased that the three of them could meet without friction, and that was enough for now.

'Are you married?' Lamont asked, when they'd grown tired of discussing football.

'I met my wife eight years ago, and we have been married for six years.'

'Kids?'

Ahmed shook his head. 'Soon. You?'

'No marriage. No kids.'

'Why not?'

'I guess I've never seen myself as marriage or parent material.'

Lamont could see Ahmed searching for a response to what he'd said, and grinned.

'I'm guessing you'd pick a boy over a girl?'

Ahmed returned the grin.

'I have seven brothers, so I relate more to boys than girls.'

They spoke for a while, drifting back to football and discussing long-term plans for the organisation. Lamont wondered if Ahmed had any access to the information network. He was presuming he did, but he would have to play it carefully if he was going to tap into it. If Jakkar learned of it, the consequences would be devastating.

'Mustafa will be pleased we've had a conversation. Next time, we'll have to invite him too.'

'If you do, be aware you will spend twice as much as you do tonight. He has a tremendous appetite, especially with curry.'

Lamont smirked. 'Maybe we'll expense it back to the company and call it a work dinner.'

Ahmed chuckled, and they finished their dessert. Lamont was tempted to get another glass of wine, but felt two was enough. He instead asked for water, along with the bill. The restaurant had a bar attached to it, and there were various people seated there. Lamont checked them out, noticing a group of attractive women laughing over a story one of them was telling. He instinctively looked around to see if they were attached to any men. He couldn't even explain why he had done it. One of the women turned and met his eyes. She wore a black dress, with dark brown hair hanging past her shoulders, and she had dark, alluring eyes. They locked eyes for a moment, and she didn't look away. Taking another sip, Lamont returned his attention to Ahmed.

'Who is she?' Ahmed noticed his wavering attention.

'I don't know. She caught my eye.'

'I'm not surprised. She's stunning, as are her friends. What do you do in these situations?'

Lamont hadn't had to work for a woman's attention in a while, but certain skills never left a person.

'Depends what I want to happen.'

'I think she wants something to happen. Come, let's buy them some drinks and see where it takes us.'

Lamont shrugged. He wasn't eager to go along, but also liked the idea of appeasing Ahmed. They had made some ground in dealing with their issues, but if they were going to be working together for any concentrated length of time, they would need to stay on a positive level.

Maybe women would help them relax.

Lamont let Ahmed make the moves. He went straight for the high-priced champagne, with orders to send it to the trio. The brunette was the most attractive of the three; the others both blonde, one taller and leggier than the other, who was curvier. A wave of anxiety shot over Lamont, like he was betraying Jenny's memory by even entertaining this. He took another sip of water, trying to force the thoughts away.

After the women accepted the drinks, they invited them to come and sit at the table. The brunette ended up next to Lamont, giving him an understated smile.

'Thanks for the champagne.'

'Thank my friend there.' He held out his hand. 'Lamont.'

'Anna,' she replied, shaking it. Ahmed was already talking at length with the blondes, leaving him to speak with Anna.

'You all appear extremely dressed up. Where's the night taken you so far?' He asked, getting right to the small talk.

'It's Sarah's birthday.' Anna pointed to one of the blondes, but he didn't bother checking which. 'We decided we'd go out to celebrate, but the first place we went to was rubbish. What are you and your friend celebrating?'

'We're working together on a project, and we were laying down the groundwork,' said Lamont. Anna looked interested now.

'What sort of project?'

Lamont grinned. 'There are NDAs in place, I'm afraid. I wouldn't want to get sued for revealing the details.'

'That sounds interesting. You've made me curious, which I imagine was your intention,' said Anna. She smiled often, which he found he enjoyed. Reaching out, he placed his hand over hers. It was a move he'd used in the past that he found helped to relax. As Anna leaned in, Lamont's mind skipped to Jenny, a twinge of guilt shocking his system. He pulled his hand away sharply.

'Are you okay?' Anna asked, her forehead creased with concern.

'I'm fine. I just went somewhere for a moment, but I'm back.'

'Are you sure?'

Lamont nodded. He'd slipped into charming mode for a moment, then the guilt had brought him back. There was an opportunity here. A woman he didn't know, who had no expectations of him. This was a chance to get his life back, and to crawl out of the pit of despair that overwhelmed him.

After some more conversation, he went for it.

'Would you like to get out of here?'

Anna gave him a surveying look.

'Are you going to make it worth my while?'

'That's certainly my intention,' Lamont replied, meeting her stare head-on. Smiling, Anna agreed. They hung out a while longer, then said their goodbyes, Lamont shaking hands with Ahmed, who winked at him. He wondered how his married subordinate would handle the two blondes, but that was on him. Lamont had done his part, and now he was leaving.

ANNA WASN'T sure what made her go back to the house of the well-dressed black man she'd known for an hour. It wasn't the sort of thing she normally did, but something had drawn her to him. He was good-looking and undoubtedly charming, but there was something behind

TARGET PART III

his eyes that wasn't quite right. She couldn't put her finger on what, but it intrigued her. He was the type of guy she would assume was married, but there was no ring on his finger and the sprawling home he'd brought her back to had no signs of any female element. It was a quandary, to be sure. The room they were currently in was a medley of dark browns, with Corinthian leather sofas and an elegant coffee table and bookshelf. There was a drinks cabinet in the corner. Lamont approached it when she'd taken a seat.

'What are you drinking?' he asked.

'I'll have what you're having,' she replied. Lamont fixed them both a gin and tonic. He'd mixed it well, and she enjoyed the taste.

'Are you single?' he asked. Anna nodded.

'Trust me, I wouldn't have come back if I wasn't. Are you?'

There it was again. There was a haunted look for just a second, then it was gone.

'Yes, I am.'

'This is a lovely home,' she said, to avoid the silence that had crept over them. Lamont was like a different man than he'd been in the restaurant. He seemed less sure of himself, more strained. She didn't know what the cause was.

'Thank you. I've lived here for a few months.'

'Where did you live before that?'

'I lived in Adel.'

'Alone?'

'No, I lived with someone.' Lamont's tone was definitely different, and she suspected the *someone* he had lived with was long-gone, and that he wasn't over it.

'Can you tell me any more about your job?'

'I'm a trader by day.'

'You must do well based on how you're living,' she said.

Lamont thought about that, and it made him wonder. To the outside world, he had everything a person could want, *so why did he feel so unfulfilled?* He thought about Ken's question at Trinidad's funeral, when he'd asked Lamont if he was happy. *Was it money that defined him, or something else?*

'I guess I do,' he said. 'Tell me more about yourself.'

'Like I said, I work in the city centre. I'm a Data Protection Manager, and I enjoy it.'

'How did you get involved in that?'

'I was a team leader in a contact centre, and I wanted a change, so I went for a position when it became available elsewhere. That was six years ago. I've been doing it ever since.'

'Let me ask you something else,' Lamont started. He seemed to have relaxed now from earlier. 'Do you often go home with strange guys you don't know?'

Anna grinned in response. 'I don't, but my friends have been telling me to take more chances.'

Lamont smiled back, but it was strained again. He didn't actually have any friends. He had people that worked with him, and people he associated with, like Delroy. Shorty had been his best friend, but they weren't on good terms. He'd lost touch with a lot of the people he'd hung out with in his twenties, and a lot of them were mutual associates of Chink's. After his death, the relationships didn't seem the same.

He wasn't sure how he felt about any of it, but he was sure he should feel *something*, nor did he understand why these thoughts were parading through his mind now. Needing a distraction, he sat next to Anna. She seemed startled by the sudden change in proximity, but didn't back away.

'I'm happy you came back with me,' he said, drawing her in for a kiss. Anna allowed it for a few moments, then gently pulled back, gnawing her lower lip as she watched him. His heart sank at the thought of rejection. A moment dragged by, neither of them speaking. Anna hadn't taken her eyes from him, but after another beat, she returned the kiss, and Lamont deepened it as they snuggled into the sofa.

K-BAR FOLLOWED Maka into the house, not knowing what to expect, as loud hip-hop music pumped from the speakers. They were on Francis Street, in a spot K-Bar recognised as a base for parties. When they entered the living room, and he heard the cheers before he was doused

TARGET PART III

in champagne, he was elated. The moment was electric, a major sign for K-Bar that he was free. Shorty was there, along with Manson and Darren, among others. Shorty embraced his friend, patting him on the back.

'It's fucking good to see you out, K. For real.'

'It's good to be out, fam. Thanks for sorting that thing for me. I wasn't sure how it was gonna go down for a while, but you handled it.'

'You're my brother. I wasn't gonna leave you in there.'

They hugged again, then K-Bar greeted the others. The celebration continued. Maka called some girls to come over. K-Bar was polite to the ladies, but couldn't move without someone giving him another drink or a spliff to smoke. Shorty watched his antics with a massive grin on his face. For him, tonight was a major sign things could get back to the way they had been.

He loved the atmosphere and enjoyed seeing people he'd come up with just kicking back and having fun. K-Bar had apparently had a hard time of it when he'd been in charge, but now he was back in his element, and everyone was enjoying the moment. Shorty felt whole with K-Bar watching his back again.

He'd discretely been putting the word out about Lennox, looking for information, but people weren't responding the way he wanted. Lennox's reputation carried more weight than his, and people seemed wary of crossing him. As hard as it was for him to admit, he didn't have the same juice anymore.

Shanice had repeatedly tried contacting him, but he'd finally blocked her number and blocked her on Facebook. He wasn't sure Adele would have told her about the threats, and he didn't care. There was no way she could pin it to him, even if she had recognised his voice. Shanice was nice, but she had outlived her usefulness.

Amy came to his mind then, as he recalled how bad he'd felt for sleeping with Shanice. It wasn't something that had happened to him before, but he wasn't sure where his relationship with Amy was going. When she had coldly told him he wasn't going to see Grace anymore after the shooting, it had felt normal, and he hadn't fought it. After he'd confessed to killing Lutel, her behaviour toward him changed, and he didn't understand why. He was a murderer, and she knew it. *Why would she even want to be near him?*

Getting another drink, Shorty tried to lose himself in the surrounding conversations, not wanting to be overwhelmed by his thoughts.

'What's going on, anyway?' said K-Bar after a while. He'd gone outside to get some fresh air and, after gulping down some water, felt better. 'Where's L?'

'I don't think he knows you're out,' said Maka. 'He hasn't really been around lately.'

'How come?'

'Who cares? He's not here, so forget him,' snapped Shorty, cutting across the conversation. K-Bar cut his eyes to Maka, who appeared unruffled by the remark. He'd heard things were frosty between the pair, but hadn't known it was so bad.

'What the hell happened with you two?' He asked Shorty.

'Doesn't matter. We're not cool, and that's that.'

For anyone else, it would have worked. Few people liked being on Shorty's bad side. K-Bar had known him too long to be worried.

'Shorty, tell me what's going on. There was no point springing me if you're gonna leave me in the dark.'

Shorty shot him a sour look, but K-Bar glanced back blankly, waiting.

'We had a fight. A proper one. We've argued and come close to fighting before, but this was different. If Akeem hadn't stepped in, one of us would have ended up seriously hurt, maybe even dead. I never thought that would happen.'

'Brother's fight, Shorty. Move on.' Secretly, K-Bar was shocked that the pair had fought. For years, they had a knack for pushing one another's buttons, but it never led to trouble. This was different, and it was worrying.

Shorty kissed his teeth, not replying. Maka saw the mood changing and switched the subject.

'Darren said Roman's doing well. Aaron's people have settled in nicely too, and they're not making any trouble.'

'What about Aaron?' replied Shorty. 'Has anyone heard from him?'

TARGET PART III

'Not since we smacked him around and dumped him in the middle of nowhere. He's dumb, but not dumb enough to come after us by himself.'

'There are plenty of other little knucklehead crews nipping at our heels. This shit with Lennox has made some crews proper brazen. They seem to think they can step up to us now.'

'Let me get out there,' said K-Bar. He wanted to prove to the crew he was still worth something after being on remand. Shorty shook his head.

'Lay low, K. We can handle the street stuff for now. Let the pigs lose your scent, then you can get back out there.'

CHAPTER TWELVE
THURSDAY 7 MAY, 2015

WHEN LAMONT AWOKE the next day, he winced, his head pounding as he glanced to his side. Anna was awake and looking at him, which he didn't like. Even the fact she was naked didn't sway him. Waking up with headaches was a regular thing nowadays, whether or not he'd been drinking. It made him irritable. Anna was still staring, her lips pinched together, fists tight.

'Do you want a coffee?' he muttered, sitting up and rubbing his forehead. Whatever answer he expected, he wasn't prepared for the one he received.

'Who's *Jenny*?'

It was as if someone had poured ice-cold water down Lamont's back. He flinched, looking away from her as he climbed out of bed. His eyes flitted around the room, wondering if she'd gone through his things while he was asleep, before remembering he had nothing with Jenny's name on.

'You said her name in your sleep,' said Anna, realising he wouldn't respond. 'Multiple times. I thought you were single?'

'I am.'

'I don't believe you, Lamont, if that's even your name. I don't believe you're a trader, so who knows what else you've lied about. Was

TARGET PART III

it worth lying to try and sleep with me?'

'I don't want to talk about it,' said Lamont, leaving the room. He stormed downstairs and through to the kitchen, splashing his face with cold water from the sink before he put the kettle on.

'What the hell was that, Lamont? Why would you walk out in the middle of a conversation?'

'I didn't want to talk about it. I still don't.'

'You don't think I deserve to know about the woman in your life after you tried sleeping with me last night? Guess that's why you couldn't get it up.'

'What part of *I don't want to talk about it* don't you understand?' snapped Lamont. He didn't want to think about Jenny while he had another woman in his house. Anna's eyes flashed with anger, but he didn't care. He was rattled and couldn't believe he'd said Jenny's name in his sleep. It was twisted on a whole new level.

'You're scum, Lamont. Don't contact me again.'

'Get the fuck out of my house,' said Lamont coldly. Anna stood her ground a moment, then after another look of disgust, flounced from the room and stomped upstairs to get her things. Nausea bubbling in his stomach, he hurried to the downstairs bathroom just in time. He emptied the contents of his stomach into the toilet until he was heaving, drawing in deep breaths.

Somewhere in the background, he heard the front door slam, but didn't move. The bodyguards would take care of her. He stayed hunched over the bowl for another few minutes, then shakily climbed to his feet. Forgoing the coffee, he headed upstairs and stood under the shower for as long as he could cope. His head was still banging, and he wanted nothing more than to crawl back into bed. He had an afternoon of meetings, though, and needed to be sharp. Rubbing his forehead once more, he went to get dressed.

'You ready?'

K-Bar turned to Shorty as they pulled up outside Marika's. He hadn't told her he was getting out so quickly, and Shorty had taken advantage of that by organising the party the previous night. After they woke up in the morning, Shorty took him to get his dreads tightened up, then for breakfast. It was Marika's day off from work, so she would be in, but the kids would be at school.

'Course I'm ready. Rika held me down when I was inside. She's a keeper.'

'I'm surprised L left you breathing after you started banging his little sis.'

K-Bar scowled. 'Don't talk about her like that, fam. This is serious.'

'Okay, man, calm down. Marika's cool. L's just proper protective over her.'

'He was. They fell out, remember? Not sure they ever really made their way back from that.'

Shorty didn't say anything. He couldn't. He and Lamont were basically going through the same thing.

'Come on. Let's get in there,' he finally said. They climbed from the car, and K-Bar tried the door, but it was locked. Kissing his teeth, he knocked.

When Marika opened the door and saw K-Bar, her eyes widened, and she flung her arms around him. His heart soared. She was as beautiful as ever, and fit nicely against him. They hugged for a few minutes, then started kissing. Shorty cleared his throat when it seemed they had forgotten about him.

'Save all that shit for after I'm gone,' he said.

'Shut up, Shorty.' Marika hugged him too. 'I'm guessing you're the reason I didn't see K last night?'

'He needed a night with the boys, and we didn't want to disturb the kids. Is everything good?'

'Everything is perfect now.' Marika gave K-Bar an adoring smile, Shorty pretending to vomit. Soon, they were all sitting in the garden with cups of tea.

'Does L know you're out?'

'Unless my solicitor or someone else told him, I doubt it.'

Marika frowned. 'What's going on?'

'I don't know,' said K-Bar. 'I'm still getting my head around things, but it doesn't appear he's with it at the moment.'

TARGET PART III

'Of course he isn't. Look at everything he's been through lately.' Marika noticed Shorty looking away with a scowl. 'What aren't you telling me?'

'Shorty and L aren't speaking,' said K-Bar, playing with his cup.

'Why would you fall out now of all times? You need each other. Can't you squash it?'

'It's not that simple, said Shorty, feeling he had repeated those words more in the past week than he had in his life.

'Course it is. He needs you, Shorty. This isn't the time to be falling out.'

'Says you,' replied Shorty. 'How many years did it take for you two to speak after you fell out?'

'That's different. He got shot, Shorty, or did you forget?'

'Look, both of you, calm down,' interjected K-Bar, as Shorty opened his mouth to retort. 'We don't need to be fighting amongst ourselves right now. We'll deal with L soon, I promise. I need to meet see him, anyway.'

Marika nodded, satisfied.

'He must be fucked up over what happened to Trinidad too. Lamont looked up to him.'

Shorty briefly lowered his head, remembering his harsh words to Lamont at the gravesite.

'*OurHood* fucked L up. It's like they turned the whole Hood against him,' said K-Bar.

'Someone needs to do something,' replied Marika, hands on hips. 'He's obviously in a bad way. He hasn't even been to see the kids lately.'

Shorty quietly listened to the pair talk, and he liked the way they looked together. Marika had always been a handful, but she seemed different around K-Bar. More composed. For someone who knew her as a bratty teen, it was nice to see her as a grown-up. She even dressed differently. More understated, less tight and revealing clothing.

Analysing them as a couple stopped him thinking about Lamont, and the guilt that occasionally slipped through. He slipped his mind to business, and all the work they still had to do in the crew. He didn't have to be cool with Lamont to use his resources.

LAMONT STILL FELT ropey even after he finished getting ready. Anna's departure had messed with his already precarious mindset. Sex was something Lamont always knew he could perform. He had a way with women, and he parlayed that into getting what he wanted from them, but if last night showed him anything, he'd lost his mojo, and that made him feel sick. He didn't want to go out and sleep with every woman on the planet, especially with how he was feeling, but at the very least, wanted to know he could.

As he left the house, he tried to put the events into perspective. He'd drunk some wine, but not enough to influence his performance. He trained and worked out, and he was in his thirties. He couldn't think of a single reason behind his *malfunction*, and that irked him.

Lamont's bodyguards fell in step as they headed for the car. None mentioned Anna, and he didn't ask.

Ahmed and Mustafa were at the warehouse when he arrived. Ahmed gave him a knowing smile, a far cry from the usual scowls he received. Their talk had done him some good.

'How was your night with Anna?' he asked, his eyes glinting. Lamont shrugged.

'I don't remember much of it. Don't think I'll be seeing her again.'

'That's too bad. You two looked good together.'

'How are we looking for today?' He changed the subject. 'The load comes in tomorrow, so I'm assuming we'll be ready?'

Ahmed nodded. 'The people are already in place, and the load will come first thing in the morning. One of Saj's old contacts contacted us today, and he wants five boxes of dark. Also, your representative, Maka, placed an order for eight boxes. Business must be improving.'

'Must be,' agreed Lamont. It was the largest order his crew had put in for a while, and he wondered what the change was. There was the possibility they had moved into some fresh territory, but it didn't matter. It meant more money for him. Maka and co didn't know about the role he'd taken, and he saw no reason to share it with them. As far as they were concerned, the *Asians* were supplying them, and that was still the case.

TARGET PART III

He spent a while talking business with Ahmed and Mustafa, then went to get some lunch at a nearby sandwich shop. He was finishing up when Marika called.

'Hey, sis. What's wrong?'

'Why does something have to be wrong for me to want to speak with my brother?'

Lamont gave her that one. They were still finding their way back, and he hadn't reached out much lately. They had reconnected at Jenny's funeral, but even that seemed like it was years ago rather than months.

'Sorry, you're right.'

'I wanted to see how you were.'

'I'm fine.'

'K's been asking about you.'

'When did you see him?'

There was an awkward pause.

'K's out. He got out yesterday.'

Lamont froze, stunned. The last time he'd spoken with his solicitor about K-Bar, they were putting a case together to have his case dismissed due to lack of evidence. Due to the reports of a witness, it was proving more difficult than expected.

What the hell had he overlooked?

'How did that happen?'

'Probably best we don't speak about it on the phone.'

'My phone is encrypted, sis. The CIA couldn't trace this call, never mind anyone else.'

'Still, I'd rather speak with you face to face. Come over later, spend some time with me and the kids. They miss you.'

'I'll come over this evening.' Lamont said goodbye and hung up.

K-Bar was out, and it was clear someone had done some work behind the scenes to facilitate that. He assumed they'd learned who the witness was and taken action, and wasn't sure how he felt about that. K-Bar murdering Naomi had been bad enough, but that was during a hectic time, and no one knew what was happening next. He would need to catch up with him and get the full story.

Anxiety churned within Lamont. The world was moving on

without him, and he felt sick over that. Nothing was going the way he wanted. He had elevated to a new level of power, but that same power had been neutered because of a war that ultimately had little to do with him. If Lennox hadn't gone after Shorty, Lamont would have never become involved in his business. Jenny would also still be alive, but he filed those thoughts away for the evening, where he would have liquor. There was nothing to be done about these things now, so he focused on what he could control. He had another person to see.

JUKIE'S WAS a mainstay in the Hood. There were many gambling spots dotted around, but Jukie's was the most well-known and respected. It was still early, but it would be open. Unless the police had shut him down, Jukie operated twenty-four hours a day and always had something going on.

Lamont headed to his spot and entered, hit immediately by the stench of body odour, hastily masked with cheap air spray. There were a few mainstays in the main room, but all the action was likely in the back rooms.

Jukie was behind the bar, humming along to a song on the radio. He perked up when he saw Lamont, grinning. Even knowing that Jukie was fairly neutral in most things that went down in Chapeltown, he felt a surge of relief to see someone in the Hood who didn't immediately vilify him. Heading closer to the bar, he firmly shook his hand.

'Good to see you, L.'

'You too, Juke. Business good?'

'Some people are staying away because of the police, but that can't be helped. Saw you at Trinidad's funeral. I was gonna say hello, but you looked preoccupied.'

Lamont nodded, accepting that. *Preoccupied* was a polite way of putting it. He had publicly argued with Trinidad's family and embarrassed himself.

'It was a tough day.'

'Truly. Trinidad was a great man. What happened to him shouldn't have happened.'

'Agreed.' Lamont bowed his head. Jukie rested his hand on Lamont's shoulder.

'It wasn't your fault, L. You need to understand that.'

'My enemies went after him to get to me. I don't see how that isn't my fault.'

'The only person to blame is the one responsible for the fire, L. You didn't do that. I can see you're not listening, though, and I doubt you came here to look at my old face, so how can I help?'

'Lennox Thompson.'

Lamont appreciated Jukie didn't immediately play dumb and pretend not to understand what he was implying.

'Lennox's people don't really stay around the Hood, and they definitely don't come around here. Last one that did got beaten with a stool by Shorty. You need to look outside the Hood if you want to find something.'

'Do you know where I should start?'

Jukie shook his head. 'If I hear anything, I'll pass it on, but people are keeping their heads down. Delroy and Lennox are playing for keeps, and no one wants to get caught in the middle of that.'

It was a fair statement and was precisely the sort of thing Lamont would expect from Jukie. He reached into his pocket and laid a stack of notes on the bar.

'You don't need to do that, L. I didn't even give you anything,' he protested.

Lamont shook his head. He respected Jukie, and knew the feeling was mutual. The old man didn't play sides, but he knew and liked Lamont, and they had always looked after one another.

'Keep the money, Juke. Keep me in the loop if you hear anything.'

'I will, L. Thank you.'

CHAPTER THIRTEEN
SATURDAY 9 MAY, 2015

BRONSON ZIPPED DOWN HAREHILLS AVENUE, turning onto Spencer Place and nearly running over a kid crossing the road.

'Watch where you're going, you little shit,' he roared over the sounds of the Drill music pumping from his speaker. Taking another turn onto Francis Street, he screeched to a stop and hopped from the car, an imposing square-headed figure in his red designer tracksuit, standing over six feet tall, with a powerful build to match. His baby mother and sometimes girlfriend, Ella, was waiting, and he hoped she had food because he was starving. He was so preoccupied that he didn't see the masked man until it was too late. The blow crunched against his jaw, and Bronson hit the ground hard. Dazed, he saw the blur of a weapon, then heard the bang and felt the searing pain as a bullet tore into his left shin.

'Keep your fingers to yourself, or next time you're dead,' warned Shorty. Stepping over the bleeding man, he hurried to his car, which sped away. A few streets away, the car stopped, and he wiped down the pistol, before dumping it down a drain. They drove to Bankside, and his luck was in. There was no one standing outside the spot he was visiting. He took off the mask, stowed another pistol, then approached. He banged on the door.

TARGET PART III

'Shorty? What are you doing around here?'

'Came to talk business. Dex in?'

The man at the door clearly didn't want to let him in, but he also didn't want to be rude, so he stepped aside and led Shorty into the living room. Two men were there, cracking jokes as they played a game of *Fifa*. One of them, a freckled mixed-race man with reddish brown hair, looked up, paling when he saw Shorty.

'Shorty, what the hell?'

Shorty pulled his gun and smacked the man that had answered the door in the side of the head. He crumpled to the floor, and Shorty held the gun on the others.

'I'm here to warn you, Dex. Once and once only; pack it up.'

'What are you talking about? What are we supposed to have done?' The freckled man replied.

'You thought you could badmouth Teflon and get away with it. I'm back now, and old rules apply. You took a few customers, made more money, but now things are back to normal. Buy from our people, or you're out of business. Same deal as that little shit Aaron. What are you saying?' His finger tightened on the trigger. Both men had been around long enough to know he didn't play when he had a gun in his hand.

'We're in. We'll buy from you lot.'

'That's a good choice. Put the word out that I'm back around. I don't care what people think they heard about the crew. We're taking back what's ours. You lot can go back to your game, but you might wanna get some help for your boy there.'

Shorty left, his work done for the day. He had put the fear of God in a few crews to show that no matter what was going on with Delroy and Lennox, these were still his streets, and they were still the best game in town. Bronson was the most brazen. He'd attempted to muscle in one of their spots, subtly thinking he could intimidate the workers into working for him. Dex was a small-timer who'd tried increasing his clientele at the expense of their crew.

The gloves were well and truly off, and word would spread throughout the Hood.

RICKY BLACK

RIGBY LEANT AGAINST his car in a parking lot in Seacroft, waiting for Terry Worthy to show. He'd left Murphy back at the office, digging into what they had unearthed about the gang war. There were over a dozen murders they had tied to the conflict, including the death of Teflon's girlfriend, and the shooting of Shorty Turner's little girl. If they had attempted to shoot back, Rigby couldn't find the link.

All the attacks were being orchestrated by Lennox and Delroy. Rigby couldn't get a line on either of them, not that it would do any good at this stage. Both men were well-trained in the ways of the street and knew better than to blatantly give orders or hold guns where people could see them. Rigby would have to wade through at least a dozen ranks to get close to Delroy in particular. He hoped Terry was taking his orders seriously.

Terry soon arrived in his Audi. Sliding from the driver's seat, he gave Rigby a cocky smile.

'Nice to see you again, chief.'

'I take it by your smiling face you have some news for me?'

'I'm still working on the gang stuff. People haven't seen Teflon around lately, and they're saying it's because he's going directly after Lenny Thompson.'

'Is that because his girl got knifed?'

'Probably. That and the barber getting roasted. Tef was proper close to Trinidad Tommy. Looked at him like a dad. Used to keep his office there and everything, probably so he could monitor him.'

'We know about the office,' said Rigby. He'd tried getting a warrant to search the place on multiple occasions, but had no probable cause. There were never any incidents on the premises, and Trinidad had been a mainstay in the community. Suddenly, Teflon being outside the barbers on the day of the two deaths didn't seem like such a coincidence. 'What are people saying about Teflon's connection to the death, or to the death of the man who was shot next to him?'

'Nowt, really. Akeem was building a nice rep as a bodyguard.'

'In what sense?'

TARGET PART III

Terry shrugged. 'He was just capable, know what I mean? That kinda thing always makes people feel safe.'

'We know he was connected to some gangs in London. Any chance any of them are gonna come up here kicking up a fuss?'

'Doubt it. Teflon always had links down there. He has links everywhere.'

Rigby was aware of this, which was part of why Teflon had always worried him. He made money for everyone he dealt with and was practised at staying out of reach. He had tidy relations with a lot of firms, but this seemed to have soured as of late. If Teflon was smart, he would dedicate time to rebuilding these relationships. Another of Rigby's worries was the street conflict overshadowing whatever moves Teflon could be making behind the scenes. He needed to get to the bottom of things as soon as possible.

'What do you have for me then?'

'I know that K-Bar and the lads had a fucking celebration. I wasn't invited, but they invited some lasses around and made a night of it.'

'Why do I care?' said Rigby, running a hand through his hair. Truth was, he did care. It still made him sick that K-Bar had taken advantage of clear disharmony within the police department, and had got himself free of his potential sentence.

'Dunno, figured you locked him up, and that you might care. He doesn't know I'm helping you lot, does he? K-Bar's a fucking psycho when he wants to be. I don't want him coming after me.'

'I'm not Murphy. I don't threaten you with someone killing you. I threaten you with you spending half your life behind bars for the sale of drugs. All jokes aside, Terry; I need more information from you. I want to know who the main killers are on each team, and where to find them.'

'How the bloody hell am I supposed to find out all that?' Terry was aghast. Rigby had no sympathy. He didn't dislike Terry, but he didn't think he was taking the potential threat of prison seriously.

'Work it out. You either help me solve this gang war, or you get us some serious dirt on your crew. I'm talking enough dirt to lock up everyone. The choice is yours.' Rigby didn't wait for Terry to reply. He climbed back in his car and drove away.

'Finally, you're here.'

Lamont gave his sister a tight smile and stepped past her into the house. They'd spoken on the phone two days ago, and in that time, she hadn't heard from him.

'Sorry. Things came up.'

'It's fine. Better late than never. Go on through, and I'll bring you a hot drink.'

Lamont's niece, Bianca, sat in the middle of the living room, her eyes glued to the television — some goofy show on *Nickelodeon*. She was a smaller version of her mother, but her eyes were darker, and her facial features more rounded. When she saw Lamont, she jumped to her feet and ran into his arms.

'Uncle L! You came?'

'Hello, Princess Bianca. How've you been?'

Lamont was made to sit with his niece, and had to pretend to be interested in the show, as she babbled and explained the characters. She curled up next to him, refusing to move even after Marika brought his drink. Showing great skill, he was able to drink it without spilling any on her.

'I missed you,' she mumbled, after he'd finished and put his cup on the nearby coffee table. Despite everything, this made Lamont smile, and he felt his heart soar. He pulled his niece closer and kissed the top of her head.

'I missed you too. Even when I'm not here, know you're always on my mind, okay?'

Bianca nodded, eyes on her show.

'How come you don't have any kids, Uncle L?' She asked, a few minutes later.

Lamont had figured Bianca to be distracted by her show, and the question stunned him for a moment.

'I don't know, baby. Guess I never figured I would be any good at being a dad.'

'I think you would make a good daddy,' she said, not even turning to look at him. Lamont blinked, feeling oddly emotional after the short conversation. He disagreed with her. The idea of being responsible for a person he'd created didn't seem natural to him. With all the issues he had, it wouldn't be fair. He loved his niece all the more for her attempt to make him feel better, and showed this by clutching her tightly until she giggled and tried to get loose.

Marika watched Lamont and Bianca together, a small smile on her face. This was the reason she'd wanted him to come and see her. She knew Bianca could make him feel better. She had him wrapped around her little finger just like Shorty's daughter, Grace, did, and he couldn't say no to either of them.

Marika felt guilt for the fallout with Lamont. She had stupidly listened to Marrion and fallen for his manipulations, escalated by their fight after Marcus died. It was mostly behind them now, but they were nowhere near as close as they once were, and seemed to walk on eggshells around each other. He seemed so different when it was him and Bianca. Unguarded, almost. It was amazing to see, and she didn't want to disturb their time together.

K-Bar and Shorty were out doing something. She didn't know what, and hadn't asked. She'd only told K-Bar to make sure he stayed out of trouble. It would be easier said than done. He was even-tempered, but seemed to get caught up in various situations. Shorty and his temper would only escalate that further if it came to it. K-Bar hadn't spoken with Lamont yet, but they needed to, and soon. Marika wanted things back to normal and hoped he could bridge the obvious gulf between Shorty and Lamont.

Soon enough, Bianca fell asleep against Lamont, and he carried her upstairs. After waking her so she could go to the toilet, and helping her brush her teeth, he carried the sleepy girl to her bed, and sat with her until she fell asleep. By the time he made it back downstairs, another cup of tea waited for him.

'You timed that well,' he said to Marika.

'It was a lucky guess. I would have microwaved it for you if it went cold.'

'Thank you, anyway.' Lamont sipped the drink and took his seat back on the sofa. Marika had already changed the channel, and was watching the evening news.

'Since when do you watch the news?' he asked, grinning.

'Sometimes it's just good to know what's going on,' Marika replied, lowering the volume and facing her brother. Bianca had revitalised him a little, but he still looked tired. There were visible bags under his eyes, and every so often, he would stifle a yawn. Clearly, he wasn't getting much sleep.

'I guess so.'

'What's been going on?' she asked.

'Nothing.'

'You look like hell.'

'Thanks. I love you too.'

'I mean it, L. What's going on? Is it Jenny?' she watched his face blanch at the mention of his former partner.

'I wish that wouldn't happen,' he mumbled.

'What?'

'Anytime someone says her name, I get this jolt, and it's like a fresh reminder she's gone. I just wish I was over it.'

'Why?'

'Why do you think? I'm here, and she isn't, and I have it weighing me down along with everything else. If she hadn't met me; if I hadn't pursued her, she would still be alive, and I have to live with that.'

'You weren't responsible for her death, L. No one blames you.'

'*I* blame me, Rika. I should have protected her, and Trinidad. They were innocents in this shit, and I let them die, so that is on me.'

'Jenny wouldn't want you to wallow. Neither of them would.'

'You can't say that.'

'Course I can. I knew them both. Maybe not as well as you did, but still. Jenny loved you, and she knew what you were. Trinidad did too. What happened to them wasn't your fault.'

Lamont didn't want to talk about it. He wanted to push it all away and put it behind him. His encounter with Anna still lingered, leaving a bad taste in his mouth. He should have never invited her back to his house, or attempted to sleep with her. Now, the guilt lingered with the failure of not being able to *perform*.

'I don't want to argue with you, but you're gonna calm down soon

TARGET PART III

and realise that I'm right. I'm making some food, and you're staying for dinner. K-Bar should be back soon, and he'll want to see you.'

He could have pointed out that K-Bar had been out a few days and hadn't looked him up, but it wasn't important. He hadn't eaten all day, and if there was one thing he knew about his little sister, it was the fact that she could truly cook.

By the time K-Bar entered, Lamont had finished his dinner and was on his third cup of tea.

'L, my bro. It's good to see you.' He had a broad smile on his face as they slapped hands. Lamont stood, and they properly greeted one another, hugging like brothers. Marika smiled at the camaraderie between the two most important men in her life.

'You too, K. You look healthy.'

'I kept my head down in there. Wasn't sure how it was gonna go, but I wasn't gonna lose my shit over it.'

Lamont nodded like he had experience dealing with prison. K-Bar took a seat, and Marika put a plate of food in front of him a few minutes later. The three of them stared at the television in silence, waiting for K-Bar to finish. When he did, Marika took his plate despite his protests.

'You two talk. I need to wash up anyway.'

'How have you been?' asked K-Bar after a few moments.

'You're the one that was locked up,' said Lamont.

'Like I said, I kept my head down. I'm sorry about Trinidad and Jen.'

Lamont nodded, swallowing down the lump in his throat. He didn't want to show weakness in front of K-Bar. K-Bar seemed to understand and didn't press the issue. They weren't as close as K-Bar and Shorty, but he had always been able to sit quietly with him, which was a nice distinction he'd always enjoyed.

'How did you get out?' Lamont asked after a moment.

'Got a message to Shorty through my solicitor. Worked out where the Feds were getting their information from, and I sent Shorty to handle it.'

'Who was the leak?'

'Do you remember Adele? Party girl who was always around town?'

Lamont shook his head.

'You'd know her if you saw her. Anyway, she was the missing link. After the Chink shit and then your shooting, we kinda forgot about her.'

Lamont didn't understand how you could forget about a potential witness, but he'd nearly died during that timeframe. K-Bar had stepped up out of necessity, so he grudgingly accepted it.

'Did Shorty hurt her?'

'Nah. Just words and a bribe. He was on some *007* shit. He used to grind her sister back in the day. Ended up getting in touch with her, sweet-talking her into bed, and then following her to the spot where Adele was staying.'

'If she was a witness, why wasn't she under surveillance?' Lamont was silently impressed with Shorty's actions.

'Who knows? I'm not overthinking it. He got word to her anyway, and she told the police she lied. Next minute I'm out.'

'I'm glad, K. I don't want it to seem like I was neglecting you. Levine was looking into it, and if it came to court, he was confident you wouldn't be convicted. Just be careful.'

'Don't worry, L. I know how to stay low-key. You don't need to feel guilty, either. These things happen, and it wasn't anything you did that got me caught. I know you would have sprung me like you did Shorty.' K-Bar's expression softened. 'What happened with you two?'

'We both said things, and shit got out of control.'

'You'll find your way back to where you were.'

'Do you need anything now that you're out? We have a package for you.'

'Maka already sorted it. Thanks for looking after me.'

'You're part of the team,' said Lamont, realising once again just how out of the loop he was. Thankfully, Maka and the others were all operating at a higher frequency and making up for his lack of attentiveness.

'Still, it's appreciated.'

'Have you spoken to Fiona?'

TARGET PART III

Some of the light in K-Bar's eyes seemed to dissipate at the mention of his baby mother.

'I tried to see Levon yesterday, but she wasn't having any of it. Threatened to call police on me if I didn't leave, so I'm keeping my distance for now.'

'Probably for the best,' Lamont agreed. Fiona was a pleasant woman with a vicious streak, and things had never been plain sailing for her and K-Bar. He could see her using his son against him as a way of keeping him compliant.

'Streets are hot at the moment. Del's making some moves against Lennox. Surprised you're not doing the same.'

Lamont didn't see the need in mentioning his current plans to K-Bar.

'Delroy's handling it.'

'I'm surprised Shorty is being calm, after Lennox popped Grace.'

'Shorty's had to do a lot of growing up lately.'

'I just need to get you two back on the same level now. There are some little crews that are talking shit and trying to nibble away at the team. Anyone said anything to you?'

'They can handle things without me,' said Lamont.

'What are you doing in the meantime? I know you. You've always got a plan.'

'I'm playing things quiet at the moment, K. I don't need to remind you to do the same, right?'

'Right.'

K-Bar continued to discuss street politics, but he tuned out. It didn't interest him at the moment. Soon, K-Bar went to sit with Marika when she'd finished washing up. Lamont watched the pair of them cuddling, as he relaxed on the sofa, his eyes growing heavy. He was asleep before he had even realised what had happened.

'Looks like he needed that.'

K-Bar and Marika watched Lamont sleep, as he softly snored.

'He looks wrecked, Rika. If I didn't know better, I'd think he was on drugs.'

'Not drugs necessarily. Drink maybe. It's been hard for him, like I told you lot the other day. He's clearly not operating at one hundred percent. I think he should speak with someone about his issues.'

'Someone like a therapist?'

Marika nodded.

'L doesn't need to speak to a therapist. He's the strongest guy I know. Give him some time, and I bet you he'll bounce back from all of this shit.' K-Bar hugged Marika against him, planting a kiss on her lips. She returned it, but deep down, she wasn't as convinced as K-Bar. Lamont was in a bad way, and she didn't think it would get better without something drastic happening.

CHAPTER FOURTEEN
MONDAY 11 MAY, 2015

LAMONT WINCED as he woke up. It was morning, he was curled up on Marika's sofa, and his phone was ringing. Sitting up, he realised she'd put a blanket over him while he was sleeping. He wished she'd woken him up and sent him home, but it was too late to think about that now. Reaching for his phone, he cleared his throat and answered.

'Hello?'

'L, it's Jukie. Did I wake you?'

'No, it's fine. Everything okay?'

'That thing we were discussing the other day. I might have a lead. I heard some people talking about a few of Lennox's guys going in and out of a spot on Jackie Smart Court. Not sure if they're planning a move or if it's a stash spot, but I thought you should know.'

'Thanks a lot, Jukie.' Lamont was on his feet now, aches and fatigue forgotten. 'What's the address? I'll take care of you for this.'

After hanging up, Lamont headed to the kitchen to make a drink and freshen up. This was potentially a tip he had been waiting for. Jukie had previously said that Lennox's people didn't stick around the Hood for fear of detection. If they were changing up their pattern, he could figure it out and use it to track down Lennox.

He was washing up his empty mug when Marika entered the

kitchen. Her hair was still wet from a recent shower, but she was dressed in a shirt and smart trousers.

'Take it you're working today?' he asked. Marika nodded.

'I finish at two. Bianca will be up in a minute so I can get her ready for school. How are you feeling?'

'I'm fine.'

Marika gave him a quizzical look. 'You said you were fine yesterday, but you passed out on my sofa and wouldn't wake up.'

'I was tired, I'm sorry. I'll sleep at my place next time.'

'That's not the point, and you know it,' replied Marika, sighing. 'Look, hang around for a bit, and I'll make you some breakfast. At least I'll know you've had one good meal today.'

SHORTY WAS in the kitchen at Amy's. He had come early so they could visit Grace, and was cooking breakfast. His purging of the streets had been flawless so far. He had pacified Aaron, Bronson, and several other crews, and had changed the perception of how the other crews looked at Lamont's organisation.

The money was creeping back up, and he took advantage, having Grace moved to a private healthcare facility. Lamont's links were wizards when it came to moving money around and making it legit, though Shorty had no idea how they did it. Not willing to forget about Dionte, he sent money to Stacey in Huddersfield. He hoped they were safe, and wondered if it was worth the risk.

'What are you thinking so hard about?' Amy entered the kitchen, stunning in a green t-shirt and black peasant skirt. Shorty checked the eggs he was cooking, and decided to be honest.

'I was thinking about Stace and Dionte. Now that we've sorted Grace. Maybe you should get out of town for a bit, just until things blow over.'

Amy shook her head. 'I want to stay close by in case Grace needs me. Are you really that nervous that something will happen?'

'Things are going on out there, Ames. They're not just gonna go away because I'm happy and our daughter is getting better.'

TARGET PART III

'Make sure you look after us then.' Amy winked, then went to get the plates and cutlery ready for the breakfast.

'Is there an *us* then?' he asked a while later, when they were finishing. The facility had more flexible visiting times, but they wanted to spend as much time with Grace as possible. Amy's face reddened at the implication.

'I think there might be something. I've always cared about you, but in the past, it never seemed we were on the same wavelength. Now, we might be.'

'What are we gonna do about it then?' said Shorty, his heart racing. 'I still want you. I've always wanted you.'

'You always wanted sex, Shorty. Don't get it twisted.'

'This is deeper than that.'

Amy looked away. 'It might be. I won't deny that. I don't think we should talk about it yet.'

'Why wait? We're both here now, so let's break it down.'

'Shorty, I just said I don't want to talk about it yet. Please respect that and let's go see our daughter,' said Amy waspishly. Shorty decided he would drop it for now, but would definitely revisit the subject. He still didn't understand what had changed other than Amy knowing the lengths he had gone to in order to avenge what had happened to Grace. It was weird to think that fact alone might have completely changed how she felt about him. He stayed quiet, waiting for her to get ready. She stood in the doorway, smiling at him.

'Are you ready to go?'

'Right behind you, Ames.'

―――――

LAMONT WAS HOME, thinking about his sister and K-Bar. They looked good together. Far more compatible than any of the men she had messed with before. He was still getting used to her changes. The argument they'd had where he'd called her a parasite, had clearly had an effect. He regretted his comments, but was pleased she'd matured.

He'd spent his day pottering around, then had a drink before heading to bed. He switched off the lights and tried to sleep, willing his body to fall asleep at a normal time.

His phone began buzzing, and he fumbled for it, answering without checking the caller.

'Yeah?'

'Hello L.'

'Charlotte?'

He could hear the smile in her voice. Charlotte was the former girlfriend of an old acquaintance, whom he'd spent time with in the recent past. Stupidly, he'd asked her on a date over a month ago, before getting cold feet and avoiding her.

'You sound shocked to hear from me, but I'm the one who has been waiting for you to call.'

'I'm sorry.' Lamont sat up in bed, wincing as he felt his bones creak.

'Are you really? What's going on, L?'

He rubbed his eyes.

'Everything,' he admitted, his head aching. His mouth was dry, and he wondered if it was worth going to get some more liquor.

'Talk to me.'

'Look, I'm sorry for getting you caught up in my twisted web, Charlotte, but trust me when I say that you're best off staying away from me.'

Charlotte said nothing for a long moment, and he waited for the click of the call ending.

'This isn't a conversation to be held over the phone. I want to see you and talk to you.'

'Char—'

'You need to speak to someone, L. I can hear it in your voice. I can come to you, or you can come to me. Choice is yours.'

Lamont closed his eyes. Sleep wasn't coming, and it was clear Charlotte wasn't taking no for an answer.

'I'll come to you.'

———

TARGET PART III

Lamont showered and threw on a t-shirt and jeans. After a quick drink, he drove to Charlotte's, two guards following in another vehicle. They would park down the street and shadow him to make sure there were no issues.

Charlotte's Chapel Allerton spot was as well-tended as it had been the last time he visited. She waited by the door, her expression unreadable as she stepped aside and let him in. Charlotte had a regal beauty, similar to Jenny; brown hair, eyes a startling shade of grey. Lamont tried ignoring this as they walked down the hallway and into the living room. It was wide and airy, with deep red sofas and throw pillows, a fruity scent punctuated by two candles at the top of a marble mantlepiece. She signalled for him to sit.

'What are you drinking?'

'Coffee if you've got it. I'd prefer to mainline it into my veins if you have the equipment.'

This got a smile. She sashayed to the kitchen, and as she walked away, he took note of the pyjama bottoms and sleeveless top she wore, then turned away. Anna had taught him he couldn't rely on that. He'd tried losing himself with her, and it had backfired spectacularly. Closing his eyes, he pushed her and their awkward night from his mind.

'You seem the sort who likes bland coffee,' said Charlotte, as she held out a steaming cup. Lamont took it.

'*Bland coffee* is fine.'

'Did I wake you?' Charlotte sat next to him, folding her legs under her. 'You sounded sleepy.'

'I was in bed, but I wasn't asleep,' he said.

'What's been happening then?'

'Nothing. Everything is fine.'

'Why didn't you contact me then?'

Lamont shrugged. 'Things got hectic in the streets, and I didn't want to get you caught up.'

'Because I'm a defenceless little girl who needs a big powerful man to protect her?'

That irked Lamont.

'Because your ex got gunned down over a street beef, and I didn't think you'd want the reminder,' he snapped.

Charlotte looked down, still clutching her cup. Lamont sipped his coffee to have something to do. He regretted his attitude, but she had asked him to come, despite his attempts to let her down gently.

'I can understand that, I guess,' she finally said. 'I suppose what I'm interested in is why you're still doing it?'

'Why would you care about that?'

'Because I'm madly in love with you,' she deadpanned. Despite himself, Lamont chuckled.

'Seriously,' she pressed.

'Because I have to,' said Lamont. 'I lost someone close to me, and I have to make it right.'

'And that means staying around the danger?'

Lamont didn't respond. He didn't need to. Charlotte continued to watch him, and he had the feeling she would survey him all night if needed. He cleared his throat.

'Why am I here, Charlotte?'

'I don't understand why you're trying to cut me out.'

'I already explained why.'

'Tell me what's going on? Whatever you're doing, it's taking a toll, L. When you were at my door, you looked like you were going to keel over.'

'I'm just tired.'

'Tired, but you couldn't sleep . . . how long has that been going on?'

'A while. I haven't exactly been keeping count,' he replied.

Do you think your state of mind might be tied to whatever it is you're doing?'

Lamont shrugged. She was probing, and he didn't like it.

Charlotte was shocked at Lamont's appearance. His eyes were bloodshot, and it was clear he wasn't in the best way. There was an air of vulnerability about him. The power he normally resonated seemed tapered, diminished somehow.

'L, just talk to me. I won't judge, I promise.'

Lamont took a deep breath, there was no way to avoid the conversation other than to leave, and he was tired of running away. Charlotte

TARGET PART III

was here and wanted to listen. Maybe if he confided in her, she would leave him alone.

'Jenny's death broke me,' he confessed. 'Everyone keeps telling me I shouldn't feel guilty over what happened to her, but I do, and I can't shift it. Every time I think I have, I get deeper into whatever hole I've dug for myself. I lost a business, and more than that, I lost a friend when Trinidad Tommy died. Time after time, he went to bat for me, and now he's gone, and the community rightfully hates me for it. So, I'm here, with no one I can really turn to, and it's no more than I deserve.'

Charlotte didn't respond immediately when Lamont finished. He felt slightly better after letting it out, but the guilt still lived deeply in the pit of his stomach, and the worrying part was that he wasn't sure it would ever diminish. He wasn't sure he would ever be normal again.

'How you're feeling is perfectly normal, L.'

The statement didn't make Lamont feel any better, and he didn't respond. Charlotte shifted closer.

'You're being too hard on yourself.'

'I'm not being hard enough. They're dead, and I'm alive, and it just feels like I've lost something. I hate feeling so fucking helpless, and I don't know how to fix it.'

Lamont's resolve nearly broke, and Charlotte wrapped her arms around him now, hugging him tightly. He initially tried to shift away from her soft touch, but she hung on, and he relented, losing himself in her slim curves, and the wildflower scent emanating from her. They sat quietly for a long while, and Lamont slowly felt himself relaxing under her tender touch.

K-BAR AND MARIKA were lying in bed holding one another, the *Netflix* movie paused in the background. It was shocking for K-Bar how easily things had returned to normal for them. They were out in the open now. Lamont knew about them and seemed to have semi-accepted it, though he wouldn't be surprised to find a *protective brother talk* in his future. He didn't mind the prospect. He cared deeply for Marika and her children, and he wanted to commit to her if she would let him. They were equals, which was a balance he'd never had in any of his previous relationships. Marika had her own baggage to deal with. Her relationship with the Manchester gangster, Marrion Bernette, had left scars that even years later, she was trying to work past. He admired her inner strength.

'Your bro looks tired lately, don't you think?'

'You want to talk about L now?' Marika giggled, highlighting the fact they were both naked.

'Seriously. I was talking business with him the other day, and it was like he wasn't even listening. I dunno what he's got going on, but it's fucking him up.'

'It's Jenny. I told you and Shorty that when we were all here.'

'This is L we're talking about, Rika. We call him *Teflon* for a reason. He's bigger than that, and he's not the sort to let murder affect his business.'

Marika scoffed.

'He loved her. I don't know what that means to you or Shorty or anyone, but this is different. You didn't see Lamont at her funeral. Her death destroyed him. He's not even close to recovering yet.'

'Is it really that deep?'

'Of course it is. Next time you see him, try truly looking at him, and then tell me what you see.'

'Shorty thinks he's shook over Lennox. He thinks that's why he's hiding out from the crew.'

'What do you think?' Marika's tone was crisp, and she knew it. Despite knowing K-Bar meant well, she didn't like the implication that her brother was being weak, and she didn't like the fact he was discussing it with Shorty, who he *knew* wasn't even talking to Lamont.

'I don't know. I saw them together, and I know L liked her, and he was ready to walk away from the game for her, but he didn't. They broke up before she died.'

'I doubt they would have stayed that way. I was friends with her, even when me and L weren't talking, and I think she may have loved him even more than he did her. She stuck by him all the way through

TARGET PART III

his recovery. A woman doesn't do that if there aren't genuine feelings involved.'

'L's rich.'

'So was Jenny. She had her own business and her own money. Plus, her parents are clearly loaded.'

'How do you know that?' K-Bar had never heard Lamont mention Jenny's parents.

'Because I was at the funeral and I met them. They're super rich. Trust me on that. Jenny didn't need L's money, and she didn't care about his status. Maybe that's why he recognised it and can't work past it?'

'I think you might be looking too much into it.'

'Maybe I am,' conceded Marika. 'Tell me about the war. What's going on with Lennox?'

'He's something else,' K-Bar admitted. 'I didn't expect him to last so long. No one did. He's basically fighting a war on two fronts. Realistically, he shouldn't have been able to go toe to toe with Delroy, never mind be able to take shots at us like he has.'

'How do you think he did it?'

K-Bar shrugged. 'I'm not sure. Len always had skills. Marcus liked him. So did Shorty back in the day. He was against drugs, but otherwise, he'd have probably been down with the crew.'

Marika mulled that one over. She vaguely remembered Lennox from back in the day. K-Bar was still talking, so she tuned back in.

'We've focused more on rebuilding than going after him directly. Delroy's people are all over him now.'

'Is Delroy in contact with L?'

'I think so. What I've told you is what people told me. I've been trying to get back up to speed with everything going on. This Shorty and L thing is stressing me out too. It's not natural for them to not be talking. He's working with the crew again, and I don't even think L knows.'

'Do you think he would mind?'

'No. L's still the one in charge. If he really wanted Shorty cut off, he'd stop paying him. I just don't think the crew is his number one priority right now, and people are noticing.'

'Can you bring them back together?'

'I think so,' admitted K-Bar. 'The timing just needs to be right.'

———

LAMONT WAS SITTING around considering his next move. He had men discreetly watching Jackie Smart Court, and they had reported seeing several of Lennox's men there. He'd done nothing regarding the spot yet, but he'd had the members of Lennox's team he'd seen there under surveillance. He didn't want to rush any of his moves. Lennox had a knack for countering, and he wanted to make sure that the moves counted.

Jukie clearly liked the money Lamont gave him for the tip, because he'd been in contact again, with another spot, this one a drop-off spot. He didn't know many details, but he had given him a name that more than made up for it.

Sinclair.

No surname, and no real profile, just a young, temperamental kid who'd been bragging about a murder he'd committed. The murder of Akeem. Lamont had flooded the Hood with men looking for him after the shooting, but he'd got away in all the confusion. Now, he was out and about, running his mouth, and Lamont wanted badly to put him in the ground.

For Jukie's trouble, he had given him three thousand pounds, and made sure he put the word out about Teflon's generosity. He admired the fear tactic that Lennox was using to suppress snitches, but cash rewards were always great for testing resolve — one reason Lamont had always paid his people well, lest they get greedy and take someone else's money to work against him.

Lamont had two spots he could move against, but one of them was helping him understand the pieces of Lennox's crew. He'd heard the name *Mark Patrick* rumbling around, but there were few details attached to the name. Lennox was clearly keeping his closest pieces to his chest, having learned after what had happened to Nikkolo. Sharma had been a great help with surveillance and tracking, and Jukie had contacted some freelancers who were always after a payday, meaning Lamont didn't have to drain the crew's resources more than he had to.

His talk with Charlotte had been a strange one, and he wasn't sure what to make of it. He hadn't mentioned his failed dalliance with Anna, but admitting how he was feeling about Jenny's murder had felt good. He'd felt clearer and slept well after eventually leaving Charlotte's that night. The guilt resurfaced in the morning, reinforcing his belief that he would never feel better. This state of mind was becoming the new normal for him, and that was a terrifying prospect. It made him want to speed up his actions against Lennox. The sooner he got his revenge, the sooner he could focus on making himself strong again.

Where he now stood with Charlotte, he didn't have a clue. He didn't want to rush into anything, and his experiences with Anna had shown him that wouldn't work. She didn't seem to expect anything from him other than to be a shoulder to cry on, but that was dangerous. His life had taught him that people weren't around forever. Whether they were killed, or they fell out, or they simply moved away, you needed to rely on yourself and be strong enough to cope with whatever life threw at you.

Lamont had been that way for a long time. He had been an island; an *army-of-one*, and now he felt like a quivering basketcase that needed his hand holding. It made him feel like a weak child, and that simply wasn't good enough.

Forcing his thoughts back to the surveillance situation, he had a decision to make. Leaving the spot on Jackie Smart Court would work for now, but he was considering giving Delroy the tip about the drop-off spot. Delroy had his own men, and was determined to go all out against Lennox's forces. It would be prudent to stay in the shadows, and let him fight off the first waves of Lennox's troops. Whether or not Delroy complied, Lamont would be the one to kill Lennox. Whatever Delroy did after was up to him.

With that in mind, he finished the gin and lemonade he'd been nursing for the past thirty minutes, then called Delroy.

'Good to hear from you, L. How are you?'

'I'm fine. I need to talk to you. It's important.'

'I'm home. Stop by anytime. I'll have a drink ready.'

TRUE TO HIS WORD, Delroy had a glass of brandy waiting when he arrived. He wasn't a fan of mixing drinks at the best of times, yet in all the years he had known Delroy, he'd never seen him drinking gin, and there was a chance he didn't stock it. He held out his glass, and Delroy clinked it. They sipped in silence.

'What do you want to speak about?' Delroy asked.

'I have a location for you. It's a drop-off spot Lennox is using. Don't know exactly what for, but I'm guessing weapons or maybe a warehouse for his people.'

'Who'd you get the info off?'

'A trusted source.'

Delroy's eyes bored into Lamont's. He put the glass on the desk in front of him.

'You don't wanna share it?'

'Not yet.'

'Why are you giving it to me?'

'You said yourself last time we spoke face to face. You need this.'

Delroy continued to watch him, clearly trying to understand his angle. Lamont waited him out, in no hurry to rush anything.

'I'll send a team to check it out.'

'Fine. One thing, though.'

Delroy grinned. 'Here we go. I knew there was something.'

'Do you know a kid called Sinclair?'

'Heard my people talking about him. He's a little psycho Lennox has running around doing shootings. We haven't caught up to him yet.'

'He's the one who killed Akeem.'

Delroy's eyes softened, understanding immediately.

'If he's there, he's yours. I'll tell my people to capture him alive, but if he won't come quietly, he's dying with the rest.'

Lamont wondered if Delroy had tried interrogating any of the people he'd ambushed, or if they had simply been killed or maimed. In the grand scheme, it didn't really matter.

'How have you been since we last spoke?' Delroy asked.

TARGET PART III

Lamont savoured his drink. 'Everyone thinks there's something wrong with me.'

'Who do you mean when you say *everyone*?' Delroy settled back in his chair.

'K-Bar, Marika . . . random women on the street,' muttered Lamont. Delroy chuckled.

'Be glad so many people care about you.'

Lamont felt a wave of shame spread through his body. Delroy was right. He doubted Delroy had anyone who cared about him the same way. He'd said his daughter hated him and his wife refused to speak to him. As sad as his life was at the moment, at least he had people he could speak to.

Delroy could read the look on Lamont's face. He wouldn't let him blame himself for something else he couldn't control.

'Don't feel sorry for me, L. I made some shitty decisions in the past, and they're coming back to haunt me. Make sure you make better ones.' Delroy rubbed his head. 'How the hell did you get K-Bar out? I thought he was looking at decades.'

'Shorty handled it. He had a word with a witness, and she told the truth about what she knew. They couldn't hold K after that.'

'Shorty sorted it . . .' Delroy rubbed his chin, eyes probing Lamont. 'How do you feel about that?'

'They're friends.'

'That's not an answer.'

Lamont blew out a breath, shaking his head.

'I don't know what you want me to say.'

'Yes, you do. Shorty coming back with a bang and helping free his best friend. Do you see that as a threat to your power?'

'No,' replied Lamont, and he honestly didn't. He liked the fact Shorty had done it, and until Delroy had mentioned it, he hadn't considered the possibility he would have an ulterior motive.

'This game of ours, it's a show, L. You know that as well as I do. For most people, especially those on the lower levels, the perception is the reality. Shorty is getting involved in your crew politics, but he can't even spare a polite word for you. Does that seem right?'

'I think you're reaching. Shorty and I both crossed the line. Regardless, he helped build that crew.'

'Maybe so, but it's still *your* crew. Without you, he'd have a record longer than my arm. They all would have.'

'You don't know that.'

'You mean, you don't want to admit that. You're in denial because you feel bad over the things that have happened, but you need to pick yourself up and get things back in line, before it's too late. How's the thing with the Asians going?'

'I had a problem, but I resolved it.'

'People not respecting you?'

Lamont chuckled at Delroy's attempts to instigate. 'Respect isn't a problem. The two people under me were proteges of Akhan.'

'Sounds awkward.'

'It was. One of them is fairly laid back, but the other guy was prickly. I took him out for dinner, and now we understand each other's position.'

Delroy had an approving look on his face.

'I'm glad it's working out for you. Is it enough?'

'I . . .' Lamont didn't know how to answer. 'I guess it's too early to tell.'

They sat in silence for a while. Lamont expected Delroy to send someone to the drop-off spot immediately, but he was more patient than Lamont had given him credit for.

'Are you hungry?'

'No.'

'When did you last eat?'

'I don't keep count of the hours.'

'You need to keep your strength up. People would probably stop going on about how tired you look if you took proper care of yourself.'

'Everyone said I look tired, not thin,' said Lamont. Delroy waved him off.

'It's all connected, and you know it. I'm gonna make us something, and we're gonna hang a little bit. I'll sort this Lennox business later.'

CHAPTER FIFTEEN
THURSDAY 14 MAY, 2015

DAYS LATER, Lamont assessed the moves that had been made. Delroy had indeed struck against the spot, sending in a team. There were four shooters there, who were caught completely off guard. Sinclair wasn't among them. Lamont didn't know if he had received pre-warning something might happen, or if he simply wasn't staying there, but regardless, he was in the wind, and this irked him.

Delroy saw it as a win. As well as wiping out the team with no casualties of his own, he had seized several weapons along with ten thousand pounds in cash hidden upstairs under the bed in the main bedroom. The money was irrelevant, but it was still money Lennox couldn't use against him.

Lamont hoped it would lead to more tips being thrown his way. He had protected Jukie as a source, and even Delroy didn't know about him. He would need to be careful going forward. If Lennox suspected where the information was coming from, he wouldn't hesitate to retaliate against Jukie with extreme prejudice.

It was after midnight, and Lamont was wide awake. He was comfortable, but couldn't sleep, and didn't even want to leave his bed to get another drink. Charlotte had told him the last time they spoke that he could contact her any time, but he couldn't ring her so late. He didn't even know how to put across how he was feeling and hated the fact he was so conflicted over this situation. He was torn between letting Delroy completely go after Lennox, and doing it himself. Delroy had as much right as he did to pursue Lennox. Two of his children had been murdered by him, and he had outright stated he had nothing else to lose.

So, why did Lamont feel he had an equal right? Why did he feel that he too had nothing else to lose?

He had family that was becoming more distant by the day, and he had associates. There was nothing preventing him from putting his life on the line in the same fashion. There was no Jenny.

Closing his eyes, Lamont searched down deep within himself, wanting to know if there was a way to walk away and leave it up to Delroy. The need for revenge remained all-consuming; he grew angrier the longer he lay there, staring at the ceiling. He felt tears prickling his eyes, wishing he was strong enough to cope with whatever was happening to him. He wished he could be *Teflon* instead of Lamont the weakling.

He thought back to a time he'd done his best to repress.

The time after his parents had died, and his Aunt had become the primary carer for him and Marika. He remembered hugging Marika as she wouldn't stop crying for their mum. Aunt Carmen had approached with a smile that, even as a child, he didn't trust and had told him she would look after Marika. When he'd told her he could do it, he had seen her eyes turn cold, and a fear glissaded through his body.

That same night, she beat him with a belt until he cried, for disobeying her. The pain faded, but that feeling of utter helplessness had prevailed, and he felt the same way now. He wanted nothing more than to bury his head and stay hidden, and the feeling frustrated him to his core. There was so much going on that it wasn't a realistic option for him.

Taking a deep breath, he wiped his eyes and tried to relax. He needed to get some rest. Ahmed had set up a meeting with another buyer tomorrow, and he would need to be present for the introduction.

TARGET PART III

The ringing phone put paid to that idea, and he snatched it up without checking the number.

'Yeah?'

'Did I wake you, Teflon?'

Lamont's blood ran cold. His stomach clenched, his mouth opening and closing.

'You've got some nerve calling me.'

Lennox sounded calm, almost too calm, which Lamont loathed. With everything going on, and the attacks Delroy had made against him, he expected Lennox to sound agitated, but he didn't.

'We need to talk, and I didn't think you would be receptive to a face-to-face meeting.'

'I'd be receptive to it. The chance to tear your head off is appealing.'

'You seem angry. Would you like me to call back in the morning after you've slept?'

'Do you think this is a fucking joke?' snapped Lamont, infuriated by his calm manner.

'Do you want to hear what I have to say?'

'Talk then. Stop wasting my time and tell me what you want.'

'Are you working with Delroy?'

Lamont didn't understand the point of the conversation. *Why would Lennox call him to ask about Delroy?*

'Is that really why you wanted to speak with me?'

'Don't avoid the question. Are you?'

'Delroy doesn't need me to take you down.' Lamont wasn't explicitly mentioning his involvement. If Lennox wasn't watching for him, it would enable him to hit harder later.

'Do you remember our last meeting?'

'Yes.'

'I told you then, Chapeltown was in a funk. Do you think it's any better?'

'You're the one pillaging the streets trying to kill Delroy's men.'

'I can't stop my people from defending themselves. He has a vendetta against me.'

'I'm not re-treading this shit.' Lamont's muscles quivered. His anger hadn't abated in the slightest. 'Tell me what the hell you want.'

'I told you at that meeting that I didn't authorise what happened to Shorty's daughter. In that same vein, my men weren't supposed to kill your girlfriend. Nor were they supposed to kill Trinidad.'

'You expect me to believe that crap? What about Akeem? Wasn't he worthy of avoiding death?'

'Akeem was a soldier. He knew the rules. I instructed my men to kidnap your girl. I needed something to calm you down, to enable you to hear what I was really saying to you that day.'

'How the fuck did she end up dead then?' Lamont knew he needed to calm down, but couldn't. This man was responsible for Jenny's murder, yet he was calmly trying to justify his actions.

'One of my men was overzealous. She was a tiger and fought for her freedom. She grabbed the knife and ended up dead in the struggle.

'And now what? You want to apologise?'

'I wanted you to understand that I'm not the monster you think I am, and that our goals are not much different. You care about Chapeltown, and so do I.'

'Trinidad cared about Chapeltown too,' said Lamont through gritted teeth. 'You had him burned alive, and for what?'

'He wasn't supposed to be in the building. The barber's was retaliation for what your people did to Nikkolo. I retaliated, but I didn't want Trinidad harmed.'

The entire conversation was surreal, and he couldn't get his head around any of it. There was no reason for Lennox to call and say these things. He couldn't understand his angle, unless it was to keep him from attacking any further. It was short-sighted. Even if he pacified Lamont, there was still Delroy to deal with.

'Do you really expect me to believe anything you say?'

'I expect you to remember my reputation. It was the same reputation that led to you meeting me that day. I have no reason to lie. Whatever is going to happen with us will happen, but it was important you knew the truth.'

Lamont didn't reply. His head hurt from processing the information. He wasn't in the right state of mind to deal with this. He felt sluggish, overly tired, and far from his best.

'You can have the one responsible.'

TARGET PART III

Lamont had zoned out, but those words brought him back.

'What?'

'The man who stabbed her. He should be punished, right? For taking her from you.'

'What's your game here?' Lamont's eyes narrowed.

'Nothing other than what I've already said.'

'I don't trust you or your setups.'

'That's up to you. Regardless, you can have the name and a location, and if you choose not to do anything with that information, that's your choice.'

'What do you want? You never give something for nothing.'

'Like I said, take whatever action you deem necessary. We'll speak again soon, Teflon. Get some rest.'

Lennox hung up. Lamont stared at the phone as if he expected it to make him appear. He didn't even know where to start with the information he'd been given. Lennox hadn't sounded at all rattled by anything that was happening, which was worrying. He couldn't fathom his angle. It took a certain level of balls to call up an enemy and calmly relay information you didn't need to give them. Even after all the hits Lennox had taken, he was still scheming.

Lamont wanted nothing more than to roll over and dismiss his words, but then his phone buzzed, and he had a name: *Ryan Peters*. There was an address too. He recognised it to be in Seacroft. Despite his conflict and the fact he didn't trust Lennox Thompson, there was absolutely no doubt in his mind about his next action.

He couldn't let the chance for revenge go.

CHAPTER SIXTEEN

THURSDAY 14 MAY, 2015

LAMONT WAS SHOCKED by his mood change the morning after the conversation with Lennox Thompson. After so little sleep combined with the drama, he'd expected to wake up in a foul, lethargic mood. Yet he hadn't. He'd climbed out of bed at 5 am, showered, exercised, then had a cup of coffee. He felt sharp and alert in a way he hadn't in a while, and it shocked him.

He was waiting on a phone call back about Ryan Peters. He'd never heard his name before, yet this man had killed Jenny. He'd extinguished the life of someone Lamont loved, and it seemed a little flat that this was him: Some loser hiding out in Seacroft, likely unaware of what was about to befall him.

There was always the possibility he was walking into a trap. He knew Lennox could be trying to set him up, but he'd had his opportunity. Only a few weeks ago, he'd had Lamont at gunpoint, with Sinclair there to pull the trigger. He could have killed him, but killed Akeem instead. Lennox had got under his skin all over again, and now he was reconsidering what he knew. He had known Lennox a long time ago through Marcus. He was a man of his word, and though he'd hurt people in the past; he wasn't indiscriminate with it. He'd told him not to involve himself. He'd told him he didn't want Grace harmed, but

TARGET PART III

wanted Shorty dead. It was possible he was even telling the truth about Trinidad.

Adrenaline spiking, Lamont did some more training before his meeting. He would arrange a meeting with Delroy later and get his thoughts.

———

DELROY SLID a drink across to Lamont. These meetings had become so relaxed that he didn't even ask if he wanted one anymore.

'I didn't expect to hear from you so quickly. You know we didn't find Sinclair at that spot, right?'

'This isn't about that. I received an interesting phone call last night.' Lamont told Delroy what Lennox had said. He listened in silence.

'He's a crafty bastard. He wanted to get in your head, and he's definitely succeeded.'

'Do you think that's all it is?' A day of meetings and work with Ahmed hadn't robbed him of the confusion regarding Lennox's potential motives. He couldn't pinpoint the exact game Lennox was playing, but the man's words had undoubtedly impacted him.

'He could be trying to draw a wedge between us. Turning us against each other is probably the best card he can play right now.'

'He made sense,' Lamont admitted, as hard as that was. He knew Lennox's rep, and *ruthless but fair*, seemed to suit him. Lennox had his own code and had resisted the money being made selling drugs, remaining in his own lane. That took tremendous strength of character.

'Len's not stupid. He wouldn't have lasted as long as he has without that. He must know he's on the ropes now. I'd lay money on that being the reason he contacted you.'

'What do I do then?'

Delroy sipped his drink, then lit a cigarette. Lamont hated the smell, but he could put up with it.

'What do you want to do?'

'I want to find this Ryan Peters guy, and I want to kill him. Right now, my instincts are rusty, though. I've made one wrong move after another this year, and I don't want to make that worse.'

Delroy scoffed, shaking his head.

'You're the smartest person I know, L. Believe me when I say that you were built for the game we play. Never doubt yourself.'

Lamont wasn't sure how Delroy's praise was supposed to make him feel, but *uneasy* fit. The game was tiresome, and lately, even the thought of playing it filled him with dread. He had a long way to go, and eliminating Peters might help in that regard.

'I have to face him. No way around it.'

'Why aren't you using your crew?'

That took Lamont out of his reverie.

'Using them for what?'

'For anything. You have shooters and goons you could send after him. I'm surprised you're not fighting me kicking and screaming to get Lennox.'

'I can't expect them to fight my battles all the time.'

'They work for you. It's *your* crew. Do you think everyone who works with me is happy to be at war? Do you think they like constantly having to watch their backs for danger from Lennox's people? I'm in charge, and they follow me. That's my privilege.'

'I think there's more to it than that with my team. I've had enough people killed.'

'What the hell are you talking about?'

'Chink, Tall-Man, Jenny, Trinidad, Akeem, and those are just the ones I can think of off the top of my head. People around me die, Del.'

Delroy scowled, and the anger made him look ten years younger.

'Maybe I should take back what I said about you being smart. Not one of those deaths is your fault, except for Chink's, and after what he did, he deserved worse.'

Lamont agreed about Chink, but it didn't make the words any easier to accept. As the person at the top, he was responsible for those below him, and he had repeatedly dropped the ball. He didn't want to think about it anymore.

'You've made a dent in his forces. I have a feeling his phone call to me is an attempt to control the situation.'

Delroy topped up his drink. 'I don't know if we're doing enough damage. Lennox has spots everywhere, and his people are extremely loyal to him. It's a war of attrition now, so I guess it comes down to who can last the longest.'

'Would you sue for peace if you had the opportunity?'

Delroy gave him a sad smile. 'Backing down isn't an option. You already know my feelings about the situation. Forget it, anyway. You've made your choice. What's going on with the crew?'

'Shorty is leading by example,' replied Lamont. Word had finally reached him about his involvement in the crew, and his attempts to retaliate against their usurpers. 'Everyone's supporting him. It's a good fit.'

'How does that make you feel?' Delroy watched him closely.

'I don't have an issue with it. Shorty has always fit in well with the crew, and they can all look out for one another. I expected him to go on a rampage and get killed going after Lennox's forces. He started out that way, but something calmed him. If I was to put money on it, I would say Amy.'

'His baby mother? Didn't think they were together.'

'They're not, but there are feelings there. I could see Grace's accident bringing them closer.'

'Is that why you haven't fought against him being involved?'

'Maybe.' He hadn't considered it. 'Either way, it's best for the crew right now. I can't focus on all areas, and we don't need any more mistakes.'

Delroy continued to study him over the top of his glass, and after a few minutes, he grew annoyed, cocking his head.

'Why are you staring at me?'

'I'm worried about you. You don't sound like yourself.'

'How am I supposed to sound?' Lamont's voice rose. Delroy shook his head.

'Get some rest, L. Whatever you do about this Peters' kid, sleep first. Don't rush into anything.'

LAMONT PUT TOGETHER a plan for dealing with the target, having people surveying his spot and reporting to him over a three-day period. He lived alone, working in and around Seacroft, selling mostly weed, but some rock too. Getting him would be easy. The smart thing would be to snatch him from his house, take him to one of their soundproofed locations, and go to work on him, but Lamont wanted to confront him face-to-face, in his own living space.

That was the plan he was going with. It was just a matter of executing it.

THAT NIGHT, Charlotte invited Lamont for dinner. She'd prepared a delicious steak, but he picked at it, not having much of an appetite. Peters dominated his thoughts; the need to confront him was hard for Lamont to shake off. Charlotte seemed to be in an odd mood too, and made little conversation, struggling to meet his eyes.

'Are you okay?' he finally asked, laying his knife and fork down on the plate. He'd managed around four bites of the steak before giving it up. Looking at her plate, she had eaten even less.

'I was thinking about Justin.'

Lamont's nostrils flared before he controlled his reactions. Despite his own feelings, and the fact he'd respected Justin, it annoyed him for a moment that he was on Charlotte's mind when she was with him.

'Anything in particular?'

'The book he wrote. The one I told you about, where he mentioned us. I was thinking about the part he wrote about me.'

'Can I see it?' He briefly remembered the conversation where she had spoken about Justin's writing, and the book he'd written in prison. She nodded after a moment and headed upstairs, coming back a few minutes later with an expensive-looking leather book, which she handed to him.

'I had it bound,' she needlessly explained. 'He gave it to me in paper form, and I didn't want to lose any pages. I still have the original.'

Lamont didn't speak as he read the book. It wasn't particularly long, and was more of a collection of thoughts than a novel, but he was gripped. He felt his stomach flip flop when he read his name. He'd

TARGET PART III

known Justin respected him, but reading it was different. When he finished, he placed the book on the sofa next to him.

'I saw Justin in a restaurant, a while before he died,' he said. 'We spoke, and I offered him a job.'

'Why?' Charlotte asked. She saw from the look on Lamont's face he was right there in the moment.

'He was good. Sounds simple, but people like Justin come around once in a while. He had poise, and he made people around him work harder. When you have someone like that, you need to cultivate it. He reminded me of myself.'

'How?'

'We both saw things a certain way. Could put our egos aside to work effectively with people. When I saw him that night, I knew there were issues with King. I even caused some of them.'

'How?'

'I knew the people who were making his business harder. Tunde and Bloon. I used them to make things difficult for him.'

'Why would you do that?'

'King was a virus. He stole his power and flouted a lot of the rules people had in place. We allowed it, but we didn't make things easy. Then, Justin got out, and he calmed down a little and put Justin in charge, but it was clear it wouldn't last long. He had a taste of being the main man, and there was no way he was going to share.'

'Did you tell Justin that?' Charlotte hadn't taken her eyes off him.

Lamont shook his head. 'I made the offer, he rejected me, and I let it go. The fact is, I understand why he had such an effect on you.'

'The night he died . . . he called me. Said I was the motivation behind his words, and that he wrote to avoid going crazy when he was behind bars. He wanted me to know how he felt, and the last thing he said to me, was to read those pages and that I would understand.' Charlotte choked back a sob. Lamont slid closer, holding her and letting her cry in peace. She had been dealing with her pain for two years, and it made him wonder how long it would take for him to improve. He was tired of the grief suffocating him. He just wanted to be better.

'I wish I was okay,' she sniffed. 'I wish I could just move on and leave the memory of him behind, but he's always there, and I'm writing my own words because I think it keeps me connected to him.'

Lamont stroked her back, enjoying the closeness as he had last time. It didn't feel as awkward as his encounter with Anna. Charlotte was broken. He was broken too. When he was around her, he felt more like a protector than a victim. Tilting her head toward him, he felt her breath catch as he stared into her eyes. His lips met hers, and the kiss instantly deepened. He was back in the zone, desire surging through his veins as he pulled her closer to him, devouring her mouth, loving her taste and feel.

Blinking, he pulled away at the same time as Charlotte. Breathing hard, they stared one another down. It went on for a moment that seemed to last forever, and he knew the magnified pain in her eyes was reflected in his own.

He wasn't seeing her. He was seeing Jenny, and he knew Charlotte wasn't seeing him. Like Anna, it couldn't work. He had once again tried to seduce his way out of feeling his pain, and once again, his body had shut him down.

'I'm sorry,' he said, letting her go. Charlotte gave him a soft smile.

'I'm sorry too. It would have been so easy,' she admitted.

Lamont rubbed her hair, smiling despite not feeling particularly cheerful.

'Friends then?'

'Friends,' she repeated.

CHAPTER SEVENTEEN
MONDAY 18 MAY, 2015

RYAN PETERS HUMMED along to a *Giggs* track, tired from another day of hustling and keeping his head above water. Money had dried up recently, and he had to work longer hours to survive. He had been ostracised from his crew after accidentally killing a woman, and didn't know how to get himself back into the fold. When he wasn't working, he stayed close to home, smoking, playing on the PlayStation, and watching whatever films he had lying around. He had a takeaway resting on the passenger seat, a cheap chicken and chips meal he'd picked up from his regular spot, and had stopped for cigarettes and a few cans from the local shop. There was nothing else for him to do but lose himself to the monotony.

As he turned onto his street, he noticed that a nearby streetlight had been knocked out, cursing the local kids. They were unruly and bored, always causing trouble, knocking over bins and smashing windows; when they weren't smoking weed or robbing houses.

Resolving to smack one or two of them around if he caught them, he grabbed his bags and shuffled his way inside after unlocking his door. Dropping the bags on the coffee table, he switched on the light and jumped back.

'What the fuck?'

A man sat in his favourite armchair, a slight grin on his face as he surveyed him. He was well-dressed in a black jumper, trousers and boots. He wore gloves and, in his right hand, was a gun.

'Hello, Ryan.'

'Who the hell are you?'

'Sit down.' The man motioned to the sofa. Keeping his eyes on him, Peters complied.

'Are you gonna tell me who you are?'

'You don't know?'

Peters frowned. 'I've never seen you before. How would I know?'

'I heard you were sharp, but I'm guessing that was an exaggeration. You don't look very smart.'

'I haven't done anything, mate. If there's a problem, just tell me so I can make it right.' Peters ignored the jibe.

'What if you can't make it right?'

Peters opened his mouth and closed it. He studied the man, racking his brain to see if he knew him from anywhere. He was well-spoken and didn't look like he was from the streets, but he held the gun on him with no issues.

'Look, I don't have any money, but you can take the TV, PlayStation, and whatever else you can find, if that will make things right.'

The man shook his head, tutting.

'What makes you think this is a robbery?'

'Why else would you be here?'

'I'm patiently waiting for you to work that out, Ryan. Use your brain — the part you haven't rotted away with drugs, anyway. You're a no-hoper in a shitty little house, with a shitty little existence. Why would I be here? Think to your sins.'

Peters was baffled. The man seemed to have a problem with him, but he was far above his level, and didn't fit his usual clientele. He sold drugs to people lower than him, and he didn't sell much. This guy looked like he was a heavyweight. Peters didn't have a patch he was working, and he had a feeling that if the man was a drug dealer, they didn't have the same customers.

It took well over a minute before it hit him. Lennox Thompson had essentially cut him loose after the kidnapping

TARGET PART III

went wrong. He paled, nausea swirling, able to taste the bile in his stomach.

'*Teflon*,' he gasped, watching the man's eyes light up.

'I've been waiting a long time to speak with you,' said Lamont, his body tensing. He wanted to beat him to death with the gun he was holding. His people were surveying the house in case it was an ambush. He wondered if Jenny was watching over him. She hadn't known his hands were stained with blood. He had kept her out of his business with Akhan, not wanting her to get caught up. Now, she wasn't. Thanks to the man currently quailing under the sight of his gun. Deep down, Lamont knew Jenny wouldn't have accepted him as a murderer, but didn't want to think about that right now.

'I'm sorry. I promise, it wasn't meant to happen. We tried grabbing her, and she fought back, struggling to get free. She grabbed the knife, and I tried to calm her down, but she was wriggling around so much that it stabbed her.'

'She was a fighter. She was better than you. Better than me too. She was mine, and you took her from me. I don't care why you were in the house. I only care about what you did, and what you robbed me of. Do you get that?'

'I'm sorry,' Peters tried again.

'Sorry will not cut it here. Do you know my rep?'

He nearly broke his neck nodding.

'Why would you risk it then? Why would you go after my woman? Didn't you think I would do anything?'

'Lennox made me. You have to believe me. Look at me,' gibbered Peters. 'I'd never have done something like that by myself. He just wanted us to hold her. If she hadn't struggled . . .' he couldn't finish.

'How long have you worked for Lennox?'

The sudden subject change surprised him, but he hastened to answer. Teflon hadn't immediately killed him. He wanted information, and if Peters could keep himself alive by helping, he would.

'Three years.'

'What sort of work did you do for him? Other than killing women.'

'I . . . I sent messages. Beat people up. Collected money and did robberies.'

Teflon nodded, absorbing the information.

'Tell me everything you know about Lennox and his operations.'

Peters' eyes widened. He wanted to be helpful, but Lennox was equally dangerous, and if he knew he had been telling tales about him, he would hurt him. He was stuck in the middle of a deadly situation, and he wasn't sure how he could get out of it. Teflon was his best bet for now. Staying alive was the plan.

'Lennox doesn't keep me close like the others. He was furious after what happened, and I've been on my own ever since. Everyone in the crew abandoned me on his word. Dunno what I can tell you.'

'Tell me what you know. If I like what I hear, I'm more likely to leave without using this.' He waved the pistol.

Another jolt of fear spread through his body. Teflon was entirely too calm, and it was even more unnerving. He didn't know how to deal with this sort of man. Teflon was a mainstay in Chapeltown and was surrounded by deadly killers who would easily take him out. The only reason he had gone after Jenny was because he had Lennox's backing, and presumed he had a plan for dealing with the man seated before him. Clearly, he hadn't.

'I . . . look, I wanna help, but I'm a nobody. I don't see how I can.'

'Do you know why I'm here?' Teflon cut through his babbling.

'Because of what happened. . . what Lennox made me do.'

'No. Well, yes, that's partly true. The main reason is because Lennox called me, and he gave me a *gift*. His words. He told me the address and the name of the man who killed my partner.' Teflon shot him a truly mirthless smirk. 'I'm here because Lennox gave you up, because you mean nothing to him. You were disposable.'

Despite the circumstances, Peters felt a surge of anger cancelling out the fear. Lennox valued loyalty, and before the incident, he'd never put a foot wrong. Lennox was practically in hiding, and there was no reason for him to betray Peters, but he had. This was his chance. Teflon wanted information, and it was his best chance to stay alive. If he could remain helpful, he would live, and then he could leave this life behind and start again somewhere else. He had nothing tying him to Leeds.

'What do you want to know?'

TARGET PART III

'How does Lennox make money?'

'He does everything. Contract kills. Robberies. Businesses pay him money to look after them. He does security. Anything that makes money.'

'Drugs?'

Peters shook his head. 'He robs them, but doesn't make money from them.'

'How do you know?'

'People talk. Sometimes people want to make money selling drugs on the side, and they try and talk him into getting involved in the drugs game. He has the contacts if he ever needed. Probably make millions if he did.'

'Why doesn't he?'

'No one knows. He doesn't even like people mentioning it.'

'After Nikkolo got murdered, who did Lennox start speaking to?'

'I was out of the fold by then, but I'd say Mark Patrick is the one he would turn to. He did some time in the army, and he's good with weapons and stuff. Everyone in the crew respects him.'

'Why wouldn't Lennox send him after my partner rather than you? He wouldn't have fucked up.'

Despite his dire predicament, he felt another surge of annoyance at Teflon's attitude. He was used to people outright dismissing him, but it didn't make it any easy to tolerate. It would be over soon. He would give Teflon what he could, then he would flee.

All he needed was him gone from the house.

'Guess he saw the job as beneath him. Mark's a weapons guy. He even knows about explosives and shit, bombs, petrol bombs, whatever is needed.'

'Sounds like the kind of man the army wouldn't want to lose. Why did they?'

'I dunno. All I know is he does well under Lennox; handles all kinds of special jobs. There are a few names that were beneath Nikkolo, but Mark sticks out.'

'I want the other names.'

Peters gave them, tempted to use them to negotiate his freedom. He was determined to show Teflon he was an asset, though, and gave the names freely, noting that Teflon made no movement to write any of the names down.

'Going back to Mark Patrick. You heard what happened to the barbers in Chapeltown?'

Peters shook his head. 'I stay away from the Hood. I've been keeping myself around here, and out of everyone's way.'

'What about *Sinclair*?'

He blew out a breath. 'Sinclair is absolutely nuts. Lennox knew his dad and brother, so he's been around him for years. Schooled him and made him into a killer. He only listens to Lennox.'

'Where can I find him and Mark?'

Peters shrugged. 'I don't know. I promise I don't. Mark will probably be wherever Lennox is, or close by. Sinclair could be anywhere. His family live in Miles Hill, so he might be around there. I'm out of the loop, and I didn't spend much time around these lot when I wasn't on the job.'

'Where did you hang out when you weren't working? I want the spots you frequent; the areas Lennox recruits from the most. I want a list of safe houses you could use.'

'The safe houses change all the time, especially with the Delroy shit, but I'll give you what I can. I just want to help,' said Peters, searching Teflon's face for any sign of whether he was to live or die. He was a closed book, his expression inscrutable. For the next twenty minutes, he spilled his guts, searching his brain for every bit of knowledge he could link to Lennox, whether it was a small rumour, or something he directly knew. Still, Teflon wrote nothing down, only prompting him to continue.

'That's it. That's everything I know,' he finally said. Teflon nodded.

'You've been extremely helpful.'

Peters waited, his heart leaping into his throat. He hoped he had done enough to earn a reprieve, but his expression gave nothing away.

'Stand up.'

Peters did it without thinking.

'Walk outside.'

'Where are we going?'

'Did I say *walk*, or did I say *talk*?'

TARGET PART III

His mouth snapped shut. Teflon stayed a few paces behind, keeping the gun out of reach. It was pitch black outside without the streetlight. Peters realised Teflon's people had likely done this to lower the chance of any witnesses seeing what was happening. Despite the late hour, people usually hung around, talking from their gardens or shouting curses at the little kids wreaking havoc. Now, the street was empty, save for the two large men standing at the bottom of the garden. Grabbing his arms, they none-too-gently dragged him toward a nondescript grey van and shoved him in the back, where another man waited.

'Get on the floor.'

Peters immediately complied, his nose to the floor of the van. It was empty aside from his captor, with nothing he could use to defend himself. Not that he intended to try. The man who had just growled at him was built like Anthony Joshua, and it was clear from his demeanour that he would like nothing more than to tear his head from his shoulders.

The vehicle moved off, and he kept his head down, panic shooting through him. Teflon had given him no sign of what he intended to do after leading him outside. He'd told him everything and hadn't held back. All he wanted was the opportunity to survive so he could flee.

Before long, the vehicle rumbled to a stop. The man guarding Peters signalled for him to stand as the van door opened. Two more men stood there, waiting for him to climb out. His heart slammed against his chest as he descended. They were in a warehouse, the largest he had ever seen. It was filled with machines and a selection of vehicles, mostly random, nondescript cars. In the middle of the room, Teflon stood, still holding the gun.

Peters stomach sank as he glanced left and right. There was no escape. There were half a dozen armed men around the warehouse and Teflon waiting for him, expression still unreadable, ready with a weapon. His chances of escape seemed slim, but he was determined to try. Teflon had kept him alive earlier when he could have killed him. He would need to work harder than ever in his life to convince him, and as he drew closer, he gathered his words, searching for something, anything that might work.

'You don't have to do this,' he said, somewhat lamely. Teflon didn't even react. He held up the gun. Peters jerked back, trying to run, but two men seized his arms, holding him in place.

'Move, and we'll break your fucking arm,' one of them growled. He immediately froze.

Teflon stepped closer, lightly resting the pistol against his thigh.

'You took the woman I loved from me.'

'Lennox—'

'Is just as responsible as you, and he will get what's coming to him. This is about you thinking you could go after what was mine. You didn't think about the consequences, or what I would do. Instead, you did as you were told, and you got the job done.'

'No, I—'

'Lennox didn't do you any favours. He didn't protect you. He gave you up because you weren't useful anymore. I don't care whether or not you wanted to do it. I don't care if it was an accident and if she grabbed the knife first. She was defending herself,' Teflon's voice rose. 'Defending herself from the men who broke into her house to take her away. I was listening on the phone. I heard her screaming and fighting, trying to get away, as I drove to the house as fast as I could. I had to walk in on her, bloody and dead, on the fucking kitchen floor. You stabbed her, and you left her there, and you really thought you had a chance at living?'

Peters' mouth was dry. He couldn't even form words. Shaking, his knees knocked together, dizzy with fear. He wasn't seeing the calm man who had interrogated him earlier. He was seeing the deadly criminal who had ruled his own empire for years, who few before Lennox had ever thought of testing. Without warning, the bile rose, and this time he threw up, emptying his stomach onto the concrete floor beneath him. The guards cursed in annoyance as the vomit splashed against them, but they still didn't let him go.

'I'll make it quick,' said Teflon. 'It's more than you deserve, but there is no reason to prolong this.'

'Teflon, please, I'm begging you, don't do this.' He fell to his knees, the movement forcing the guards to let go. He crawled forward, not

TARGET PART III

caring that he was kneeling in his own vomit. 'I'll go away. You'll never see me again. I'm sorry about your girl! Please don't do this.'

Lamont's face was bloodless with intense rage. His breathing intensified. He couldn't believe Jenny's killer was begging in such a disgusting manner. He felt no sorrow; didn't care that he had been duped into doing it by Lennox Thompson. All he felt was the anger he had bottled up from the moment Peters had entered the house earlier in the evening. This weasel, this pathetic excuse of a man, had robbed him of Jenny. He raised the gun.

'No!' Peters screamed, foolishly trying to grab the weapon. Scowling, Lamont's finger tightened on the trigger, and there was a loud bang that echoed around the building. The bullet went through Peters outstretched hand, slamming into his chest. It threw him backwards, and he crumpled to the ground. Stepping forward, Lamont emptied the rest of the clip into him, still squeezing the trigger long after he'd run out of bullets. He yelled, startling the men present, breathing hard as the smoking gun trembled in his hands. The first bullet would have surely killed him, but the stream that followed had removed all possibility of survival.

For a full two minutes, Lamont stared down at his body, then turned to the men present, who were all gawping.

'Take care of this,' he ordered, striding from the spot without another glance at the dead man.

CHAPTER EIGHTEEN

THURSDAY 21 MAY, 2015

'I HAVEN'T BEEN HERE in a long time.'

Marika had the day off, and when Lamont called around, asking if they could spend some time together, she'd readily agreed. They'd run a few errands, then went for some lunch, and were now at the graves of their parents. She turned to her brother. He was dressed for the warm weather in a crisp t-shirt and khaki chinos.

'When was the last time you came?'

'Two years ago. The day after that dinner party you had. Auntie and I got into an argument, and I stormed out and got drunk. The next day, I came out here and spent some time.'

Marika remembered the night. She had announced her relationship with Marrion, hoping to get under Lamont's skin, but the argument had taken all the attention from them. Looking back, she didn't even know why she invited her. She loved Aunt Carmen and accepted she was hard work, but had long since given up on getting her and Lamont to make peace. Aunt Carmen was the catalyst for their next disagreement. Fuelled by grief over Marcus's death, Marika and Lamont argued, and he had called her a parasite. Other than another argument after an attack at Marika's that she wrongly accused him of orchestrating, they hadn't spoken for almost two years.

TARGET PART III

Marika learned of his shooting and, even through her grief over Marrion, had cried over her big, strong brother, laid up in the hospital and barely alive. She spent time with Jenny, watching over him until he recovered, and then she stopped coming.

It wasn't until she was dealing with Aunt Carmen without Lamont around, that she realised just how hateful the woman was. She was bitter about everything and utterly spiteful towards her family. Marika's children loathed her, and many family members made excuses to avoid spending time with her. She still loved her, but their relationship had definitely changed in the past few years.

She doubted Aunt Carmen had been to the graves since their parents had been buried there. She had certainly never taken them.

'Why did you stay away for so long?' she asked.

'I couldn't face it. Sometimes I would come, and I'd stare at these pieces of stone and speak with them, and then I'd feel guilty, like I knew they wouldn't be pleased with my life choices.'

'I think they would be happy as long as you were,' Marika replied. It seemed like the right thing to say.

'I think I'm happy,' he said. 'I feel better than I have in a while.'

When Lamont said that, Marika glanced at him. He seemed more focused and locked-on than he had recently, more like his old self, and certainly better rested. His eyes were clearer, and as he turned to meet her gaze, he had a small smile on his face that seemed to encompass him and make him appear younger. Lamont had never lost his looks. He was a *Jones* like her, and they were a good-looking family, but his sadness had diminished them. Now, he was her brother all over again, and he seemed in that moment to stand taller than ever.

'Have you been sleeping?'

Lamont nodded, his smile widening.

'I've been sleeping well for a few days now.'

'Why?' Marika asked. Turning from the grave, he held out his hand for her to take, like when they were kids.

'Good things are happening,' he said, as they walked away. He wouldn't tell Marika about Peters, but since he had killed him, Lamont felt freer, his burden of guilt and despair removed. The bullets he pumped into the killer's body had been cathartic.

The morning after the deed, he'd woken up after a solid eight-hour-sleep, and gone for a run. He'd had a stitch and felt exhausted, but it was a pleasing pain, and a sign things were on the up for him. Lamont hadn't heard from Lennox, but assumed he would know about the death. The Jackie Smart Court address remained under surveillance. He had people in Miles Hill, keeping an eye out for Sinclair and discretely asking questions about the young killer. He reached for his phone, but remembered Marika had made him turn it off earlier when it wouldn't stop ringing.

It was all ending. Delroy had Lennox on the ropes, and he had his head back in the game. When his people put the pieces together, they would make a last move against Lennox, root him out of his hiding place, and it would all be complete.

———

LENNOX WAS in his safe house, reading over some *OurHood* documents. The organisation hadn't been the same after Malcolm's murder, and didn't seem to have the same pop. Malcolm had been a tremendous waste of potential. He was the perfect man to feed Lennox's propaganda about the local dealers, but had fallen apart when he'd sent him after Jenny Campbell. Lennox considered it one of his biggest failures. He'd been warring with Delroy but took advantage of several schemes to ruin Teflon's position, just in case. Breaking up Teflon's relationship was one, but Malcolm had fallen for Jenny and, after her murder, confronted Lennox just as he was set upon by Eddie Williams, seeking revenge for the murder of his brother Winston. Malcolm had died in the confusion, and Lennox escaped with his life after murdering Eddie.

With Malcolm being found alongside the son of a major drug kingpin, it put *OurHood* under an ugly spotlight. A few stalwarts continued to lead the charge, attempting to keep the narrative fixed on police brutality and its effects on the streets of Leeds, but fewer people were getting involved. Even Trinidad's murder had been overlooked and marginalised.

He was leaving the organisation to wither. It served little purpose anymore, and Delroy was moving the goalposts. His people were out

TARGET PART III

in force, suffocating the Hood to draw him out. If it wasn't them, it was Teflon. His people were subtle and just surveying, but the pressure was still there. Shorty was still out there, apparently leading Teflon's crew, which likely meant rumours of a rift between the pair had been exaggerated.

When Lennox's phone rang, he put the papers to one side before answering.

'Speak.'

'You hear about Ryan?' said Mark Patrick, getting to the point.

'Which Ryan?'

'Our Ryan. Peters. Someone killed him. Probably Delroy's lot, right?'

'Right,' lied Lennox. He'd known about the murder the day after it happened and was surprised it had taken Mark so long to contact him. Peters had messed up, just as Lutel had messed up by shooting Shorty's daughter. The only punishment for such acts was death. Without Shorty around, Lennox was sure he could have negotiated with Teflon down the line, but he'd been forced to escalate the conflict further.

Mark had also messed up when he didn't check if Trinidad was in the building before destroying it. By all rights, Lennox could have killed him too, but had held off on that action. Unlike the others, Mark was too useful to be wasted in such a fashion. He needed him to keep the ranks focused. He'd heard the grumbles about the ongoing war, and the team were chafing under the conditions, constantly having to watch out for ambushes. Lennox spent most of his time reading or thinking, his discipline serving him well. It stopped him making the silly moves others had made.

'Do you want me to investigate? They left him out in the open, so I guess they're sending a message.'

'Don't bother. Keep everyone focused, and stick to the plan. Understand?'

'Understood, boss. I'll keep you posted.'

Hanging up, Lennox went back to his reading.

After leaving Marika, Lamont called Maka.

'Boss, long time no speak. Tried calling back earlier, but your phone was off. Are you still wanting that meet?'

'Yes. I want Manson, K and Shorty. Darren too, if you think he's needed.'

'You know about Shorty . . . helping out?'

'Of course I do,' replied Lamont. 'I'll leave it to you to organise a time and place.'

'No problem. I can handle that. Are you alright?'

'I'm great.'

Maka paused. 'You sound it. Compared to how you were last time, you sound different. Sharper.'

'I'm feeling it, fam. Set up that meeting, and we can talk about it more face to face.'

'Got you.'

Lamont hung up with a smile on his face. The last time he'd felt like this had been the morning after Akhan's death. There had been the sense then that his life was going to change, but this was different. He'd shown Peters true power that night. He had played God with his life and strung him along, making him believe he could live. It had been part of his plan. If he believed he was going to die, there was the chance he would be less willing to give any information on his crew.

Lamont had manipulated him, told him of Lennox's betrayal, and left the slight hope open that he might be allowed to walk away. The death had changed something in him. It had brought his older, more composed self back to the surface, ready to finish what he had started. From there, he would get the crew back in line, and everyone would make more money.

With the war over, there would be no reason for Jakkar and Stefanos to keep him out of the loop any longer. The police would move on to new targets. Everything rested on getting Lennox out of the way, and he was making it his number one priority. He would share his information with the crew, and they would work together with Delroy's crew to finish the job once and for all.

TARGET PART III

SHORTY SAT by Grace's bedside, holding her hand. She'd woken a few times over the past week for short periods, but there was still a long way to go before she would recover. To his relief, she seemed to thrive under the more personalised care. He couldn't take his eyes off her. Watching her breathing rise and fall was tranquil. If Grace had died, Shorty knew he would have completely lost it. Until he'd gone to see Amy to leave her his money, he had been ready to ride the path to the end, killing any of Lennox's men he saw in front of him.

Amy and the thoughts of being a proper father to Grace had pulled him back from the suicidal edge. He hadn't spoken with Amy in a few days, and had hoped to see her when he visited Grace, but she hadn't come yet. They would normally make the trips to see Grace together, but he had a feeling she was avoiding him. Their conversations had been shorter since he had told her his feelings and let her know he wanted something real between them.

A growing part of him felt she was trying to let him down easily, and it hurt. He recalled the comments she had made a while back about dating other people and believed he had been slow in picking up the signs. It was a bitter pill to swallow. He loved the thought of something real taking place with them, but Shorty was who he was, and she knew that. Whether they were together, he would always be a part of Grace's life, and when it came down to it, that was all that mattered.

Maybe he needed to move on too.

After sitting with Grace for another hour, Shorty placed a gentle kiss on her forehead and left, turning his phone back on when he left the facility. He had numerous messages from Maka, and called him back as he walked to his car.

'Yes, Shorty. Everything good? I tried you a few times.'

'I was with Grace. I don't keep the phone on, just in case. What's going on?'

'Teflon wants a meeting.'

'Okay. Why are you telling me?'

'He wants you there. Mentioned you by name.'

Shorty frowned. They hadn't spoken since their argument at

Trinidad's funeral. He couldn't think what he would have to say, and wasn't happy at the idea of being around him.

'I don't need to be there.'

'You're needed, fam. The moves we've made recently are down to you, and that needs to be recognised. You don't need to speak, but at least show up so we know what's what?'

'When are you meeting?'

'Tonight. Haven't arranged the place yet.'

'Can't do tonight. Let me get back to you with a time.'

'Cool. Let me know.'

CHAPTER NINETEEN
FRIDAY 22 MAY, 2015

FOR THE SECOND time in as many meetings, Rigby met Terry Worthy alone. It was barely past nine o'clock in the morning. Murphy was back at the office doing paperwork and covering for Rigby, who had been ordered off any investigations into Teflon and his crew. Despite the spate of shootings and attacks, they couldn't tie them to any of it, and all the intelligence received suggested he and his crew weren't directly involved. Rigby would have had his usual disdain for meeting with Terry if it wasn't for one key difference: Terry had requested it, and that told him he had something good to share.

When he arrived, Terry already waited, a broad grin on his face. His posture differed from the last meeting, and Rigby could have sworn he looked like he had just been laid.

'Good to see you, Rig.'

'You too. Why are you so happy?'

'For once, you're gonna be kissing my arse, mate, I'm telling you.'

'We'll see. Do you know where I can find Delroy Williams or Lennox Thompson?' Rigby hoped he did. They were sure these were the two gangs responsible for waging war in Chapeltown, but there was no direct proof other than hearsay. They couldn't question them based on circumstantial evidence, and had no witnesses.

That being said, the policy regarding witnesses was currently under review. Rigby had gone over Reid's head and submitted a letter to her boss, showing how the department had messed up pertaining to the misuse of Adele Chapman, and how it would look if the press was to stumble onto this fact. He'd heard nothing back directly, but the station had been awash with talk of DCI Reid being summoned to a meeting. It was a minor victory, but one, nonetheless.

The bodies were still dropping, though. A body had been found a few days ago, one Ryan Peters. He was affiliated with Lennox's crew, but no one was claiming credit for his death. He had been shot multiple times, including once through the hand, suggesting he'd tried to stop the bullet. It was a brutal killing, and the body had been moved, meaning they didn't know the original location, making it harder. Thankfully, Rigby and Murphy weren't on that case.

'No, mate. No one does. They're giving their orders and staying out of the way. No one wants to get caught in the middle of that.'

'Why have you called me here then?'

'I don't have anything on Teflon, but he's not really involved in the running anymore. Like I told you last time, Shorty and K-Bar are running the crew.'

'Where is Teflon then?'

'Fuck knows. No one, and I mean no one, is seeing him. He's on the missing list.'

'How is that not causing a panic?'

'K-Bar's back. It's reassuring people. Him and Shorty were always a bloody double act, and now they're running the show.' Terry spat on the floor. He could tolerate K-Bar, but had never liked Shorty, and knew the feeling was mutual.

Rigby gritted his teeth. The mention of K-Bar made his blood boil. The way he had smiled in his face before his release made him want to knock all his teeth down his throat. He didn't like to make things personal, but getting something on K-Bar would make him infinitely happy, and he had few reasons for such an attitude these days.

'Okay, so you have nothing new.'

Terry waved his hands and said, 'slow down, mate. I told you I have something you're gonna like. The difference with K-Bar and

TARGET PART III

Shorty is that they're not as squirrelly as my mate Teflon. Much more inclusive, if you know what I mean. They're comfy too; like to have their big meetings in the same spot.'

Rigby's smile stretched the corners of his mouth. It was impossible to survey places if you couldn't definitively prove the targets were using them to discuss criminal business. Teflon and his contemporaries never had meetings in their houses, or anywhere with any frequency. They had safe houses dotted all over, and homes of mutual acquaintances they could use if they saw fit. If they were getting lazy and using the same spots, it would help with the probable cause.

'Seriously?'

'Serious. Dunno if you know the name *Darren Lyles*, but he's the little bastard in charge of recruitment. Me and him go way back, and I took him for some drinks the other night. We had a chat, and I pumped his ego a bit, told him about how well he was doing. He was telling me about some new faces, bragging really. There's a kid named Roman, who they're all in love with. He's got a partner he runs around with . . .'

'*Keith*. I know the pair,' interrupted Rigby. Roman and Keith were smarter and had more common sense than the average little shits. If they were learning under Teflon and his crew, it would only make them more dangerous. 'How did they get those two on board?' He continued.

'According to Darren, they helped them with some problems they were having with local crews. They slapped a few people around and put the word out that Roman and co were under their protection. Now, they're paying a percentage and getting access to Teflon's product. I guarantee Teflon's stuff is the best on the streets. It always sells.'

'You can't tell me anything about where he's getting his supply?' asked Rigby, though he was sure of the answer. At one point, it was alleged Teflon received his supply directly from Delroy Williams, but those days were long gone. He'd apparently hooked up with some new heavyweights, but all inroads into investigating the chain had led nowhere. It was one of the things he'd planned to pump K-Bar for information on once he had worn him down.

'Okay, so Shorty and K-Bar are switching things up, Teflon is on holiday, and Darren is hiring thugs to keep the crew going into the next century?'

'Pretty much. Things are different now. Teflon kept everything on a need-to-know basis. Shorty and K-Bar are cagey, but nothing like Teflon. They're giving people chances to prove themselves and get more involved. It means that just by being around certain people, I'm in the know like never before, meaning I have a list of hideouts and locations for numerous people tied to the crew.'

Rigby's smile grew. He gave Terry a lot of crap, but he had come through for them with this information.

'C'mon, let's sit somewhere so you can tell me all about it.'

'I wanna know what I'm gonna get first. I've done you lot a right service here, so it should wipe clean my old record, right?' said Terry.

'That would depend on where the info leads. Is there nothing you can tell me about Teflon, or about the street war?'

'No, boss.'

Rigby nodded. He was satisfied with what he had. He needed to sell his boss on the information, and he wasn't her favourite person after his previous actions. Locking his car, he climbed into Terry's Audi, keeping his head low as he pulled off at speed.

―――

'DETECTIVE RIGBY. I understand you have some information for me?'

Reid folded her arms, her eyes boring into Rigby's.

Hours had passed since his conversation with Terry Worthy, and the information was extensive. There were more than a dozen locations, some storage for product and weapons. There was a list of spots that were used for meetings, along with various hideouts for soldiers. A year ago, he would have already been surveying the properties and getting warrants, but this was a different time. It would have been difficult even without him being on Reid's shit list, but now it would be near impossible. It wouldn't stop him from pushing as far as he needed to.

'I met with one of my informants. He contacted me and asked for a meeting, claiming to have vital information.'

TARGET PART III

'That's great. What did he tell you about the war?'

Rigby paused. 'Everyone knows the players involved, but there is nothing tying Lennox or Delroy to any illegal activity. Both men are well hidden and are giving their orders likely through buffers to avoid any direct links.'

Reid frowned. 'If that is the case, then what is the purpose of this meeting?'

'My informant had information pertaining to Teflon's crew.'

'That would be the crew you were specifically instructed not to investigate?'

'I stuck to that, ma'am. I haven't investigated them, but my informant is part of the crew, and had relevant information. There have been restructures which have led to laxness in certain areas, namely *security*.'

'Get to the point.'

'The point,' continued Rigby, ignoring the rudeness, 'is that I now have a list of locations linked to the crew. I'm talking safe houses, storage spots, places where they hold meetings. This is everything we need.'

'It doesn't involve the main Chapeltown conflict. That is our mandate. To stop that war by any means necessary. It is not our mandate to look into other criminals that have nothing to do with it.'

This wasn't going well. Reid's demeanour was the same, but her words implied she was growing tired of the conversation. He had to push deeper.

'This lead could be the one that nets us the whole thing, ma'am. I still believe Teflon and his crew are involved in the war, and I want to prove it. Shorty's daughter was shot. Teflon's partner was murdered. His business, co-owned with Trinidad Tommy — a man beloved in Chapeltown — was blown up. These incidents connect to the wider issue, and with more pieces behind bars, I will prove that. All I need is a little more time, and warrants and resources for the locations. Give me ninety-six hours and if I have nothing, pull them back. Do this, and we will break the back of the Chapeltown gangs and restore confidence in the area, in our officers.'

Reid didn't reply for several long moments. He didn't turn away, continuing to meet her gaze until finally, she coughed into her fist.

'Ninety-six hours, and not a second more, Detective Rigby. You will have whatever pieces you need but hear this: if this investigation leads nowhere, I promise your career will never be the same afterwards. Do you understand?'

'I do, ma'am. Thank you.'

SHORTY KNOCKED on the door of the address he'd been given, glancing around as he waited for an answer. He hadn't been to Little London in a while, but he'd never liked the area. Unlike Chapeltown, which was full of energy and always bustling, little London felt bleak and sterile by comparison. A few seconds later, the door opened, and a woman smiled at him. Her milk chocolate skin complimented her white blouse, curly black hair tumbling past her shoulders. He'd forgotten how beautiful she was.

'Hey, Shorty.'

'Sienna. How've you been?'

Sienna smiled warmly.

'I heard about your daughter. I'm so sorry, Shorty. I didn't think Lutel would be capable of such a thing.'

'She's alive, and that's all the counts,' said Shorty, remembering Lutel's face before he put a bullet in him. Torturing and killing him had made him feel good, and he only wished he'd had longer to make Lennox's lackey suffer. 'Why did you ask me to come see you?'

'Come inside. Can't really speak about these things on the doorstep,' she said. They sat in the living room. It was cosy, though cramped, with bookshelves, two tables, and a selection of trashy magazines, books, and DVDs. Sienna invited him to sit on the sofa, and she sat next to him. Neither spoke for a moment. Shorty wondered what her game was. He'd become involved with Sienna a few months ago after meeting her at an *OurHood* meeting. They'd gone out a few times, but she had a jealous ex named Lutel, whom everyone feared. He'd started running his mouth about Shorty taking liberties with his

TARGET PART III

woman, and this culminated in a fight at Jukie's bar, which Shorty easily won, beating the man unconscious with a bar stool.

Undeterred, Lutel fired back, literally, shooting Grace instead of Shorty. He retaliated by killing Lutel and his accomplice, but not before learning of Lennox's direct involvement. With everything that had happened since, he had forgotten all about Sienna, until she had contacted him out of the blue.

'Go on then, what is it?'

'It's about Lennox.'

CHAPTER TWENTY

FRIDAY 22 MAY, 2015

SIENNA HAD SHORTY'S ATTENTION. He leaned forward, brow furrowing as he waited.

'Lennox never spoke much around me, but I knew him through Lutel. I know a girl who used to deal with him.'

'Deal with him how? She was his girlfriend?' Shorty hadn't found a single thread he could pull on surrounding Lennox. He had no family they could get to, and before now, had been linked to no women. This was a massive development.

'Yes. That's why I contacted you. I want to help.'

'Can you put me in touch with her?'

'I wanted to talk to you first.'

'About what?'

'About us.'

Shorty said nothing. They had barely gotten off the ground, and he'd forgotten all about her until she contacted him. It wasn't worth alienating her, so he needed to be coy.

'Is there an us?' She pressed.

'Honestly, I don't know. I went to a dark place after my girl got shot, and I didn't want to know anyone. I certainly wasn't thinking about the future.'

TARGET PART III

'What about now?'

'Things are getting better, but there's still work to do. If you wanna talk more after things get sorted, I'm willing to have that conversation.'

Sienna shifted closer to Shorty, and when their lips met, he didn't pull away. Instead, he deepened the kiss, his hand entangled in her hair, pulling her ever closer before finally pulling away. Sienna smiled.

'That was some kiss. I'll be in touch,' she said. He nodded. The kiss hadn't made him feel good. Instead, he felt hollow. Amy still hadn't spoken to him, and rather than act as a distraction, the kiss only made him more frustrated with the circumstances.

———

LAMONT'S good mood carried on into the next day. He had again slept without issue, and woken up fresh and alert, handling some business with Ahmed, who had become much more receptive to him. They were due to go out for dinner again soon, with plans to invite Mustafa.

There had been no repercussions for killing Peters. His men had been meticulous in dumping the body, and the local news was linking it to the ongoing *Chapeltown War*, suggesting it might spread throughout Leeds.

Ahmed had made some cryptic comments about Jakkar and his displeasure with the lack of resolution in the conflict, but Lamont hadn't responded. When Lennox was taken out, the war would end, and he believed they were close in that regard. He had used the information given by Peters, Jukie, and other sources, along with intel from watching the Jackie Smart Court property, to narrow down where Lennox might be hiding. He didn't think he was in Chapeltown or any of the surrounding areas, but Cross Gates was a possibility as he'd had a base there before. Lennox also had links in Garforth, and his people were investigating these. No one had found Sinclair yet, but they had found some other little knuckleheads he associated with, and they were being watched.

It was early evening when he made his way to Kate's house. They hadn't spoken since Jenny's funeral, but he had made her a promise at the grave site, and part of it had been fulfilled. She was with Tek, an old friend of Lamont's, when he arrived. Predictably, Tek grinned when he saw Lamont and greeted him with a hug.

'Good to see you, mate. I'm sorry about Jen. I was stuck outta town and couldn't make the funeral.'

'It's fine, bro. I appreciate it regardless.' Lamont noticed Kate behind Tek, giving him a searching look.

'Tek,' she said. 'Can you go to the shop and get me some cigs, please?'

'Sure. L, you want anything?'

Lamont shook his head. Patting him on the shoulder, Tek left. Lamont and Kate went to stand in the back garden.

'This isn't a random visit, is it?'

'I wanted to give you an update,' said Lamont.

'How have you been doing with everything? I feel like I lost a part of myself, L. I really do. She was beyond my best friend, and not having her hasn't got any easier.' Kate rubbed her arms. Lamont hung his head. He felt exactly the same way, and that was the hardest part to overcome.

'I know how you feel. Getting used to her not being there hasn't been easy.'

Kate gave him a shy smile.

'It's okay to miss her. You loved her.'

'Ryan.'

'Ryan?' Kate blinked, confused.

'The man who stabbed Jenny. That's his name.' Lamont watched Kate processing this information, her eyes going through a host of different emotions, widening as she realised the significance.

'He's dead?' Her voice croaked.

'Yes.'

Lamont didn't add any more, and Kate didn't ask him to. She flung her arms around him, and his shoulder was wet with her tears as she sobbed. He tightened his hold on her, and for a moment, it felt like Jenny was there with them. They stayed like that even as Tek appeared in the doorway behind them. He locked eyes with Lamont, knowing there was nothing romantic about the moment. With a nod, he went back inside. Tek had known Jenny longer than Lamont, but he knew

TARGET PART III

they cared for her as much as anyone. He wouldn't intrude on whatever was happening between them.

Lamont was in no hurry to let Kate go. This was someone who had been just as affected as him. He remembered how crumpled she had looked at the funeral. He had done this for her as much as himself, and she hadn't judged him for it. Lennox was the last piece. Lamont didn't mention his name. If it reassured Kate to think it was over, he was okay with that.

'What happens now?' Kate mumbled as they finally broke apart. She wiped her eyes.

'I don't know,' he said.

'I know you loved her, L, but you shouldn't hold back. Live your life to the fullest. That's what she would have wanted.'

'I think she would have wanted to still be alive, and the rest is just conjecture,' said Lamont. Kate sounded like the rest; hopelessly naïve and trying to predict the actions of a dead person. The fact was, he still had some debt to pay back, and he intended to do so.

'I knew Jenny since we were kids, L. I don't deny what the two of you had, and it's so sad it only lasted a short while, but put this behind you and move on. It doesn't hurt her memory; I promise you that.'

Lamont didn't reply. He took his phone from his pocket, noting Maka had tried calling him.

'I need to call someone back,' he said to Kate.

'Stay for dinner. Please. We'll have a few drinks and relax, listen to some music.'

'I think I'll need to jet. I've been waiting on this call,' replied Lamont. Kate nodded and went inside, leaving him in the garden. He called Maka back.

'Are we on?' he said. He'd been waiting days for Maka to get back to him.

'Tomorrow. It took me a second to get everyone together. I'll drop you a message with the location.'

'Catch you then.' Lamont hung up, once again reminding himself that he was almost at the end.

Kate was lighting a cigarette when he entered the room. She looked up and gave him a small smile.

'My plans have changed,' he said. 'If you still wanna chill, I'm down.'

'What do you feel like eating?' she asked, her smile widening.

K-Bar and Marika were curled up on the sofa, drinking wine and half-watching TV.

'I saw L the other day,' she said, giving up on the boring action movie completely.

'The *invisible man* . . . what's he saying?'

'We went to visit our parents' graves,' replied Marika. 'He looked well. I don't know what changed, but he seemed lighter, like he didn't have the weight of the world on his shoulders for once. When you spoke, did he say anything to you about how he was feeling, or what was going on?'

'You know your bro better than me, Rika. He takes *secretive* to a whole new level. Doesn't talk when he doesn't have to.'

'Something happened, I'm telling you. It's like he got laid or something.'

'Maybe he did. Not exactly difficult for him, is it?'

'His girlfriend died like a month ago. Do you think he could do it?'

'Maybe. Probably. Hard to tell what's going on with your bro.'

Marika sighed. 'Whatever it is, I'm glad it happened. He looked so much better.'

'I hope that means he's ready to get locked onto the crew, because people are grumbling about him not being around. He's losing face on the streets the longer he avoids dealing with people. They need to see him out and about, leading, or they'll lose even more faith.'

Marika pulled away from K-Bar, eyes flashing. 'My brother's mental state is more important than the streets.'

'That may be the case for you, but we came up in those same streets, and me, L, and Shorty, we've been playing that game since we were kids.' K-Bar wasn't backing down. 'Fact is, if he doesn't step up in a major way, our way of living could be done.'

TARGET PART III

'I thought you guys were winning now? You said Shorty was leading.'

'Shorty is like me. He's more of a tactician, but it's easier to smack someone over the head than to be diplomatic. He's doing well now because we're putting ourselves out there on the streets, slapping a few jokers around, but we need the thinkers like L. That's where he shines. He sees three moves ahead, and right now, we're only making one. The crew still looks vulnerable, and if we don't fix up, people will try us again.'

Before Marika could open her mouth to reply, K-Bar's phone rang. Grumbling, he checked the number. 'It's Shorty. Better take this,' he muttered, before answering, 'what's up?'

'I'm outside. Need to speak to you.'

'Now?' K-Bar was relaxed and hadn't intended on going anywhere. Shorty's response was to hang up. Kissing his teeth, he clambered to his feet and smoothed out his trousers.

'Gotta go,' he said. 'Don't wait up. Could be a late one if it's business.'

'Okay.'

Giving her a quick kiss, K-Bar grabbed a hooded top and left the house. Shorty's ride was outside, the engine running. He climbed into the passenger seat and slapped hands with him. Shorty immediately drove away, eyes on the road.

'What the hell? You couldn't have come for me in the morning? I was rooted.'

'This couldn't wait, bro. I need to meet someone, and I want you to come with me.'

'Who are we meeting?'

'Lennox's ex-girlfriend.'

'What ex?' K-Bar's eyes widened. He couldn't recall Lennox ever being linked to a woman on a serious level.

'Remember Sienna? The one I smacked up Lutel over? She's setting up this meeting with me and the girl.'

'Why?' K-Bar frowned. It didn't sound right.

'Says she felt bad over what happened to Grace.'

'And she's only just contacting you now? Sounds dodgy, fam.'

'Why do you think you're watching my back? Are you strapped?'

'No. I was chilling on the sofa, bro. You didn't even say where we were going.'

'Check under your seat.'

K-Bar pulled out a Glock and checked the weapon. It was lighter than expected, but he could make it work. In their younger days, they'd trained with whatever guns they could get their hands on, determined to have the edge in any encounter. It had been years since he had used one, but he would manage.

Neither man spoke the rest of the way. K-Bar recognised the area as Meanwood and hoped there wouldn't be trouble. He had been cool with the older, established gangs in the area, but the newer gangs were as bad as the Chapeltown ones, and they didn't respect anyone.

They parked up outside a pale bricked, semi-detached spot. Both men had their guns by their sides in case of an ambush. Shorty knocked on the door, and when Sienna answered, he gave her a tight smile.

'Hey, this is my boy, K-Bar. He's watching out for me.'

'Didn't you trust me?' Sienna was almost pouting, but he wasn't in the mood for it.

'We're warring out there. We don't travel light. Is she here?'

Sienna nodded, leaning in for a kiss. Shorty tensed, but returned it. K-Bar gave him a weird look but said nothing. In the living room, a slim, brown-skinned woman perched on the sofa, wringing her hands together. She met their eyes, then looked away. Shorty could understand why Lennox would be taken with such a beautiful woman.

'Julia, this is Shorty, the guy I was telling you about.'

Julia's eyes immediately flitted to the guns they were holding.

'I'm not gonna hurt you,' said Shorty, trying to reassure her. 'It's just for protection.'

Julia nodded, but didn't look relieved in the slightest. Sienna made them all cups of coffee, and they sat in uncomfortable silence. Shorty was waiting for Julia to start. He exchanged a look with K-Bar, who yawned and scratched his eyebrow.

'Jules, these guys are cool. I promise. Tell them what you have to say. Please,' said Sienna.

TARGET PART III

Julia took a deep breath, resting her hands on her thighs.

'I . . .' she cleared her throat. 'I've known Lennox a long time. We met when I was sixteen. He was twenty, and he swept me off my feet. I . . . he wasn't especially romantic, but he was honest and tough, and said what was on his mind, and I fell for him.'

Shorty listened, but grew more annoyed by the second. He'd figured Julia would have information, not some bullshit love story. He again glanced at K-Bar, who shook his head, silently cautioning him to be patient.

'For a while, we were fine. My mum didn't like me being with an older guy, so he moved me into a flat, and he would stop by now and then, but things were different. He was out in the streets building himself up, and he didn't always have time for me.'

Shorty could relate. A lot of his dalliances had fizzled out because he needed to be in the mix, making things happen in the streets.

'I never heard about him disrespecting me with women, but I knew at the same time I *didn't* have him, if that makes sense.

'I was naïve and didn't really understand how deeply he was entrenched in the crime life. Soon, he got locked up, and I was a mess. I didn't know how I would cope, but somehow I kept the flat and kept going. He sent me money, and I dropped out of college and got a job. There were visits, and he looked well, even behind bars. In the visiting room, I saw how much people respected him, and it was strange.

'When he got out, he flew me to Egypt, and for the entire holiday, he was attentive and loving, and any misgivings I'd had were ironed out. He sucked me back in.'

It was a nice tale, but Shorty would go ballistic if there wasn't an endpoint. K-Bar pinched his chin, leaning in, and Sienna looked moved by the tale that she had probably heard before.

'Back in Leeds, he was back out there in the streets, and he seemed harder, more closed-off than before.

'We started arguing, and I guess I thought he would listen to me when I said he was changing, but he just said I could accept him for who he was, or I could leave.' Sienna gathered herself. 'I loved him and couldn't imagine not being with him, so I stayed. He wasn't around anymore, though. He was in and out of town, doing deals. I'd find guns hidden in the flat, along with packages of money, and it all grew too real for me. So, I left.

'I expected him to chase me and beg for me back, but of course, he didn't. I didn't hear from him for a few years, and I moved on, but then he sought me out. By this time, I was in another relationship with a guy I liked. Lennox had my heart, though, and soon I was cheating on my partner with him.

'Eventually, we tried again, but Lennox was way different now. He had gone from strength to strength in the crime game. He wanted me to move in with him. Mentioned marriage and taking care of me, but when I fell pregnant, I saw the other side. He told me I had to get an abortion, and I was terrified. Deep down, I knew if I didn't, he would kill me and the baby. I did it, and then I left again. Again, he let me, and again, he went to prison.

'He stayed away for four years now, and our paths randomly crossed when I was out with Sienna. She was with Lutel at this point, and when I saw Lennox, all the old feelings came rushing back. I remember him saying I was under his skin,' Sienna's head bowed slightly, but she composed herself. 'We slept together for a while longer, but we drifted apart, and here I am,' she finished.

'What the fuck was the point of that?' said Shorty, unable to hold back. He had listened to her entire pathetic tale of love for no reason.

'Shorty!' hissed Sienna. 'That's my friend you're insulting.'

'Do you lot think I came here to listen to her recount some love story? This is real-life shit.'

'You think I don't know that?' snapped Julia. 'It may not mean much to you, but even my being here is tearing me apart inside. I gave him years of my life, pieces of my soul. I'm here to help.'

'Why did you want to speak to us?' Shorty decided moving past the melodrama was the best bet. K-Bar straightened behind him.

'Lennox will never let me go. I'll never have a life of my own because he's always out there, waiting to prey. Sienna told me about what he ordered done to your daughter. It can't go on. You need to stop him.'

'We're working on it.'

TARGET PART III

'I have an address. Lennox stays there. He likes it because it has sentimental value. We lived there on and off for a few years.'

'When was the last time you were there?'

Again, Julia lowered her head. 'Valentine's day.'

Shorty felt a wave of euphoria surge through his veins. That was only a few months ago. It meant the house was still in circulation, and Lennox wouldn't know they knew. He shot K-Bar a look, seeing the same level of understanding etched onto his friend's normally inscrutable face.

'Do you know who I am?' Shorty asked, wanting Julia to understand what she was essentially engineering by giving them the address.

'I know you're dangerous, but I also know you love your daughter, and he should pay for what he caused.'

'Where's the house?'

'Garforth. I'll write down the address for you.'

They didn't stay much longer. Shorty suffered through another hug and kiss with Sienna, then they drove away.

'What a story,' said K-Bar.

'Fucking nonsense is what it was. Can't believe we're gonna get Lennox on the back of his ex feeling unfulfilled.'

'Who are we gonna get to scope out the spot?'

'I'll do it myself,' said Shorty instantly.

'I don't think that's a good idea, fam,' said K-Bar. 'When are you gonna find the time to do that, anyway? We're deep in the streets, and Roman and that lot need a firm hand. They're not ready yet.'

'You can monitor them. I'm doing this.'

'You don't need to do it by yourself. We can use people for this. Bring L in on it and come up with a proper plan.'

'We don't need L, and I want to do this myself. Lennox nearly killed my daughter, and it has to be me that finishes him. Not L, and not that motherfucker Delroy.' He pulled the car to a stop on a quiet street and glared at K-Bar. 'I need you to support me. If it was the other way around, you wouldn't even need to ask, and you know it.'

K-Bar couldn't deny that. As much as he wanted to tell Shorty to use the crew, this was who he was.

'Okay, I'll go along with it, fam.'

SHORTY SPENT all night watching the address, hoping he would find Lennox Thompson and end him early. He left his surveillance at four in the morning, and no one had shown in that time.

The meeting with Julia had been weird. From everything he knew about Lennox, it was strange to imagine him getting caught up with a woman and almost having a child. He wondered how being a parent would have changed Lennox. Ultimately, it was pointless to think about. He needed to get a few hours of sleep to be sharp for the meeting later. Being around Lamont wouldn't be easy, but he would handle it. There were things that needed to be said. Sienna was another matter altogether. She was attractive and seemed interested, but she wasn't Amy, and he couldn't shake that.

Heading to his spot and collapsing on his bed, he quickly drifted off to sleep.

NAVEED ARRANGED a meeting room for the crew in the back room of another club. They arrived separately, dressed in *going-out* clothes. Naveed had prepared the room accordingly. There was a chocolate brown sofa, along with several smaller love-seat style seats. Bottles of brandy rested on a tray, along with glasses and ice.

'Did you want food?' he asked. Lamont shook his head, and the rest followed suit. Maka and Manson sat on the sofa, making a start on the brandy. Shorty wasn't drinking, and neither was Lamont. He glanced at Shorty, who scowled back. It would not be easy, but he couldn't give up now. Not when he was so close to the end.

'We're all here then, L,' said Maka. 'Are you gonna tell us what this is about?'

He nodded, assessing each man before he started speaking.

'I won't rehash all the things Lennox has done, but he hurt people close to me, and I made it my mission to learn more about him, and the

TARGET PART III

people working for him.' He locked eyes with Shorty again, seeing his old friend wasn't convinced. 'Ryan Peters, the dude that was killed in Seacroft. He did a job for Lennox. It was supposed to be a routine kidnap job, but the woman fought back. She grabbed a knife, he fought with her, and ended up getting stabbed.'

'Jenny,' said Shorty, putting the pieces together. Lamont nodded.

'He's dead now. Before he died, he mentioned the name *Mark Patrick*. He's the one doing all Lennox's running around. He also mentioned a shooter. *Sinclair*. He gunned down Akeem on Chapeltown Road.'

'Sinclair . . . Never heard of him,' said Manson. Maka looked equally confused.

'Delroy is focusing on shutting down whatever people he can find. I want us to focus on finding this pair. I have men on it, but with our experience, we can do more. K-Bar, you and Shorty are trackers. I want you to go deep underground and smoke them out. Use whatever people and resources you need to do it.' Lamont waited for them to reply. Shorty spoke first, as expected, but his words threw him for a loop.

'Where've you been?'

Lamont blinked, confused by the question.

'What?'

'You've been hiding, doing your own thing, completely ignoring the crew. We've been holding things down, stopping the gangs on the street from pushing us out.'

'I know. I—'

'You come here after all this time, giving us a little speech, trying to get us back in line. It's all about you and your fucking agenda. Typical you, fam. Not caring about anyone or anything but what *you've* got going on. You don't give a shit about the crew.'

'That's not true, Shorty. Lennox is the single biggest threat to this crew.'

'Is he? Or are you?'

'What are you talking about?'

'I'm talking about this! You never letting people in on what's going on. Just expecting them to fall in line.'

Lamont's eyebrows rose. '*Fall in line?* Shorty, taking out Lennox was always the goal.'

'Why haven't you done that then?'

Lamont's mouth fell open. He was familiar with Shorty's temper tantrums, seeing him fly off the handle over the smallest things. This was the other side. The strategic, tactical side of Shorty's personality. It was influencing the room. K-Bar hadn't said a word, but he was nodding along with Shorty now.

'He's in hiding, Shorty. We haven't located him yet.'

'Nothing to do with you being scared of him?'

'I'm not scared.'

'Explain it then. For once in your life, no sneaky shit. Lay it on the line and tell us why you haven't gone after him.'

'I'm cautious, Shorty. That caution has benefited the crew many times over. When you're at the top, making the decisions, it's different. It's all on you, and you have to pick the right moves.'

'Exactly. That's why I'm here. I've had to decide, because you walked away and left Maka and Manson in the lurch. You left K-Bar to rot, and I had to get him out. Where the fuck were you?'

'I . . .' Lamont didn't have the words for the first time in his life. Shorty shook his head, recognising the indecision.

'Guess that's more *caution* from the boss,' he said. 'You were nowhere. You hid in your house, and you didn't care what was going on around you. That isn't leadership. We all put ourselves on the line for the crew, and you know what? You don't have the heart anymore. Maybe you never did.'

Lamont looked at each man. Shorty and K-Bar had been alongside him when he started the crew. Maka and Manson had come into the fold later, but this was the first time all pieces had been united so clearly against him. K-Bar stared at him with something akin to regret. Maka and Manson watched him like he was the enemy. He supposed he was now.

Had he been outplayed? Was this Shorty's plan all along?

Ultimately, it was still his crew. He still controlled their supply, but he had wanted them with him on this. He saw them taking down Lennox together and mending old fences.

TARGET PART III

'Shorty, whatever is going on between us, those are our problems. It doesn't affect crew business.'

'Our problems have grown bigger. You were about one thing: Lennox is a problem, but after he dies, things are gonna change, whether or not you want them to.'

Shorty stood up and left the room. One by one, each man followed, leaving Lamont sitting there, trying to work out what had just happened. He and Shorty had done most of the talking, but the divide was clear, and his crew supporting Shorty spoke volumes.

Lamont poured a drink, a leaden feeling in his stomach as he contemplated the mistakes he had made lately. Instead of gaining centre, he and Shorty were further away than ever.

CHAPTER TWENTY-ONE

SUNDAY 24 MAY, 2015

THE FOLLOWING DAY, Lamont was still mulling over the disaster of a meeting. Shorty's words had resonated, and he couldn't work out exactly when he took his eye off the ball. He'd known Shorty was helping the crew, but he fully hadn't known to what degree. They were right about his lack of focus. He was determined to kill Lennox, but there was something wrong with him deep down that he couldn't put his finger on.

Lamont was supposed to be more powerful than ever, yet he didn't feel it. He had a loose alliance with the most powerful crime boss in the county. He'd avenged Jenny's murder. Grace was recovering, and he had more money than he could spend. Despite those wins, he felt desolate, and he hated it.

After spending some more time sulking, he went to see Marika again, hoping she would make him feel better. Charlotte would have been useful, but he was giving her space after the way their last encounter had ended. He and Marika were at least on a loving level again, and he was pleased she was back in his life and doing so well. Maybe being around her would influence him.

Lamont knocked on the door, smiling tightly when K-Bar

answered. He wore a vest and tracksuit bottoms, and was holding a protein shaker.

'Easy, L. Everything good? I just finished a workout.'

'I came to see Marika. Is she in?'

K-Bar shook his head. 'She's at work. Come in, anyway. I think we have some things we need to say.'

Lamont could have pointed out that it was his sister's house and that he didn't need to be invited in, but didn't. He sat on the sofa as K-Bar disappeared from the room, returning with a flannel which he used to clean his face. He remained standing, and the silence stretched on for a minute. It was comfortable despite the circumstances, as it usually was with K-Bar.

'What's going on, L?' K-Bar finally said.

'You'll need to be more specific,' said Lamont.

'That meeting yesterday. You could have said more to Shorty. You basically let him control the crew, and I don't for a second think you didn't know he was running it all along.'

'Maybe it's for the best. I didn't say anything because he's making the right decisions. It would be silly to overrule that.'

'You two are best when you're deciding together.'

'I can't see that happening. Shorty can't get over what happened with us. Maybe I can't either.'

'You need to keep talking to him, L. Shorty can be stubborn. You're the same way, and you two need each other.'

'I tried. I apologised, and every time I see him, we end up antagonising one another further. He can focus on the crew, and I'll focus on Lennox. Maybe somewhere down the line, we'll meet in the middle.'

K-Bar finished his protein shake, still holding the container and frowning at Lamont.

'You're the mature one. I know it's tough, but you have to keep making the moves until you get through to him. I ain't telling you nothing new here. You know how to get to Shorty.'

'I used to. Me and Shorty haven't been right for a while, and everything that's happened over the past few years has only made things worse. So, I'll focus on what I need to. I have leads for Lennox's men, and I'll follow them. That's all I wanted to tell the crew last night, but you guys supported Shorty instead.'

'Don't look at it like that. You're still our boss, and you could have forced the issue, but you didn't.'

'If I had, what would you have done? Would you have supported me, or gone with Shorty?'

K-Bar didn't answer, not that he expected him to. The answer was obvious. He might be the boss, but Shorty had got K-Bar out of prison, and he had known him longer. Shorty had worked with Maka and Manson when they were struggling, and used that to push the crew forward and stop the vultures from swarming. It wasn't an even situation.

'Do you have a line on Lennox?'

'Not yet,' admitted Lamont. 'Mark Patrick is probably the best bet. He's the one Lennox apparently keeps the closest, so he'll know how to find Lennox. I have a few safe houses that need searching, so we'll see. Delroy and his people are pushing at the crew, so I need to touch base with him and see where he's at.'

For a moment, Lamont was sure he saw something in K-Bar's eyes, almost like a gleam. He blinked, and it was gone.

'I'll watch Shorty for now. You're right about the street stuff. Meeting got out of hand last night before we could go into it, but the money is finally on the up. We're reloading soon too, and we're gonna get twenty.'

'Twenty boxes? Do you have the moves lined up to offload it?'

'We've discussed it,' said K-Bar. 'It's more than we normally move in a week, but we've got the crews back in line, so we'll knock it out easily.'

Lamont was uneasy about the increased order. It was likely the crew had the infrastructure to move it, and it meant he would get paid twice, as both supplier and boss, but it was a tremendous risk.

'What about the police activity?'

'We'll wholesale it mostly, so it'll be out of our hands. Still gonna be a lot of profit, and it's worth it. The more money we make, quicker we get back to where we were, especially with Delroy being distracted with Lennox.'

TARGET PART III

Lamont couldn't deny the merits of the plan. The police activity had eased as of late, as it always did with the authorities. All you had to do was wait them out. They had budgets and quotas they needed to justify, and surveillance and long-term investigations were expensive. He had made a career out of out-waiting the police, and it seemed to work for his crew too.

'Be careful. There's a lot still going on, so eyes in the back of your head. How's it going with my sister?'

'She's a rider, L. Held me down while I was on remand, and we've been close since we got out. Everything is out in the open now, and I've cared about her for a long time.'

'She's changing. In a good way. She seems a lot more focused,' admitted Lamont.

'She's come a long way, L. That fight you lot had made her realise she had to stand on her own two feet. Worked hard on her CV so she could land a job, and then worked hard in the job to establish herself. She had a rough start. Wasn't used to working, and she had that funky temper. Few times she came back shouting she was gonna quit, but she didn't.'

'A while back, she told me she was studying too, because she wanted to understand money,' said Lamont.

K-Bar beamed, his pride evident. 'She wants to open her own salon. She's been talking about it for a while, and she's working on the qualifications. I'm gonna back her when she's qualified.'

Lamont grinned. Despite his off mood at the start of the day, the thought of his little sister making big moves was something to be pleased about. It had taken her a long time to grow up, but she was making up for it with excellent decision after excellent decision.

'That's amazing. I'm proud of her.'

'That's what she wants. You're always saying we should diversify and invest, so it'll be good for that too. Doing something solid with the money we're making. She really wants you to be proud of her. All the stuff that happened with Marrion and the Manchester boys . . . the guilt has lingered with her. She doesn't talk about it much anymore, but it's obvious.'

Lamont felt a jolt at the reminder of the group that had nearly ended his life. They'd had inside help, Chink pulling their strings in Machiavellian fashion, but they had still almost succeeded, taking advantage of the gaps in the crew to launch their attack.

Two years later, they were still picking up the pieces.

'I never blamed her for that.' Lamont hated the thought of Marika blaming herself. She'd shown bad judgement, but so had he. He hadn't properly communicated, then he'd argued with her when they both needed one another, pushing her further into the hands of the enemy.

'Have you ever actually said that to her?' K-Bar asked.

Lamont didn't reply.

DESPITE PLANNING to conduct more surveillance on the spot Julia had given, Shorty hadn't returned to it. He and K-Bar were putting the finishing touches on their order. It had been his idea to order big and spread it around the Hood. He wanted to show all the other crews they were still the biggest, and the profit from moving twenty boxes of food would put them in an entirely different league.

Maka and Manson had said little, but K-Bar agreed with it being a good idea, and had even agreed to be in charge of the delivery. Since their last meeting, he had spoken with Sienna a few times. She was pushing for something more to happen with them. Shorty couldn't shake Amy, though, and if he could work things out and build a future with her, that was what he wanted to do.

Despite this, Sienna was more up front, and he dug that. He didn't have to work hard to understand what was on her mind, and she was more like him. She understood Chapeltown, having grown up there. Amy was an outsider and had grown up entirely differently. Shorty had always looked at her as *better*, but saw Sienna as more on his level. He couldn't work out whether that was good, and that conflict made his head hurt.

Right now, he was getting his weaponry together so he could move on the house tonight. He planned to go in after dark and was carrying both a pistol, and a small knife he'd stashed in his sock. He'd considered going in heavy with a shotgun, but ultimately decided against it.

TARGET PART III

Depending on how many people were there, he could move quicker with a handgun. It was a risk worth taking.

K-Bar called him an hour later.

'Everything in place for the delivery?' Shorty asked.

'The spot is ready. We'll make the calls as soon as it lands. Me and Maka will handle it. Manson and the others will await the calls, and they'll do the drop-offs. A few spots are ready for pickups too. They'll sell out quick. Streets are congested, but we have the best goods, and people know that.'

'Good shit. We'll move this quick and reload again. After that, we can sit back and focus.'

'How's your thing going?'

'I'm going in tonight,' replied Shorty. K-Bar hesitated.

'I don't like the sound of that, Shorty. Put it off til tomorrow, and let me go in with you.'

Shorty was tempted. K-Bar was deadly, and with him, the mission would be a piece of cake. He could handle it, however. He didn't need K-Bar. If he could get Lennox tonight and put two bullets in his head, the headlines tomorrow would probably distract from the kilos of drugs flooding the streets. It would work better for them to make the moves all at once.

'I've got it covered, K. Chill.'

'You've been doing your surveillance then? Do you know what to expect?'

'I've done this shit before. Don't worry about it. Focus on what you need to do.'

'Okay, fam. Make sure you ring me if you need me.'

'Count on it.' Shorty hung up, already envisioning what he was going to do with his cut of the money. Most of it would go to Amy for Grace's care, and a significant portion would go to Dionte and Stacey in Huddersfield, but there would be plenty left over. In the old days, he'd have spent it on clothes, jewellery and nights out, but he wanted to be more conservative now. If the past few years had taught him anything, it was that it was essential to have money in reserve. If he was arrested again, he wouldn't be able to rely on Lamont to get him a solicitor. He would need to do it himself.

Thinking of Lamont made him recall the meeting. He couldn't put his finger on what was wrong with Lamont, but he'd expected more resistance, and was still surprised he'd given in so easily. He hadn't even cared about Shorty essentially stealing the crew from him, which he supposed made sense. Lamont had been trying to run away from the crime game for years, even before Jenny was killed. *What reason did he have to still be doing it now?*

Shorty kissed his teeth, scowling. The last thing he wanted was to think about Lamont. Clambering to his feet from the sofa, he went hunting for his weed and Rizla, wanting to relax and distract himself.

CHAPTER TWENTY-TWO

SUNDAY 24 MAY, 2015

'WHY DID you allow it to happen?'

Lamont and Delroy were talking on the phone. Needing a second opinion after his conversation with K-Bar, he had called Delroy, filling him in on the meeting and aftermath.

'He needed it more than me.'

'Are you sure?'

'Shorty has done well keeping the crew in line. Fact is, they weren't a priority for me. I just assumed everything was okay, and it was.'

'I've asked you this before, and I'll repeat it now: what do you want? What's the end game for you?'

Lamont considered his reply. The line was encrypted on both ends. It was the only way they felt comfortable speaking to one another over the phone, yet freely admitting his intent to murder someone was ridiculous.

'You know what I want. I want the same thing you do.'

'I think you let Shorty have the crew because you don't actually want to deal with running it anymore.'

'That's not it,' Lamont disagreed. 'I need to get my head in the game. I've been second-guessing myself for the longest. The desire for revenge has gone nowhere, and I figured it would have by now. I guess with Lennox out of the way, that will fix itself.'

'It's not that simple,' Delroy started. Lamont heard him take a deep breath before he continued. 'I would kill to walk away now. Getting up every day, motivating the troops, and trying to keep everyone out of prison is tiresome. I don't have the stamina for it anymore.'

'You should leave it all behind now then. Why wait?'

'I can't.'

Lamont waited for Delroy to add more, but he didn't.

'You want to retire to Grenada, right? So, go.'

Delroy laughed darkly.

'Grenada is a pipe dream, L. All along, I've known deep down I'll never go back. I built land, sent money back home for decades, because that's what I was supposed to do, and because I fucked over many people when I was there. Truth is, I will never leave Leeds.'

'You don't know that.' Lamont didn't like to hear Delroy doubting himself. They had become even closer lately, and he wanted him to achieve his goals.

'L, please hear this if you forget everything else I've told you: Walk away — for real this time. Don't worry about what you *think* you're leaving behind.'

'It's not that simple, and you more than anyone should realise that,' Lamont argued.

'It's as simple as you want it to be. You talk about fixing things and getting back to your old mindset, but that's not you anymore, and your actions lately have proved that. Killing yourself for the streets won't fix that broken part of you.'

Lamont said little more after that, hanging up a short while later with more questions than answers. Delroy was speaking from a different place, but Lamont didn't believe what he said, and wasn't sure Delroy did either. Delroy clearly didn't want him around, and it was likely it was influencing what he wanted from Lamont.

For that reason, he hadn't told Delroy the results of his interrogation of Peters. He didn't know if Delroy knew of Mark Patrick and his role as Lennox's street general, but like the Jackie Smart Court spot, he kept it to himself. They both had the same goal, and whoever

TARGET PART III

got to Lennox Thompson first would kill him. It was as simple as that.

SHORTY PARKED up the road from the Garforth spot, checked his weaponry, and headed down the road towards the house, hiding behind cars and keeping out of sight. There were no guards when he'd done his brief surveillance, but his caution was justified. There was a man outside the house, smoking a cigarette and looking at his phone. Even if he'd looked up, he wouldn't have seen Shorty, who was well concealed. He would need to get past him to get in the house. Securing his gun, he crept around to the left side of a car directly outside the house. The man had his back to him, and he grabbed him from behind, then turned him, sinking his knee into the man's stomach, hearing the whoosh of air being driven from the man's lungs. He followed it up with a crushing blow to the man's jaw. He was out on his feet.

Shorty dragged him into the garden, dumping the gun he carried, and taking his mobile phone. He was tempted to kill him, but decided against it. He had equipment to break into the house but, based on the guard outside, tried the handle instead, grinning when it opened.

Quietly closing it behind him, he took stock of his surroundings. Music was playing upstairs. Someone was in the house, and his heart raced, imagining the look on Lennox's face when he walked in on him. He searched downstairs, gun in hand, ready to shoot anyone he saw. He found no one and silently padded up the stairs. The light was on in one bedroom, so he positioned himself outside the door and wrenched it open, dipping low and charging into the room.

The music was playing from a Bluetooth speaker beside the bed, but the room was empty.

Before Shorty had time to process, he heard a noise from behind and narrowly shifted his weight as someone barrelled into him. He slammed into the wall, the gun spilling from his grasp. Whirling around and to his feet, he glanced at the muscular, smiling man by the door.

'Long time no see, Shorty,' the familiar man said. Shorty tensed.

'Derrigan. Figured you were dead.'

———

'WHAT WAS TEFLON SAYING THEN?'

K-Bar and Maka were sitting in the back of the van, looking at the product. They'd picked it up from the usual spot and loaded the bricks without issue. The warehouse was a distance away, but Maka had previously made the trip and foresaw no issues.

'How do you know I spoke to him?' K-Bar hated the vans they used for transport. They weren't comfortable, and with him being long-limbed, he had no legroom. The van hadn't been properly cleaned out and had clearly been used for another task, meaning there was a lingering odour that grew stronger the longer they were sat there. He and Lamont had talked for a while, with Lamont leaving to attend a meeting. He wasn't sure what to think of the conversation. There hadn't been a real agenda for the meeting, and Shorty and Lamont's ongoing vendetta had quickly hijacked it.

'Just a guess. You're the calm one, so it makes sense he would speak to you.'

'He didn't really say much,' K-Bar admitted. 'He's kinda just leaving Shorty to it and letting him do what he's doing.'

Maka wiped his face. 'That meeting was mad. I thought they were gonna get into another scrap. Think they'll ever make up?'

'I dunno. When I got out, I thought I could talk them around, but Shorty will barely discuss L, and L's doing the whole *hanging back and waiting for him to calm down thing*.'

Maka kissed his teeth. 'Never thought they'd fall out. Maybe Tef's way is the best way. You know what Shorty's like he when he's pissed off.'

K-Bar did. Better than anyone. Shorty could be the coolest guy on earth, and then a second later, he'd want to fight everyone in the room. He had a hair-trigger temper, and for the longest, Lamont had handled him. Somewhere down the line, it all fell apart.

'I'll have another go at them. We need the team at full strength.'

'L's not gonna do anything until he's sorted Lennox. Maybe we're best staying out of it for now.'

K-Bar shrugged. Maybe Maka had the right of it.

'D's doing excellent work with those local crews. He's working well with that Roman kid.'

Maka grinned. 'Roman and Keith remind me a little of you and Shorty. Roman keeps Keith calm, and Keith wants to go around splitting everyone's skulls. It cracks me up.'

'We need to do something more with them. Let them have the shine and take the risk. This is a young man's game. We both know that.'

Before Maka could reply, they heard a burst of gunfire, and the van veered out of control. Neither man had a chance to move before they were sent hurtling from their seats, smacking the hard floor of the vehicle. The bricks of product rained down on them. K-Bar struggled underneath a makeshift pile, his head aching. He squinted, just able to make out a car in front of them. The driver was slumped over the seat, bleeding and unmoving.

'Maka,' K-Bar hissed. 'Are you okay?'

'Shit . . . my ribs are fucked,' Maka gasped. 'The fuck happened?'

More gunshots cancelled out Maka's words, smashing through the front window, peppering the back. They ducked back down as several packs of drugs exploded under the bullets, showering them in powder.

'We need to get out of here,' K-Bar shouted.

'Are you mad? We don't even know how many of them are out there!'

'Doesn't matter. I ain't staying here to die.' K-Bar crawled forward and, hearing a lull, hoped for the best and opened the van doors. A man stood there, an automatic weapon by his side. He hadn't expected K-Bar to open the van and stupidly gawped. His hesitation cost him his life. K-Bar's bullet smashed through the top of his head, sending him tumbling to the ground. He grabbed his weapon.

'C'mon,' he yelled to Maka. They were on the Ring Road near Moor Allerton. There were woods nearby, and he kept his head low and made for them. Maka was behind him, panting as the gunfire started up again, bullets whining all around them. Gasping, Maka took cover behind a tree.

'You strapped?' K-Bar called. He could just about make his comrade out in the darkness.

'Yeah. Only got a little pistol, though.'

'I'll cover you. We need to hold them off and call for backup. We should have had a fucking car trailing us. I didn't even think.'

'Doesn't matter now. Call Shorty.'

'Where the fuck are you going?' A voice yelled. 'Stay and fight, you pussies.'

'Do you recognise him?' K-Bar asked. Maka didn't answer as he tried dialling. He cursed when it went to voicemail. He tried calling twice more, and the same thing happened.

'He's not answering.'

'Fuck. Call Sharma and tell him to get some people together.'

'We don't even know where we are.'

'We're near Moor Allerton. We'll hold out here until they come,' said K-Bar, recognising the area. Saying a prayer he would live to see Marika and the kids, he took a better position and lifted the gun.

———

DELROY SETTLED into his favourite chair with a glass of brandy. Business was done for the day, and with every passing hour, he was ready for it to end. He realised more and more just how empty his life was, and how little substance he had. He'd tried reaching out to his estranged wife, but she still wouldn't speak to him.

Earlier, he'd visited the graves of his sons, both dead before their time. He'd stared at the headstones with a growing sense of guilt and failure. They'd had no opportunity to be anything but his lieutenants. He didn't hide the life from them, and when they showed an interest, he schooled them and taught them the game.

Winston had a wife and kids, but Delroy wasn't allowed to see them anymore, and hadn't since the funeral. Eddie was a hothead with far too much to prove, who was never the same after Winston's murder. He'd tried to end Lennox Thompson's life, but had ended up dead too.

As he contemplated his life, Delroy wondered if keeping Lamont out of the loop was a smart thing. He'd wanted him to get involved earlier in the conflict, but now he was keeping him at arm's length, trying to make sense of the reasons. Lamont was an asset to any organisation. He'd made no secret of his desire to have him on his team, but lately, he'd realised just how damaged Lamont was. He wanted him to be better, more than he wanted to utilise him. The deaths of so many close to him had changed him, and he was trying to push ahead, ignoring the surrounding signs to slow down. They'd shared some tough words on the phone, and he hoped he took it to heart. Once Lennox was in the ground, they could both move on.

Staring into the glass at the dark liquid, his phone rang. He scowled. His men knew not to bother him late at night unless it was life and death. When he checked the number, his heart soared. It was his daughter. Snatching the phone, he hastily answered.

'Alicia?'

It wasn't her.

'I almost feel bad for this call, after hearing that optimism in your tone,' a man said, his tone mocking.

Delroy closed his eyes, his world crashing down around him. This was it. The game was over.

'Lennox.'

'You recognised my voice then? I'm touched. We haven't exactly spoken much in the past.'

'If you touch her—'

'Save it. You're not in control here.' In the background, Delroy heard the muffled sounds of Alicia struggling. His shoulders slumped. 'I want to see you. Now. Don't bring anyone else. If you do, I promise what I do to your beautiful daughter will not be quick.'

'Where am I going?' Delroy growled, fury making his words shake. Lennox had crossed the line going after his daughter. He didn't know how he had tracked her down, but if survived, the gloves would well and truly be off. He would tear apart anyone who even looked like Lennox.

Mocking tone in place, Lennox gave Delroy the address and hung up.

A__aron was loving this.__ His team had laid in wait for the van, and taken out the driver. Gary had failed. Aaron had ordered him to secure the back of the van to prevent whoever was in the back from jumping out. Now, he was bleeding out on the floor.

'J-Star,' he said to one man, 'you're coming with me. Grab two more guys, and let's go kill these fuckers. There can't be more than three of them. You lot stay here and secure that van for when the backup comes.'

J-Star signalled to two men, and they hurried toward the woods. Aaron grinned, his heart hammering. He had been waiting to get his revenge on Teflon's crew. He had been minding his own business when they'd jumped in the middle of his beef with Roman, beating him down and forcing his crew to abandon him. He'd licked his wounds for a time, letting his injured arm heal, before an opportunity presented itself. Now, he was going to wipe out the whole crew. Following his people, he kept his gun raised, his smile only widening.

'T__hey're coming after us__,' said K-Bar. His heart raced as he kept the gun raised. Maka had tried calling Manson, Jamal, and Sharma, but he couldn't connect to anyone. K-Bar didn't know how many enemies there were. Other than the gun he'd stolen, he had his pistol. Maka only had one handgun. They'd had no time to come up with a plan. Despite everything, his adrenaline was skyrocketing. Apart from his assassination of Big-Kev a few months back, he hadn't been in a fight like this for years, and he'd missed it more than he realised. They were outnumbered and outgunned, but it didn't matter. All that mattered was the here and now.

'Get behind me,' he said to Maka. Maka shuffled over just as the gunfire started again, narrowly missing him. K-Bar let go a quick burst with the rifle, moving to another tree nearby, bullets smashing into the surrounding trees. If one caught him, he was done for. He didn't even

TARGET PART III

have a vest on. The team had grown lax, having made the runs so many times without issue. If they survived, he would need to rectify it.

The two teams traded shots. K-Bar needed to be careful not to run out of ammunition. He saw one assailant stupidly step out of cover and put two bullets into his chest. The man dropped, and another man foolishly ran toward the fallen man. K-Bar made quick work of him too.

'J-Star,' he heard the voice that had taunted them earlier yell. 'Don't make the same mistake as those idiots. Stay in cover.'

Another voice – *J-Star* – shouted his understanding.

'Maka, start running. I'll cover you,' ordered K-Bar. They couldn't afford to wait around any longer. No backup was coming. There was no way to get to the drugs in the van. He didn't know how they were going to explain it to Lamont or Shorty, but right now, they had to go.

'I'm not leaving you,' said Maka.

'Go. I'm right behind you.'

Maka started running, kicking up mud and twigs in his haste. Bullets followed him, narrowly missing. K-Bar followed the muzzle flash in the dark. He raised his gun, waiting for the opportunity.

AARON WASN'T SMILING ANYMORE. He didn't know exactly who'd been in the van, but it seemed like *Rambo* was tearing them apart. The person was skilled, and he guessed it was Shorty or K-Bar. They were the most well-known of Teflon's lot, and they were killers. He regretted not planning the ambush properly. Now, three of his men were dead. He and J-Star had fired guns before, but never to hit anybody. They had fired at cars and windows, but he'd figured it would be easy to use those same skills in a gunfight. Now, he realised how silly that was.

There was no turning back now, though.

Hearing scuffling sounds from ahead. He fired wildly, determined to hit the running target. He didn't hear or see the bullets that hit him, but they caught him in the neck, stomach, and shoulder, spinning him around before depositing him on the floor. His gun fell from his hand as he gasped for life. There was utterly no chance. He was aware of J-

Star screaming, but it sounded like it was coming from miles away. Trying to sit up, it was to no avail. His eyes dimmed, and his life ended on the rough ground.

K-Bar lowered the rifle. He had picked off the man shooting at Maka, then his comrade right after. The rifle was low on ammo, and he wiped it down and dropped it, gripping his handgun and following Maka as they crashed through branches and undergrowth. He couldn't hear any more gunfire, but it wasn't worth doubling back to the van. The people in the woods hadn't been the best shooters, but it didn't mean there weren't more of them waiting. As he followed Maka, a leaden sensation engulfed his stomach.

Why couldn't they get hold of anyone else?

DERRIGAN GRINNED AT SHORTY, before he slowly shook his head.

'Not yet, Shorty. I've been waiting for you to come. I know you've had the address for a while.'

Shorty looked around the room, looking for anything he could use to get an advantage. He and Nicky Derrigan went way back and had even once fought after an argument, with Shorty narrowly winning. That was well over ten years ago, though, when he was younger and more reckless. Derrigan looked solid as he stared him down, a half-grin on his face. Shorty had been well and truly set up. He didn't know if they had trailed him, or if Julia and Sienna had sold him out, but he was leaning toward the latter.

'Where's Lennox? Is he too scared to step to me?'

Derrigan's smile widened. 'Why would he need to do that? You're not on his level. He has more important business to handle tonight. You're not the only one getting dropped.'

'He's got you doing his dirty work then, like a little lapdog?'

Derrigan sniggered, unaffected by the insult.

'He's paying me a lot of money for my services.'

'Who set me up?'

'You always had a weakness for pussy. Must be why you ended up

TARGET PART III

saddled with kids. How's your daughter, anyway?' Derrigan's grin was truly sinister now. 'Heard she had an accident.'

Enraged, Shorty charged him, which was what he'd wanted. He planted his feet, able to absorb Shorty's momentum, then flung him to the ground, kicking him twice while he was down. Shorty forced his way back to his feet as he took a step back.

'I'm not a kid anymore. You got sloppy, Shorty. There's no way you're winning this.'

Shorty moved forward, faking left and sailing in with a right. Derrigan slipped the hit and drove his elbow into Shorty's back. Shorty cried out in pain but moved quicker than Derrigan expected, kicking him in the stomach. Derrigan doubled over, and he caught him with a vicious knee to the face, exploding his nose. He went for a punch, but Derrigan grabbed his hand, driving his free hand into his stomach, grinning as he felt the air leave Shorty. He hit him twice more, then shoved him onto the bed. Mounting him, he moved Shorty's hands, catching him with two unguarded blows to the face, then dragged him to his feet and threw him into the wall. Unable to get his hands up, Shorty's face impacted against it, blood pouring from his broken nose. Derrigan was all over him, allowing no time for recovery. He drove a fist into his kidney, the blow sending him to one knee.

'Lennox played you and your stupid crew,' he taunted. 'You never even saw it coming. I wasn't sure about Lennox when he hired me. Figured he had big dreams but would get dropped, but he saw what everyone else didn't. You and your team are washed up. Delroy's too.'

Shorty struggled to stay upright. He was in tremendous pain, dizzy from the blows to the face and kidneys. He couldn't let Derrigan win, and he again went forward, putting his hands up, ready to box. Derrigan took the bet and threw a sloppy hook. He ducked under it and caught him with an uppercut that knocked him back. He kept up the pressure, hitting him twice more, but the blows weren't enough to put Derrigan down, who was both bigger and stronger. He grabbed Shorty in a bearhug, and Shorty yelled, feeling the air being driven from him, putting pressure on his already injured kidneys and ribs. Drawing his head back, he brought it down on Derrigan's already injured nose, making the man howl in pain.

He expected him to back up, but Derrigan instead kicked out, catching his already injured ribs and sending him to his knees. He followed up with a boot to Shorty's face, sending him crashing to the floor.

'You're done, Shorty.' Derrigan kicked him twice more in the ribs, feeling them shift under his feet. Kicking him onto his back, he looked him in the eye, then brought his boot down on the same injured ribs.

Shorty heard a noise that sounded like a scream. It took him a few seconds to realise it had come from him. He was fading, struggling to stay conscious. It hurt to breathe, and he couldn't focus. He couldn't give up. This was for Grace and Dionte. For Jenny and everyone Lennox had harmed. He couldn't let it end here.

Derrigan looked at the beaten man. He hadn't expected Shorty to present such a challenge. He was older, and hadn't trained as hard over the years as Derrigan had. He was still breathing, and Derrigan had a job to do. Wrapping his hands around Shorty's throat, he squeezed with all his might. Shorty struggled, but Derrigan was too powerful to overcome. He was in so much pain, and for a moment, he thought this was it. The intensity grew, but he fought it, unwilling to go down like this.

Still struggling, he jerkily reached for the knife he'd stored in his right sock, and fumbled to get it free. He needed to hurry. A little more pressure and he would be done. His eyes wanted nothing more than to close, but he fought through it, flicking open the knife and jabbing it into Derrigan's thigh. Derrigan yelled, letting him go. Shorty kicked the man off him, then threw punch after punch at him while he was distracted. He went for the gun he'd dropped earlier, grabbing it just as another man burst into the room with his own raised. Shorty was quicker and put the man down for the count with two shots. Derrigan had already started moving, and by the time the second man hit the floor, he'd limped through the open door.

Wincing in pain, Shorty was about to go after him, when gunfire shattered the windows behind him. He dived back to the floor, his body screaming at him as he crawled along, praying there was no one waiting outside the door. He charged into another of the upstairs rooms, which was thankfully empty. There were loud voices and footsteps thundering up the stairs. Shorty didn't know how many were coming, but he couldn't stay and fight his way out. He was barely staying upright as it was. Wildly looking around the room, he saw it was a makeshift bedroom. He could try to barricade the door, but it would take too long and wouldn't last. If Lennox's men didn't get him, the police would. He couldn't risk it. There was only one option available.

As the voices grew closer, he fired a shot at the window in the room, shattering it. Taking a deep breath, he ran to the window as quickly as he could and hurtled through it. He heard shouts, but couldn't stop to think. He slammed down onto a shed roof, his already damaged ribs impacted as he rolled onto a dustbin, then to the floor with a thud. Shorty took a few seconds, his body not wanting to move after everything it had taken, then he shifted to his feet and limped towards a fence leading to the next garden, barely climbing over.

He couldn't wait around. There was no telling what the men would do. He had no choice but to keep moving.

CHAPTER TWENTY-THREE
MONDAY 25 MAY, 2015

DELROY DROVE himself to the meeting spot. It was a ramshackle house in Bankside, with metal bars on the doors and windows. Two sullen men waited for him. When he climbed from the car, they roughly patted him down, then marched him into the house. It galled him to be treated with such disrespect, but he would take it. Alicia was all that mattered.

Inside, he was led down to the cellar. There were a set of tools propped in a corner. The floor had been wrapped in plastic; the sight making him nauseous. It was a sign he wouldn't be getting out alive. Straightening his shoulders, he stepped into the room. His heart broke when he saw Alicia sitting on the floor, gagged, with her legs and arms secured. She looked at him with terrified, tear-stained eyes. She favoured Elaine so much, with her beautiful features, dark eyes and round face.

Lennox leant against the wall, a pistol in his hand and a small smile on his face. He was a wiry, hard-faced man, with cold eyes, despite the smile. Delroy couldn't place him. He couldn't recall the last time he'd seen him.

'Delroy. Thanks for coming. Feels weird being face to face after spending the year trying to kill one another.'

TARGET PART III

'Let Alicia go. You don't need her anymore.' Delroy wanted to charge Lennox and wring his skinny little neck, but three men were nearby — not counting the two who had led him down here. They were all armed, and any attempt at a rescue would lead to him being cut down. He needed to be smart.

'It's touching how much you care,' said Lennox with false sincerity. 'If it wasn't for you, she wouldn't be here. I wouldn't have been forced to murder her brothers. This is all on you, Delroy, and you know it.'

Delroy shot a look at his daughter, seeing the pain in her eyes at the reminder of her brothers. She had blamed him for it, and he doubted what was happening now would make her feel any less angry.

'There's no need to drag this out. You got the drop on me. Let her go and do what you will.'

Alicia screamed and shook her head, the sound muffled by the rag in her mouth. Lennox glanced at her, then focused his attention back on Delroy.

'I want you to understand why I'm doing this. Why I win. I'm not led aside by emotional attachments. I go for what I want, and I take it. You're probably wondering how I got you here?'

'I don't care,' snarled Delroy. Lennox was unfazed.

'Yes, you do. You were betrayed. Like so many, you only ever look forward. You were consumed by finding me and never looked to those around you that you marginalised and ordered around. The drug life got you. For decades you polluted Chapeltown, and now I'm going to fix it.'

'You're no better than me,' said Delroy fiercely. 'You might be anti-drug, but you're a thug and a butcher.'

'Just like you,' said Lennox. 'You're forgetting, I grew up in Leeds. We grew up on stories of the *Williams Crew*, and the power you guys had. You killed your way to the top, so let's not pretend you're any better than me.'

'None of this matters. Let her go. You have me.'

'That's not enough. Thanks to my inside man, I know where several of your spots are. My men have already moved in to take the drugs. I want the money too.'

'You're not getting a thing.'

Lennox raised an eyebrow. 'You're not sounding like a loving father right now. Why do you think she's here? You're going to do what I say, or I promise you, I'll cut her to pieces while you watch.'

This was too much for Delroy. With a bellow, he charged, but was easily intercepted by the guards. He tried fighting free, but a sharp blow to the back of his head stunned him, sending him to his knees. Alicia tried to scream and struggle again, but it was to no avail.

'Like I said: you're going to do as I say,' repeated Lennox. 'Make the right decision. Show your daughter you care and give me the information I want. How many spots do you have for collecting money?'

'A dozen,' spat Delroy. The money was collected from these spots and laundered, but they kept the pattern loose in order to fool anyone who might be watching.

'Give me the addresses. No cowboy shit, either. I have someone watching your wife, and if I set them loose, you'll wish she was dead.'

Anger flashed in Delroy's eyes, but he again tried calming himself. Getting angry wouldn't help anything, and he didn't want them focusing their attention on his wife or daughter. Listlessly, he recited the addresses. Committing important information to memory was a must at his level, and he rarely wrote anything down he wouldn't want to be discovered. Lennox handed the list to a man, who immediately left the cellar. Facing Delroy again, he smiled.

'You did the right thing, Delroy. Take peace in that as you die. Before that happens.' Lennox nodded, and one of his men stepped forward, putting the gun to Alicia's head.

'No!' roared Delroy, but his words were lost over the bang. Alicia's head slammed forward as she hit the ground, blood billowing around her. 'You motherfucker!'

'Be thankful I made it quick, Delroy. Your time is over, and mine now begins,' said Lennox coldly. Gun raised, he aimed it at Delroy's chest and fired three times, smiling as the kingpin slumped forward, dead. He took stock of what he had done, and what it would mean.

The war was over. Delroy Williams had lost, and he had won.

TARGET PART III

'Is everything in place?'

Rigby ran his hands through his hair as he awaited the response. The best practice was to conduct raids first thing in the morning. Based on the information Terry had provided, the work of the intel team and the surveillance on various locations, it was determined that this was the best time to act. Rigby had noticed how different Teflon's team seemed. They had increased their reach, new members flourishing in their ranks, but appeared less disciplined. Their surveillance on one location had seen buyers going to the spot directly for pickups, with no attempts at subtlety. He knew this was the lack of influence Teflon apparently had on the crew at present. He hadn't been able to make any headway into what Teflon's intentions were, but deemed them to be serious if he was essentially abandoning the crew he'd built up.

'Everything is in place over here, chief. Just waiting for you to give the word.'

The operation was a joint one, with several stations involved, and a detachment of armed police. They were hitting half a dozen locations. Four locations housed product and money, and the other two were well-frequented safe houses. Reid had put Rigby in charge of the operation. Her reasoning was two-fold. If it was successful, she would take the credit; if it wasn't, he would be thrown under the bus. She hadn't been joking when she'd said his career was on the line, but Rigby found that didn't bother him. It was worth the risk.

'Hit the spots,' he said firmly.

Manson, Darren, Roman, and Keith were in a safe house on Leopold Street, smoking a spliff and drinking liquor. It hadn't been planned. They had held a quick meeting earlier and ended up staying. K-Bar and Maka were supervising the delivery, and they would be in place to ensure the product got to where it needed to be as quickly as possible.

When the door came off the safe house, they were sluggish in moving as they were overwhelmed by officers. Manson leapt to his feet, ready to fight.

'Manson! Don't,' said Darren. Manson tensed and allowed himself to be forced to the floor. They were secured and read their rights, then hauled away as multiple officers began tearing into the property.

Darren wore a brave face, but on the inside, he was panicking. There was no way the police should have known about this spot. There were locations they used to hang out, but this one was off the grid. There were guns on the property, along with drugs and small packets of money. All in all, it didn't present a positive picture.

Sharing a look with his comrades, his stomach lurched as he realised Maka and K-Bar would have no idea what was going on.

THE RAIDS WERE AN UNDISPUTED SUCCESS. They swarmed the locations without interruption, capturing men, product, money, weapons and an assortment of mobile phones and communication devices. It was a better haul than Rigby could have hoped for, and he knew it would damage the organisation likely beyond repair. The downside was the fact he had hoped to grab K-Bar, but he hadn't been at any of the locations.

For a moment, Rigby wondered if he'd had prior knowledge of the raids, but believed if he had, he would have told his people. They had kept the raid quiet for that reason, knowing there were many leaks in the departments. Everything was on a need-to-know basis, and it had worked like a charm. Back at the station, he grabbed a coffee. There were a host of interviews he would need to conduct. He needed to meet with Reid and debrief her on the operation, and there was paperwork he needed to complete. It was a tremendous amount of work, but this was the best chance Rigby had to finish Teflon's organisation once and for all. The piping hot coffee scalding his lips, he checked his phone for messages.

'Rig.'

Rigby faced Murphy. He hadn't been involved in the raids, with enough people already involved to not warrant his involvement. Instead of wearing a pleased expression, he appeared stunned. Rigby straightened.

'What's happened?'

TARGET PART III

Murphy shook his head.

'Chapeltown, mate. Everything has gone nuts.'

LAMONT'S HEAD buzzed from the news being spread. Delroy and his daughter Alicia had been murdered in devastating fashion. It was monumental news. Lamont couldn't fathom it. He'd figured Delroy had Lennox on the ropes and never imagined he would retaliate in the way he had. Something wasn't adding up. For Lennox to make such a move suggested a level of backing far beyond what Lamont had worked out he had.

Had he made a mistake somewhere?

All Lamont could do was look at his phone as various people tried to call him. There was no one worth talking to yet. Lennox had made a huge move, and his name was ringing out. Everyone in the know knew who was behind it, and killing Delroy's daughter had been ruthless beyond measure. Lamont knew Alicia Reynolds back in the day. She was a sweet girl who had refused to be involved in the family business. She even used her mother's maiden name, shunning the Williams name completely.

How had she been caught up? How had Lennox found her?

Lamont's immediate thought was that someone had betrayed Delroy. Pouring himself a drink, he turned off his computer and went to sit in the living room. He flicked on the television, but didn't watch it. TV was never the distraction for him it was for others. He was considering reading a book when his phone rang again, and this time, he answered, recognising the number.

He didn't speak, waiting for them to go first.

'Are you really not going to talk?'

'Figured you called for a reason, Lennox. How can I help?'

Lamont could practically feel Lennox's smile on the other end. He stowed his anger. It wasn't the time, and there was nothing he could do without knowing where he was.

'Guessing by now you've heard what happened to Delroy?'

'How did you do it?'

'I'm better than him, Teflon. Better than you too. This proves it. You had your thing with him years back, but you couldn't finish him. I could.'

'You called to gloat, then? Seems beneath you.'

'Does it? You don't know me, Teflon. You only *thought* you did. How many warnings do I need to give you before you learn your lesson? Your missus got it. Trinidad got it. Akeem. Still, you keep coming at me — an enemy that you can't figure out. All I wanted was to be left alone.'

'For someone who wants to be left alone, you sure do a lot of damage,' replied Lamont, refusing to be affected by Lennox's mentioning of Trinidad and Jenny. He didn't need those feelings weighing him down again. Not when he was so close to the end. All he needed to do was find and execute Lennox. Delroy had done most of the groundwork, and now he could take over and finish the job for good.

'I was forced to. By you. By old man Delroy. By those pathetic losers who work for you. None of you *are* or *were* good enough, and now, it won't matter. Because this is my time.'

'You can't beat me, Lenny. I am not Delroy Williams. I'm not a tired old man just wanting it to end. You stayed away from me for a reason these past few weeks. Delroy seemed easier, right?'

Whatever response Lamont was expecting, laughter wasn't on the list. It wasn't a snicker, either. This was a full-on belly laugh that lasted several seconds. His brow furrowed as it hit him for the first time that Lennox still hadn't explained why he had called.

'Delroy was unfinished business. The only reason he lasted this long was because you and your people stuck your noses in. You may not be tired, Teflon, but you are more than broken down. Shuffling around, keeping your head down because the people in Chapeltown don't like you anymore. I could have taken you out when I had your barber popped. Could have had you blasted at the old man's funeral. Like your mentor, you're still here because I have allowed it.'

'What's stopping you then? Let's finish this once and for all,' said Lamont, hoping Lennox took the bait. He was far too calm and controlled, and he didn't like it.

'I don't move when you tell me to. I am as independent as it gets, and everyone will learn that fact. Let's get down to business. I will tear your crew apart. If there's anyone left, anyway. They ran into some problems earlier, so I'm awaiting confirmation.'

'Bullshit,' replied Lamont. 'This act may work with the people dumb enough to follow you, but you're playing in an entirely different league now, Lennox. As I said to you earlier: I am *not* Delroy Williams.'

'No, you're not. I won't refute that. What you are is on borrowed time. You still don't get it, Teflon. It's almost sad, really, to be undone by the same mistake twice.'

With those words, Lamont's stomach plummeted, his blood turning cold.

'What have you done?'

'Not me. *You*. You did this. Leaving key pieces unprotected on the board once again.'

'Stop fucking talking in riddles and tell me,' snapped Lamont.

'How many innocents have to suffer before you get the message? Doesn't matter now. When you work it out, just remember; this time, it wasn't an accident. You got her killed.' Lennox hung up.

Lamont stared down at the phone, heart hammering against his chest. He felt like he couldn't breathe, his throat constricting. There was a chance Lennox was posturing, but he didn't believe it. There was no reason to call Lamont to gloat. He had done something, something that would deeply affect Lamont. Something involving innocents. With a jolt of realisation, it hit him.

Amy.

Hurtling to his feet, Lamont ran from the house, summoning his bodyguards. They zoomed down the drive, driving towards Roundhay as fast as they could. He had his phone to his ear, trying to get hold of everyone. He couldn't reach Amy, Shorty, K-Bar, Maka or Manson, and every time he tried them, the pit of despair in his stomach only grew. There was no way Lennox could reach all of them in a single night. They were well-trained and experienced. They would see his men coming.

The truth was, Lamont thought, as he hunched forward, willing the driver to go faster, he didn't know his crew anymore. Somewhere down the line, he had lost sight of them. Even when they sided with Shorty after their last meeting, he did nothing to rectify the situation. He had been so blinded by his need to take on Lennox that he'd put them on the back burner. They had proved they could look after themselves. The crew could run without him.

Lamont took a deep breath as the car sharply turned onto Amy's street a short while later. It was quiet and undisturbed, but that meant nothing. Before the vehicle had even screeched to a stop, he rushed to her front door, his heart in his throat. He tried the front door, but it was locked, which stunned him. He began banging on the door until he heard Amy's voice.

'I'm coming; calm down!'

Lamont vibrated on the spot, muscles tense. He needed to make sure she was okay. He had tried Shorty four more times, but each time it rang through to voicemail.

'You're okay?' he gasped when she'd unlocked the door. Amy wore a red dressing gown over pink pyjamas. Her hair was bedraggled, and as she stood there glaring, she stifled a yawn.

'I was fast asleep until you started banging on the door like a madman. What's happened?'

'I thought . . .' Lamont wasn't sure what to say. He was still trying to relax. The scene with Jenny bleeding on her kitchen floor had burned into his mind, and he'd been sure he would arrive to see a similar scene.

'L, what's going on? Tell me?'

'Have you heard from Shorty?'

Amy paled, shaking her head.

'What's happened?'

'Probably nothing. Go back to bed. I'll call you if anything happens.'

'L . . .'

'Seriously. Everything is fine.' Lamont ran a hand through his hair, trying to force a smile onto his face. Eyeing him suspiciously, Amy nodded and closed the door. He hurried down the steps and skidded to a halt, surprised to see Jamal — one of his soldiers — standing by his bodyguards.

TARGET PART III

'What's going on?' he asked.

'Has anyone been by?'

Jamal shook his head. 'I've been out here all day. Shorty asked me to watch over her. Said he had something to do. What's happened?'

Lamont wasn't listening. Something had jumbled in his mind when he'd seen the enforcer. Lennox's cryptic words had pointed toward Amy, but it wasn't just Amy who fit them. There was another woman, someone closer to Lamont, and like a selfish fool, he had completely overlooked his own family.

'Marika!' he shouted, getting back to the car. 'Drive!' he screamed, giving the driver the address.

ALL THE WAY to Marika's, Lamont said a silent prayer. He tried convincing himself that Lennox was sending him on a wild chase all over Leeds for no other reason than to be entertained. Until he pulled onto Marika's street and saw the flashing blue lights. The crime tape. The neighbours watching a particular house.

Marika's house.

'No,' he moaned, nausea bubbling in his stomach. He forced away the sickening feeling and hurried from the car.

'Marika!' he yelled. 'Rika!'

There were several officers stationed around the crime tape. He could see people dressed in white going to and from the house. As he grew closer, he saw the destruction, and it made his heart lurch all over again. This wasn't a knifing. The downstairs and upstairs windows had been completely shot out. Even in the dark, he could see bullet holes littering the brickwork. An officer stepped into his path.

'Sir, you can't come any further. Please step back.'

'My sister is in there. My niece and nephew. I need to get in.'

'Sir, this is a crime scene,' the officer said firmly. 'Please, you cannot come any further.'

'What the fuck happened to my sister? What happened to the kids?' roared Lamont. The officer met his eyes sadly, shaking his head.

'I'm sorry, sir. I can't give you any details. I . . .' he glanced around, pointing at an overweight man talking to two other officers. 'Tanners' is the officer in charge. You can try speaking with him, but I can't promise he'll help.' With an apologetic look, he took a step back. Lamont hurried over to Tanners, who had his back to him.

'Are you Tanners?'

Tanners turned to face him. He had a fleshy, jowly face, a pockmarked nose and pale eyes. 'Who's asking?'

'That is my sister's house. No one is telling me what's going on,' explained Lamont, his jaw hard and his tone sharp.

'What's your name.'

'Lamont Jones. My sister and her two children live here. Are they okay?'

Tanners blew out a breath, but continued to meet his eyes.

'The kids went with Social Services. It's standard procedure in these situations.'

Lamont closed his eyes, knowing what Tanners was saying, even before he said it.

'Your sister was shot multiple times. I'm sorry to say that she was dead before we got here.'

Lamont fell to his knees, uncaring of who was watching. His chest tingled. He felt numb. He couldn't believe it. It had to be a dream. Marika couldn't be dead.

Not his little sister.

'I really am sorry, Mr Jones. Is there anything you can tell us about this situation? Anything at all that will help us catch the people responsible?'

Lamont lurched to his feet, not even trying to stop the tears that were pouring down his face. He turned on his heel and stumbled towards his waiting vehicle, ignoring Tanners calling after him. Marika was dead. His little sister had been gunned down, and it was all his fault.

CHAPTER TWENTY-FOUR
MONDAY 25 MAY, 2015

HOURS AFTER BEING DRAGGED away from Marika's, Lamont was home, mulling over the utter destruction. The feelings he had over Marcus's, Jenny's, Akeem's, and Trinidad's deaths had been magnified. His heart ached. Since her birth, he had looked after Marika, only growing closer to her after their parents died. He had silently promised them at their funeral that he would keep looking after her.

Now, that promise had been shattered. Marika had been gunned down because, once again, Lennox had wanted to get to him. He had reached out and ripped away someone else that he loved, and left her children without a mother.

Earlier, Lamont had spoken to his cousin, Louis, about getting the kids from where they were being held. He didn't know where their father was, but Louis agreed to pick them up. Staring at his phone, Lamont felt the tears prickling his eyes, and for the first time since he was a child, he broke, tired of holding back his emotions. He cried until he was physically spent, then wiped his eyes, overwhelmed by the depths of his grief. This was stark and utter failure, and his family were right to blame him.

Lamont had never truly taken Lennox seriously. He'd hated him after he killed Jenny, but he had never truly seen him as a challenge. His lackadaisical attitude had cost him dearly. Lennox had a game plan from the beginning. He hadn't been intimidated by Lamont's reputation or what he might do in revenge. He had even tried making him compliant by giving up the location of the man responsible for killing Jenny. He had wiped out Delroy Williams, killed his daughter, then eliminated Marika too. Just because he could.

Lamont felt something he hadn't in forever: True and utter doubt. Lennox had been moves ahead of them for months. He had stormed to the top of the crime pile, doing exactly what he'd said he would. Delroy Williams had been an institution for decades, and Lennox had wiped out him and his family. It was ruthless and beyond impressive.

A fresh wave of sorrow hit Lamont. He and Delroy had their differences, but despite everything, he saw him as a friend. They'd grown closer lately, and he had seen Delroy's pain. They were kindred spirits, Delroy an older, broken version, who had lost his family and had a dream of returning home that he knew would never come to fruition. Like Trinidad, he'd put his faith in Lamont. They had seen something in Lamont purely beyond what he saw in himself. They saw a man who could rise above and open doors. It was overwhelming.

Lamont needed an exit plan. Lennox had made it clear he was coming for him now, and he would either need to fight back, or escape. He had more than enough money to survive anywhere in the world. Maybe the change of atmosphere would be good for him.

Lennox's levels of clout were off the scale now. Lamont knew how it went. He had gone through the same thing back in the day when he had made big moves. People would fall at his feet to appease him, and what he said and did would set the new standard.

Lamont felt weak. He should have pushed through his issues and been stronger, instead of wallowing in his pain. Now, his niece and nephew had lost their mother over a situation he should have rectified. There was no way around it. From the moment he had bumped into Nikkolo in the club in January, he'd known Lennox was up to something, but he hadn't acted. Deep down, Lennox was just another thug for him to out-think and remove from the equation. When Jenny and Trinidad were killed, he'd had more to pay him back for, but it had

TARGET PART III

never been full-on. Something else always came up. Lennox had taken the hits and the threats, appearing weaker than he was. Like last time, he had countered in spectacular fashion, and changed the entire landscape of the streets.

LAMONT'S PHONE had been ringing on and off all evening, and he couldn't ignore it any longer. He couldn't sit around and wait everything out. Whether he wanted it, the end was approaching. Snatching up the phone, he jammed it to his ear.

'Yeah?'

'L, fucking hell. I've been trying you for ages. Shit's deep, fam. We got rushed doing the pickup. Police rushed bare of our spots. Most of the team got locked up.'

Lamont listened, his stomach lurching as it hit him that K-Bar didn't know about Marika.

'Who are you with?'

'Maka. We're lucky. They were trying to kill us. I tried getting Shorty, but he isn't answering either.'

Lamont rubbed his eyes. Crying had taken it out of him, but he couldn't back away now. K-Bar needed him, and he needed to be the one to tell him what had happened.

'I'm coming to you now. Where are you?'

LAMONT TRAVELLED with a team of four bodyguards, another man trailing. He kept looking over his shoulder, expecting to be ambushed. The guards were quiet and diligent, ready to act in case of danger. K-Bar and Maka had gone to a safe house near Easterly Road. The guards took up positions around the house, and he knocked and entered. The pair were in the living room. Both men looked fatigued, but appeared injury free.

'I'm glad you're both okay,' said Lamont. Maka had a bottle of whisky and was pouring it into a glass. In the time Lamont watched, he downed the contents and re-poured. K-Bar yawned, a selection of mobile phones next to him, along with a gun within reach on the weathered coffee table.

'It's mad, L. Everyone is talking about Delroy. Lennox wiped him out. Even took out his daughter. I dunno who came for us. Could be any little drug crew. We dropped a few of them, but we were outgunned. We were lucky to escape.'

'K—'

'We need to regroup, find out who got locked up and who snitched. I'll track the people who robbed us and tear them apart myself. We can't let anyone get away with violating us. They got twenty boxes, and they were waiting on the roads for us.'

'K—'

'Shorty going missing is dodgy too. We had a line on a spot Lennox might have been at. They might have trapped him.'

'K-Bar.'

Finally, K-Bar realised he was trying to speak, and stopped talking.

'Why would Shorty go to a spot of Lennox's alone? Lennox ambushed us last time. We lost Grimer, Rudy, and he got shot.' Lamont motioned to Maka.

K-Bar blew out a breath, not immediately answering.

'He said he could handle it. This is Shorty we're talking about. He's qualified.'

Lamont thought that was beside the point, but there were other things to discuss, and K-Bar would not like the news he gave him.

'Marika is dead.'

Maka's head shot up, and he stared at Lamont, incredulous. K-Bar frowned, looking confused. His mouth opened and closed, then opened again.

'What?'

'She . . . Lennox shot up the house. I got there too late, and he . . .' Lamont couldn't finish, his voice breaking. Maka clambered to his feet and put his hand on his shoulder.

'I'm sorry, bro.'

Lamont nodded, but kept his eyes on K-Bar. He stared blankly

TARGET PART III

ahead, then without a word, he shot to his feet and grabbed his gun, heading for the door. Lamont blocked his path.

'K, calm down.'

'Get out of the way.' The icy chill in K-Bar's voice made the hairs on his neck stand on end. K-Bar hadn't earned his reputation by accident, and he was aware of this.

'Put the gun down. We need to discuss this.'

'Get out of the way, or I will kill you!' K-Bar aimed the gun at him.

'K, what the hell are you doing?' said Maka. He didn't move, and neither did Lamont.

'I'm gonna do what we should have done in the first place and put a fucking bullet in Lennox's head. Move. Now.'

Lamont shook his head, knowing that he was putting himself in immense danger. K-Bar was beyond reason, but he would try. He *had* to try.

'I'm not moving, K. We need a proper plan for Lennox.'

'That was your damn job,' snapped K-Bar. 'You're the smart one. You haven't even fucking checked in lately, so the least you could do was deal with him, instead of hiding like a pussy.' He stepped closer, all-but jamming the pistol against Lamont's face, his finger tightening on the trigger. His words hurt, but Lamont forced them aside. K-Bar had the right to be hurt, just as Trinidad's family had. He couldn't take that away from him.

'I'm with you, K. He killed my sister, and my girl. Your pain is my pain, fam. We need a plan, and I'm here, ready to work with you.' He paused. 'Believe in Teflon.'

The moment dragged on, Maka's eyes flitting between the pair, the tension spiking. Finally, K-Bar sighed, lowered the gun, and slumped into a seat, tears spilling down his face.

'I loved her,' he mumbled. Lamont too, had tears in his eyes, unafraid of showing his emotions. Not now. He placed a hand on K-Bar's shoulder and squeezed. He and his sister had been nowhere near their old level of relationship, but she was the connection to his parents. They had been through so much together, and now she was dead over something she had no involvement in.

K-Bar placed his hand on Lamont's, and they stayed like that for some time, united in their grief and giving each other strength, until Maka hesitantly spoke up.

'What's the plan? We're gonna have people out there who aren't gonna know what to do. Add to that, we got licked for twenty boxes. I don't even wanna think what that's going to cost us.'

'Don't worry about the cost,' said Lamont, straightening and facing Maka. 'Find out who has and hasn't been locked up. I'll ring my solicitor to get the ball rolling on that end. For now, all dealing is suspended until things are in order.'

'What am I telling people?'

'As little as you can for now. We don't know what Lennox knows, but we know he's coming. There's nothing holding him back.'

'The spots getting hit at the same time . . . gotta be a snitch, right?'

'It's likely,' admitted Lamont. 'They would have to be well-placed to have hit so many areas too. Keep everything to yourself. K, you're with me.'

Finally, K-Bar looked up, his posture defeated and his eyes red.

'Where are we going?'

Lamont had his answer ready. He was tired of the facade, and there was one thing he needed more than anything else right now.

'To find Shorty.'

'I GUESS that prick Mack wasn't as useless as he looks.'

Lennox had an oily grin on his face. He was with Mark Patrick, sipping champagne in a safe house in Halton Moor as they listened to the reports coming out of Chapeltown. The news about Delroy's death had spread quickly, and everyone knew who was responsible.

Mack had done his part and given them a trove of information about the organisation in exchange for his payoff. Lennox had taken advantage of the petty grudge he had against Teflon's team and had parlayed it into success. His information about Delroy's daughter, Alicia, had been a masterstroke. Lennox hadn't even known he had a daughter, and based on the fact she went by a different surname, he imagined that was by design.

'Forget Mack. It's gonna work,' he said to Mark, still grinning. 'This is the breakthrough we've been waiting for. It took longer than I wanted, but Delroy is dead, and his team is ours.'

'Teflon is still out there.'

Lennox waved his hand, spilling liquor on himself in his excitement. 'Teflon is a broken man. We took out his business partner, his girl, and now his sister. Eventually, he has to get the message and just back off. If he doesn't, we smack whatever is left of his team and take his shit too. This is what victory looks like, Mark. Savour it, because these levels of win do not come around too often.'

'Are you sure about Teflon?'

Lennox's grin faded, his eyes suddenly boring into Mark's. Mark nervously looked away. He hated meeting Lennox's dead eyes for too long. He was combat trained and had been around all types, but Lennox put out a deadly vibe that was like nothing else he'd ever come across.

'I gave him Ryan.'

Mark frowned. 'What the hell does that mean? You sold him out?'

'He sold himself out. I sent him to kidnap Teflon's missus, and he killed her instead. He was dead the second it happened.'

'Weren't you going to kill her anyway?'

Lennox shrugged. 'I wanted her because I knew she would keep Teflon from making a dumb mistake. In the end, I lost Nikkolo because Teflon's people tracked him down. Ryan had to pay for his idiocy.'

'So, you gave him to Teflon?'

'Think of it as a litmus test.' Lennox put his glass on the table in front of him. 'I wanted to see what he would do, and analysed how he did it. Ryan was shot multiple times.'

'So?'

'So, Teflon has enough hitters that know how to do a clean job. One, maybe two taps to the head. Quick and clean. The fact Ryan had multiple bullet wounds, suggests rage.'

'So?' Mark was utterly nonplussed. He wondered if Lennox was losing it.

'*Rage* is an emotion I know how to handle. Shorty was furious after his daughter got popped. He walked into a trap, got a few of his guys killed, and they ended up running off with their tails between their legs. Rage makes you do stupid shit. Speaking of Shorty, has Derrigan checked in yet?'

'No. Maybe Shorty got him,' said Mark. Lennox's eyes narrowed.

'Derrigan was confident he could handle Shorty. If he hasn't, I won't be pleased.'

'Want me to send some people to look for him?'

Lennox picked up his drink again. 'Go for it.'

———

When Derrigan was finally led into the room, he was limping, his face bruised. Lennox looked him up and down.

'What happened?'

'He got away.'

'How?' Lennox's eyebrow raised. He rubbed his jaw. Derrigan picked up the bottle of champagne and drank from it, making a face. Mark glared, but he didn't notice. 'We had a fight. I was winning, then he got the better of me.'

'A fight?' Lennox shook his head. 'I told you to kill him, not have a scrap. What the hell were you thinking?'

Derrigan shot Lennox a sharp look. 'My methods are my own. I wanted to finish Shorty alone. He has a rep. Killing him will be good for future business.'

'You failed. Well done.'

'I'll finish him.'

'You playing *Rambo* has messed up the plan. Your ego cost us the chance to get rid of a deadly enemy.'

'Like when you had your little toy soldier shoot Teflon's bodyguard when you could have finished him?'

Lennox's face paled. Mark's mouth fell open. He had never heard anyone speak to him with such open disrespect. Lennox didn't speak immediately. He locked eyes with Derrigan, neither man backing down. Seconds passed before he spoke.

'Teflon was a broken man after his girlfriend died. The hits ever since have worn him down further. There is a strategy there. We knock

TARGET PART III

all the pieces off the board, then we deal with him. Shorty is a different sort of animal, which is why I wanted him dead. Lutel fucked up, and now you have too.'

'I told you, I will handle it. I don't need to be micromanaged. You sought me out, and you paid me what you did because I'm the best.'

Lennox's eyes hadn't left Derrigan. 'Don't make me regret hiring you.'

'I hope you're not threatening me.' Derrigan's voice was equally cold.

'Call it a reminder of your duties.'

Derrigan finished the bottle, wiping his mouth and dropping it on the table.

'Do you think Teflon got to the top by being weak? Overlooking him is daft.'

'He got to the top because of people like Marcus. I respected Tall-Man and how he played the game, but Teflon has made a life out of getting everyone else to do his dirty work. His team are washed up, and they didn't adapt, which is why we defeated them with simple methods and carved through their organisation. I want you worrying about Shorty. Not Teflon. He will come for you. He's not the sort to let things go.'

'I'll handle him. No mistakes.'

'Good. For now, make sure the troops are accepting of the new regime. Everything goes through us. We'll crush the holdouts who dare to go against that.'

When Derrigan left, Lennox turned to Mark.

'Send her in.'

Mark left the room, returning with a nervous-looking Julia. She stood in front of Lennox, wringing her hands, but meeting his eyes. He gazed at her for a long time before he spoke.

'You did the right thing,' he said softly.

'You didn't give me a choice when you threatened to murder my best friend if I didn't get her to help set up Shorty. Sienna cares about him, you know,' replied Julia.

'The feeling isn't mutual. Shorty doesn't care about her. He never did.' Lennox dismissed her words.

'What do you know about caring for people?' said Julia, her voice growing stronger even under Lennox's intense stare. 'People are just things you force to your will.'

'What use are they otherwise?' Lennox shrugged, acknowledging her words. Emotions and love led to people making mistakes like the ones Teflon, Shorty and Delroy had made. They had allowed emotions and love of other people to lead them, and had been destroyed because of it.

'I pity you.'

Lennox had never seen such a look of disgust on Julia's face. He didn't like it.

'I don't need your pity. You're nothing but a Hood slut,' he spat.

'If that's true, you should be able to let me go.'

Lennox's eyebrows rose before he broke into laughter. 'Do you really think I care about you?'

The look of disgust on Julia's face only deepened. For the longest time, Lennox Thompson had been her world. She had lived for making him happy, but now she saw the real him. There was no humanity left within him. He was simply a dangerous void who cared about nothing and no one. Her heart had truly hardened against him, and she would never view him with love again.

'Can I leave now?'

'You can. Warn Sienna I will kill her slowly if she breathes a word of what happened to anyone, and I promise you that you'll beg for what I do to her before I finish you too.'

CHAPTER TWENTY-FIVE
MONDAY 25 MAY, 2015

IT WAS WELL after four am by the time K-Bar and Lamont pulled up outside Amy's. For Lamont, it felt like a lifetime since he'd hammered on the doors, thinking she was in trouble.

Jamal waited at the gate for them. Lamont had left another two men nearby, just in case Lennox tried something. Jamal nodded when he saw him. Despite the late hour, he still looked alert, something Lamont didn't share. He felt like he'd aged ten years in the past few hours and wanted nothing more than to go to sleep. There was still a lot to be taken care of, and so he would persevere.

'How long since he showed up?' Lamont asked the bodyguard.

'About thirty minutes. Didn't say much. Just argued with his missus.'

'Go home and get some rest,' said Lamont. Jamal shook his head.

'I'm good, L. I don't need to be anywhere.'

'You need to sleep. You've been out here for hours, and I have other people watching the spot. I'll get someone to ring you in the afternoon to let you know what's happening. Watch your back. We've taken some hits tonight.'

Jamal patted him on the shoulder, then went to his car and drove away. Lamont glanced at K-Bar. He had spoken little since they left

Maka, and Lamont knew what was going through his mind. He prepared himself for the meeting ahead. It would not be easy.

Amy looked pale and drawn when she answered the door to Lamont and K-Bar. She hugged both men.

'He's upstairs.'

They traipsed up the stairs after her. Shorty was laid up in the spare bedroom, his face heavily bruised, annoyance and pain etched into his face. He glanced from Lamont to K-Bar.

'She made me lay up in bed, even though I'm fine.'

'Please ignore him,' Amy started. 'He has fractured, possibly broken ribs, along with a collection of bruises and injuries that he won't tell me about. Not only that, he refused to let me call an ambulance.'

'I told you I'm fine.'

'Stop saying that!' Amy erupted. 'You're clearly not fine, Shorty. Before you run off and do these things, please remember you have two children you need to stay healthy for. You two can deal with him. I'm going to bed.'

'Shorty, what happened?' K-Bar asked, after Amy had slammed the door behind her.

'I was stupid. Didn't do the homework on that spot, and I got rushed.'

'Where did you get the intel for this spot?' asked Lamont. Shorty glared at him, but answered.

'Lutel's ex. We had a thing a while back, and she reached out. Put me in touch with Lennox's ex, who gave me and K-Bar the info.'

Lamont wanted to point out how stupid it was to rely on their intel, but he didn't. That wasn't why he was there.

'Who rushed you?'

'Derrigan was there.'

'Nicky Derrigan?' Lamont's brow furrowed. 'He doesn't work in Leeds anymore. Hasn't for years.'

'Lennox paid him a lot of money to change his mind. We got into a fight. I got the drop on him, but had to shoot my way out.'

'You're not the only one,' said K-Bar, recounting the ambush on the drugs van.

TARGET PART III

'I can't believe all this happened in a single night,' said Shorty, wincing in pain.

'That's not all. Lennox took out Delroy Williams tonight. He killed him, his daughter, and . . . he sent people after Rika, Shorty. She's dead.'

K-Bar's mouth tightened. All the anger on Shorty's face immediately vanished.

'I'm sorry, L. You too, K. I can't believe he went there.' His eyes lingered on Lamont.

'I fucked up,' admitted Lamont. 'I believed Delroy when he said he could finish Lennox.'

'Lennox is a different animal,' said Shorty. 'There's a reason everyone, including Tall-Man and Reagan, respected him. He's ruthless. He's been in and out of prison most of his adult life, but always kept his crew strong.'

'Speaking of crews, ours is fucked. Police raided five or six of our spots. Proper coordinated effort. Maka is looking into that, but Manson was definitely arrested.'

'Shit,' cursed Shorty, shaking his head. 'What the hell?'

'We lost twenty boxes. People died, and half the crew are probably behind bars. I can't think of a time things have been worse.'

'I can think of a few times,' said Shorty softly. He and Lamont shared another look, and Lamont knew this was his time.

'I'm sorry, Shorty.'

Shorty's eyes remained hard, but he hadn't completely disregarded Lamont's words, which he took as a good sign.

'I shouldn't have accused you of being responsible for Jenny's death, and I definitely shouldn't have insinuated Grace's shooting was your fault. There's only one person responsible for both. Lennox has infected Leeds. He's gone too far, and we have to stop it.'

'What the fuck do you think we've been trying to do? Me, you, the crew, even Delroy's soldiers. We were all trying to take him out, and he played all of us.'

'We were blinded by revenge, Shorty. I know I was. Len took from me, just like Leader took from me thirteen years ago. Like my Aunt took from me. I thought it would fix me.'

Shorty's face softened slightly. He and Lamont had been friends for nearly thirty years, and he didn't think he had ever heard Lamont talk like this.

'... Rochelle broke me a long time ago. She seemed to get me, and I fell for her. The first girl to ever show me any sort of affection. After she crushed me, I was adrift, selling weed with you, wondering what it would take for me to evolve.

'And then we stepped up, and *I* stepped up, and I had something I could get behind. Money would open any doors I wanted, and I would be successful, and I would make myself worth something.

'You know what, though? I was still nothing. I had money and status, but I was still hollow, and all the things and jewellery and champagne, didn't fix me. It was just the best facade we had. I got hurt by a girl once, and I decided it would never happen again. I got women because I didn't care about losing them; they sensed that hole in me, and they tried to fix it, and then they would flee. Jenny was a way out. She was beautiful and had her own brain, and she took no shit from me, and it felt like, despite the crime life, I'd found an equal to stand alongside.' The words poured from Lamont. He couldn't even filter them.

'Why didn't you?' Shorty spoke for the first time, his voice low, yet decidedly less hostile than it had been.

'Why didn't I what?'

'Walk away with her. You were gonna, and then I got out of prison, and you were still here. She wanted you to walk away, and that's why you lost her; because you didn't.'

Lamont hung his head. Shorty was correct, but it still hurt to hear. There would always be a pain associated with Jenny, and the possibility of what might have been.

'I couldn't walk away. I was blackmailed and forced to stay in the game.'

'You what?' Shorty's eyes narrowed.

'You remember Akhan, the supplier?' Shorty nodded. 'He had something over me, and when I limped into his office after my shooting, I told him I was walking away. Ready to pay whatever cost was necessary, but he played his trump card, and I was trapped.'

'What card? What are you on about?'

'Reagan,' replied Lamont. Shorty looked more confused than ever. He had hated Ricky Reagan when he was alive, and hearing about him when he was dead was even worse.

'What about him?'

'I killed him.'

Shorty's eyes widened. His mouth fell open as he gawped from K-Bar to Lamont, unable to believe what he had just heard.

'You?'

Lamont nodded.

'How? You're not that guy. You kept us around, so you didn't have to get your hands dirty.'

'You weren't there.'

'What the hell happened? I thought Tall-Man dropped him?'

Lamont filled them in on the specifics of the night Reagan ambushed him in the barber's two years ago, and their vicious fight.

'You got the better of Reagan?'

'I was lucky. Marcus cleaned it up, and I figured that was the end. I'd even let myself forget it, until Akhan revealed he knew, and threatened to go to the police.'

'How the hell did he find out?'

'Chink told him.'

'I knew it!' Shorty jerked upwards, then winced as the action put pressure on his injuries. 'I told you all along that he was no good.'

'It doesn't matter now, Shorty. What matters is that I couldn't walk away, and I couldn't tell Jenny that I was a murderer, so I had to deal.'

'Why couldn't you tell her?'

'Would you tell Amy?'

'I *did* tell Amy,' Shorty retorted. 'I thought it would make her hate me, but it didn't. It seemed to help fix things between us.'

Lamont blew out a breath. 'I couldn't take that same chance with Jen. As much as I wanted to, we were on borrowed time after that. Then she died anyway, and I'm still here.'

'Akhan's not around anymore, though, is he?'

'I killed him too.' Lamont felt nothing as he told Shorty, save for a slight amusement at the shock etched onto his face.

'Darren told me about some mission with some Asians, and some robbery. Is that what you're talking about?'

'He tried double-crossing me, and we wiped out his people, and then I finished him.'

'I can't believe it,' Shorty rubbed his face. 'You're telling me you've dropped two bodies?'

Lamont shook his head, remembering Ryan Peters begging at his feet.

'The man who stabbed Jenny. Ryan. I got him too.'

'Who the hell are you?' exploded Shorty. 'You're the guy . . . you talk and negotiate. You don't kill.'

'My back was to the wall, and I reacted. The fact is, I barrelled ahead after Lennox because that's the life we're in, and you have to get revenge, or everyone thinks you're weak. Like you lot told me repeatedly, it's about the message.'

'Yeah, so?'

'Revenge won't fix me, Shorty. It won't heal Grace, or bring Marika, Jenny or Trinidad, Akeem or Delroy, back to life. I can't hide behind it anymore. I can't hide behind the game, or the rules. Lennox has to go. For the good of everyone.'

There was a long silence after he finished, and both felt as if a weight had been lifted from their shoulders. Lamont had filled in so many blanks for Shorty. He knew why he had remained, and though he would never come to grips with the fact his friend had murdered three men, he understood. He knew why it had been a secret, and he knew why Lamont was hurting in the way he was.

'It wasn't all on you, L. I shouldn't have made out it was. I talked shit about everyone around you dying because I wanted to hurt you. You weren't responsible for any of the deaths.'

'You weren't responsible for Grace's shooting,' said Lamont.

'Course I was. She was with me. If I hadn't smacked around Lutel, she wouldn't have got shot.'

'That makes it Lutel's fault, not yours. You wouldn't have put her in danger and taken her out if you had known that might happen. Amy told me you tried to cover her body with yours. How many people would ever do that?'

TARGET PART III

'I love her.' Shorty swallowed down the lump in his throat.

'You love both of them,' corrected Lamont. In the background, K-Bar sniggered, the first noise he'd made during their conversation. There wasn't much for him to say. He didn't want to ruin the much-needed talk between two of his closest friends.

'Where the hell did things get so fucked with us? I think I resented you for years. Thought you looked down on me, and I never knew how to bridge the growing gap between us. It's probably why I was always snapping on Chink; you two seemed to get each other, and I was just lost.'

'We — the three of us in this room — started the crew, and you lot put me in charge. I thought I was better because I didn't run around shooting people. Fact of the matter is that it was a collective effort. When the chips were down, I needed you lot every time, and somewhere down the line, I squandered that.'

'We all needed each other,' said Shorty. 'Tall-Man would kill himself again if he saw how we fell apart.'

'You're right. We tried making the crime life fit around our lives, and I should have walked away a long time ago. It wasn't just about Jenny, or Rochelle or Rika. It was about me.' Lamont took a deep breath. 'I've felt guilty over what we do, the entire time, telling myself that by trying to regulate things and by giving the crew *rules*, it made what I did less deplorable. I didn't need to do it, Shorty. I made enough money within the first few years to comfortably do something else, but I didn't. Even beyond that, I tried influencing the decisions you and others were making, because I thought I was right, and that you should listen to me above everything else. I made mistakes, and some of those mistakes led us here.'

'It's not just you. We've all fucked up,' said Shorty. 'Here and now, you can walk away. Leave the streets to us and get yourself out of the line of fire. Like you said, you've got the money, and the Feds haven't tried to arrest you, so they probably can't connect you to any of this.'

Lamont shook his head, not even considering this for a moment.

'Lennox is dangerous, Shorty. We can't leave him unchecked. He doesn't care about Chapeltown. He cares about power, and that will sink the community even further if we do nothing about it.'

'What are we doing next then?' K-Bar finally spoke. 'I still need to put a bullet in Lennox's head.'

'We all have a grudge against Lennox. I have a few theories, so let's talk.'

———

LAMONT'S PHONE rang again just after nine. He'd left Shorty to get some rest, and they were meeting later to talk with K-Bar and Maka.

'Hello?'

'Lamont, we need to talk. Immediately.'

It was Stefanos. Lamont gripped the phone tighter.

'Where?'

'Come to my home again, please.'

'I'll be there soon.'

———

STEFANOS WAITED at the top of his drive as Lamont pulled up. His expression was strained, his face pinched with stress. Lamont imagined he looked the same.

'I heard about your sister. I'm truly sorry about what happened. I know you loved her.'

'Thank you,' said Lamont, not knowing what else to say. It seemed to be enough for Stefanos, who led him to his office. Jakkar waited there, fastidiously dressed in a grey suit. His jaw was tight, his eyes boring into Lamont's. Lamont had never seen him look anything less than composed, and it was strange to see.

'Sit down,' he said to Lamont.

'I'd prefer to stand.' Lamont didn't like the hostile environment. He saw the demand to sit as Jakkar trying to dominate the conversation, and he would not allow that to happen. Stefanos slipped into a seat near Jakkar, shooting him a reproachful look that he ignored. Jakkar kept his eyes on Lamont, waiting for him to speak, but he calmly waited him out. Frowning, Jakkar spoke.

'I hope you have some answers regarding what has transpired.

TARGET PART III

Your men were ambushed and robbed of our product. Chapeltown is up in arms over the murder of Delroy Williams, and even now, several smaller crews are vying for power. Lennox Thompson has done massive damage to the stability, and to compound the situation, you've had multiple arrests in your organisation. You messed up, Mr Jones. Not only that, you have failed to live up to your reputation, and I would like some answers.'

'My sister died.'

Jakkar's expression was quizzical. He looked at Stefanos, who remained stone-faced.

'I don't see the relevance.'

'Of course, you don't. The relevance is that I've lost more to this life than I can put into words. You want answers? I told the pair of you that Lennox was a problem, and I asked for resources so I could finish him before he could do too much damage. You refused to allow it. You gave me a promotion, but hobbled my resources. My answer is that I'm tired, and that the *reputation* of mine you spoke of, is bullshit.'

'What do you mean?' interjected Stefanos.

'I lost family, friends and lovers to a game I've been reluctantly playing my entire life. I'm done with it. With all of this.'

Now Jakkar spoke, paying no attention to Stefanos.

'I'm not Akhan. I won't blackmail you, but understand that by walking away, your relationship with myself will be severed, as will any link your crew has to our product.'

'Some things are more important. I thank you for the opportunity, regardless.'

'There is still the matter of the drugs that were stolen from you. Half were paid for, meaning there is still a substantial bill outstanding,' said Jakkar. To the surprise of both men, Lamont shrugged.

'Send me the bill, and you'll have the money within twenty-four hours.' He shook Jakkar's and Stefanos's hands, then left. Lamont was approaching the front door when he heard footsteps following. He didn't pause, heading for his ride.

'Lamont.'

He turned to face Stefanos, who remained in the doorway.

'What are you going to do?'

'Clean up the mess.'

Stefanos ran a hand through his hair.

'And after that? What are you going to do without Jakkar's supply?'

Rather than answer, Lamont climbed in, and his bodyguard drove away.

'ALL IN ALL, A SUCCESS.'

Reid had an enormous smile on her face, and it was strange for Rigby to see. Murphy had caught him up on the happenings in Chapeltown, and he had been stunned beyond belief. The actions would have ramifications in the streets for years to come. It wasn't the time to ruminate, however. He needed to deal with Reid first.

'We got at least five kilos, around nine grand in cash, several mobile phones, and plenty of weapons, along with a few big names such as Manson and Darren. No one is talking yet, but with these situations, it's usually a free-for-all of who can give people up the quickest.'

'You did great work, Detective Rigby. You went with your instincts, and it paid off. I noticed we didn't nab Lamont Jones, Keiron Barrett or Franklin Turner. Are you confident the people we have in custody will connect them?'

'I think it's a strong possibility,' replied Rigby, unwilling to guarantee it. This was the best chance they'd had in a long time to connect the dots, and while he was optimistic, he had been burned going against Teflon's crew previously.

'Fine. The Williams situation. What do we know?'

'Delroy Williams was murdered, along with his daughter, Alicia Reynolds. His body was dumped on Chapeltown Road near the Landport building. We're canvassing for witnesses, but it's early days at this stage. The next few days will be telling.'

'I'm putting Murphy and Peterson onto that case. You will remain at the station and prepare the evidence for the subsequent interviews of Teflon's people.'

Rigby straightened in his chair, not pleased with this decree.

TARGET PART III

'Ma'am, with all due respect, me and Murphy could do a better job out there learning the situation. Can Peterson not do the interviews?'

'Detective, you are the one who made it clear how important capturing Teflon was to the betterment of our city. I want you to make sure we get everything and more from the interviews. Murphy can handle the Williams case.'

TERRY WAS LYING IN BED, his arm around the shoulders of a blonde he'd met a few weeks back. He'd been on and off the phone all day, learning more about what had happened to Delroy's crew. For the first time in a long time, he was happy with the moves he had made. He had hedged his bets in working with the police and had stayed out of the limelight with the raids, putting him in a fantastic position to move up the ladder. All he needed to do was wait out the storm.

'Are you working today,' the blonde asked. Terry shook his head.

'Got the message to stay off the streets until someone contacted me. The bosses will put their heads together trying to work out how to solve this.'

'The Delroy guy that died . . . he was big time, right?'

'The biggest. There'll be wars now that he's dead. I know at least two teams that are getting guns together, ready to shoot it out for that top spot.'

'Doesn't that worry you?' She asked, snuggling closer to Terry, glad she was connected to such an important man. He'd plied her with champagne and drugs when they met, and had bragged about his connections to big-timers in Chapeltown.

'Course not. Whatever happens, love, I'm fine. I'm connected to everyone, so whoever wins, they'll support me.' Pulling her close, he was ready to return to what they had been doing earlier, when his phone rang. He checked the number, and it was blocked.

'Yeah?'

'It's Murphy. Need to speak to you, right now.'

'Can't it wait? I thought we were done?'

'Meet me at the car park in Harehills. You know the one. You've got twenty minutes, and then I'm coming to your house.' Murphy hung up.

Seventeen minutes later, Terry pulled up next to Murphy's car in the car park. He was with another man Terry had never seen before. He was tall and bespectacled, with sandy brown hair.

'Who the hell is he? Where's Rig?' Terry jerked his thumb at the newcomer, who gave him a cold look.

'Don't worry about that. Tell me about what's happened lately,' said Murphy.

Terry shrugged. 'Don't you already know? It's been everywhere. Lennox finally got Delroy. Wiped out his daughter too, and now a few of his goons are going around the Hood, forcing away dealers. A few of the little dealers are also gunning for that top spot, so shit's getting bad.'

'I need names. What's your boss saying about it?'

'I haven't spoken to him. Half the crew is locked up, so he'll definitely be in touch, mate. Be patient and let me work.'

Murphy scowled, gripping Terry by the front of his jacket.

'Listen, you little mug. I ain't Rigby. Get out there and find out exactly what is going on. Don't care who you need to speak to, or how you do it. Get me something quickly, or your entire world changes. Don't test me.' Giving him a last look of disgust, Murphy and the other man drove away.

Terry spat on the floor, furious. He'd always tried to be respectful, but Murphy had never shown him anything but contempt. He knew Rigby didn't like him, but he was still polite and reasonable in what he asked for. There was nothing he could do. Murphy was vindictive enough to make life hard for him if he didn't cooperate, but he swore this would be the last time.

Climbing into his Audi, he zoomed away, not noticing the car parked nearby. The driver made a call on his phone.

'Maka, you were right. Terry's the snitch.'

CHAPTER TWENTY-SIX

TUESDAY 26 MAY, 2015

'ARE YOU SURE?'

Maka, Lamont, Shorty and K-Bar were in Jukie's backroom. He had been kind enough to let them use it on short notice, and tried to decline the money Lamont gave him, to no avail.

Ever since the raids, they had moved around when needed, not staying in the same spots for too long. They could hear the shouts of a domino game going on next door. The room comprised a table and numerous spindly wooden chairs. On the table rested a bottle of whiskey and four glasses. None of the men had partaken, however. It had been a long few days, and fatigue was clear in all of them. They had rested sparingly, working on putting their plans into action. Lennox's influence was spreading, and it wouldn't be long before they were pushed out completely.

'Positive. I had someone watching him as soon as we had that first meeting. Someone high up had to be the one to give the pigs that info. Worthy was a match. He knew just enough to give up a few spots, but couldn't really implicate any of us directly. My guy saw him meeting with two officers. Didn't recognise them, but one of them was a ginger.'

'*Murphy*,' said Shorty. Lamont recognised the name and description too, knowing the detective to be a partner of Rigby's. Rigby had wanted to lock him up for years. It struck him that Terry might also have an inkling that he was behind the murder of Ricky Reagan. Regardless, he had violated, and would have to be dealt with.

'Do you think Terry knew enough about Delroy's operation to give him up to Lennox?' K-Bar asked.

'Definitely not. Terry's slippery, but not to that level. I spent enough time around Delroy to know he was always surrounded by bodyguards. His mansion was like a fortress, but someone knew enough about him to realise his daughter was the weak link. Alicia didn't even use the family surname. She was well-hidden, but they got to her anyway.'

'What are you thinking happened?' Shorty waited for Lamont's response. He had seen him theorise like this so many times in the past, and his insights were usually accurate.

'My guess is they snatched her to force Delroy to deal, then murdered the pair of them.'

'Who do you think gave them up? Delroy lost a lot of pieces this year. Who was he keeping close?'

Lamont cycled through the active names he knew in Delroy's organisation. Most were solid and dependable, and worshipped the old man. One name stood out.

'Mack.'

An ugly smile appeared on Shorty's face, and even Maka and K-Bar chuckled at the sight of it. Shorty's history with Mack was well-documented. He and Marcus had nearly killed him previously after he'd made threats against Lamont.

'Let's go get him.'

'We need to know where he is first. I'll speak to Jukie and see if he has anything for us. You guys can move onto *Step 2* without me.'

———

SEVERAL DAYS after Marika's death, the family held a gathering. The funeral would take place next week, but it was decided beforehand that the family would celebrate how much she was loved.

TARGET PART III

To say Lamont didn't want to go was a vast understatement. He didn't get along with much of his family at the best of times and accepted he had unresolved issues where they were concerned. He was determined not to hide away anymore, and this was the first step.

The last few days had been spent locked away with Shorty, Maka and K-Bar, ironing out a plan to go against Lennox. He had asked K-Bar to attend the gathering with him, but K-Bar declined, stating it was a family thing.

Lamont arrived at his cousin Louis's Harrogate home just after seven in the evening. He sat in the car an extra few seconds, staring into space, composing himself for the night ahead.

'Everything okay, sir?' his driver asked.

'I'm fine. Ring me if you need anything.'

He stepped from the car, smoothing imaginary creases from his black shirt. He'd matched it with some black trousers and shoes. His fingers brushed across his old gold watch for reassurance, then he made his way inside after knocking once.

Lamont was the last to arrive, as he'd expected. The family were gathered in Louis's living room, and there was already very little space. There was a picture of Marika that had been placed on a wall, as soft music played in the background. Lamont's eyes narrowed when he saw Aunt Carmen sitting in a chair, surrounded by people, pleased to be the centre of attention. Her eyes flitted to his, and he held her gaze until she looked away.

After doing the rounds and greeting people, he made a beeline for his niece and nephew. Bianca clung to him, and he held her tightly. She was still coming to terms with what had transpired. She and Keyshawn had been in bed when the shooting started. Keyshawn had run to her room and dragged her to the floor. They heard gunfire, screams, and then silence. It had been Keyshawn who had discovered his mother's dead body. She had been shot three times in the back, and once in the back of the head. He kept Bianca from seeing it, then called the police.

Lamont had seen them as soon as Louis secured temporary custody, and had told Keyshawn how proud he was of him. He still felt that pride even now, as he squeezed his nephew's shoulder.

Keyshawn's face was an emotionless mask, and it was disconcerting for Lamont to see. He would help him push through if it was the last thing he did. Maybe speaking to a professional would help.

'Princess Bianca,' he said, lifting her so she could wrap her arms around him in a tight hug.

'I want to stay with you, Uncle L,' she whispered.

'That's fine. You can stay with me while I'm talking to the grownups.'

Bianca shook her head. 'No, Uncle L. I want to stay with you. Forever.'

Lamont's heart wrenched in his chest. No child should have to go through something of this magnitude. The sadness in his heart for his dead sister mingled with the joy of his niece wanting to stay with him. He hadn't considered where the kids would stay. Louis was happy to have them, but he was married and already had two children of his own. The more Lamont considered it, the more he wanted it to happen.

'I told you I wouldn't leave again,' he murmured. Bianca clutched him tighter. Keyshawn gave him a look, showing he'd overheard.

'Let's go outside,' he said to his nephew. 'Bianca, go play with your cousins for a few minutes.'

Bianca didn't like it, but did as she was told. Lamont and Keyshawn made their way to the front garden. Keyshawn stared at the floor, kicking at the ground with his shoes. Lamont watched him for a moment, still shocked at the similarities between them. Keyshawn reminded him so much of himself that it was uncanny.

'How are you doing with things?' he started, somewhat lamely.

Keyshawn shrugged. It was the level of answer he'd expected, yet he persisted.

'Is Louis looking after you?'

'Yeah.' Keyshawn finally found his voice, but added nothing else. Lamont continued to watch him. He was toeing a line between not wanting to make his nephew uncomfortable, but also wanting to avoid what had transpired during his own upbringing. Lamont vividly remembered being ignored by his Aunt in the aftermath of his parent's death. There was no opportunity to properly grieve or show his emotions. He'd needed to be strong for Marika, and it was clear early on that Aunt Carmen didn't want to hear him complaining. He wouldn't allow that to happen to Keyshawn.

'I wanted to tell you once again how proud I am of you. The way you've looked after your sis during all of this is fantastic, and I hope you realise that.'

Keyshawn nodded, and silence descended on them again.

'Why did she die?'

The question threw Lamont for six, and he was unsure how to answer. Despite his maturity, Keyshawn was still a child, and he couldn't tell him what had transpired.

'A bad man went after her,' he finally said.

'Because of you?'

'Because he wanted to hurt your mum,' said Lamont delicately, before adding, 'he wanted to hurt me too.'

Again, Keyshawn nodded.

'Your sis said she wants to live with me.' Lamont paused to see if Keyshawn would react. Other than glancing Lamont's way, he didn't. 'What do you think about that?'

'I . . . don't want bad people shooting at us anymore.'

Lamont hung his head, his heart breaking all over again. Straightening, he pulled his nephew in for a hug.

'I promise you, that won't happen, K.'

Keyshawn stiffened at the beginning of the hug, but slowly relaxed into it. After a few minutes, they composed themselves and headed back inside.

Lamont kept his distance from Aunt Carmen, but felt her eyes on him several times throughout the evening. Drinks were made available, and she consumed her fair share. It was almost ten in the evening when the conversation took a sudden turn. Bianca had already gone to bed, but Keyshawn remained up, playing on his mobile phone in the corner. Lamont was nearby, listening to Louis talk about his job. Aunt Carmen and Aunt Pat were holding a loud conversation that he did his best to tune out until he heard words that chilled his blood.

'I'll take them. I raised Rika, and I raised her right. I'll do the same with her kids.'

'That's not going to happen.' Lamont's voice carried around the room, ending all conversations. Keyshawn glanced up at him, but he kept his eyes on Aunt Carmen. The sight of her drove him to rage as it always had. He'd told her the last time they spoke, that he would never see her again, but he'd been forced to break the vow. Her eyes were bleary as she glared at him.

'Excuse me?'

'Keyshawn and Bianca will never live with you. They're going to live with me.'

A low murmur broke out around the room after his declaration.

'You must be crazy, Lamont. Why on earth would the kids live with you? It's your fault their mother is dead, dragging her into your crazy mess.'

Louis opened his mouth to defend him, but froze when he saw the expression on Lamont's face. The family all knew what Lamont did. They knew his background, but few had ever seen him like this. The cold fury in his eyes as he stared down his Aunt was chilling, sending shivers down their spines.

'Keyshawn,' Lamont started, his voice level despite his rage, 'go upstairs, please. Take your cousins too.'

Keyshawn didn't argue. He took the hands of his younger cousins and led them from the room.

'You vile excuse for a woman,' he said to Aunt Carmen, still speaking in the same level tone. 'You didn't even have the common decency to speak softly around Keyshawn? Do you really think I would ever expose my niece and nephew to your awful parenting?'

'You're ungrateful. You always were. I went without so that you and your sister would have everything you needed, and never received any thanks for it. I refuse to be judged by a disgusting criminal.'

'I'd rather be a criminal than be the things we all know you are,' he retorted, taking great pleasure at seeing her face pale. 'Whatever I am, I would never mistreat or abuse those children, and I doubt that is something you could say with any honesty.'

'L . . . maybe we should—' Aunt Pat spoke up, but Lamont silenced her with a vicious look.

'No. You all let this woman do what she wanted. You let her take my sister and me without considering what would be best for us. That's bad enough, but you went one step further and practically ignored us. You kept your heads buried in the sand because, as far as you were concerned, it wasn't your problem. Do not interfere any further.'

Aunt Pat's mouth opened and closed. She looked at her husband for his reaction, but he was equally stunned. None of them knew how to deal with this side of Lamont. Aunt Carmen's chins quivered as she shot her nephew a look of loathing. It didn't matter. He'd said his piece, and no one in the room would stop him from getting what he wanted. Without another word, he went outside again to get some fresh air, needing to be away from his family. He took several deep breaths, trying to calm himself.

The comments about being responsible for Marika's death still stung, but he was working past it. He wasn't to blame. Lennox Thompson had decided to leave her kids without a mother. Lamont didn't know where her baby father was, but he would track him down in due course, and ensure there were no roadblocks in him being named the carer for his niece and nephew.

'You really got some stuff off your chest in there, didn't you?' Louis headed out and stood next to his cousin. They had similar features, but Louis was shorter and thicker around the middle. His hair was also thinner on top, but he had the piercing eyes and facial features many of the Jones' shared.

'Sorry for bringing all the drama to your house,' said Lamont, running a hand through his hair.

'Don't worry about it. Wouldn't be a family gathering without an argument.'

They both chuckled, comfortable in the silence.

'You're right, you know,' Louis said, moments later. 'You're the best one to look after them. I think you need Bianca and Keyshawn as much as they need you.'

Lamont didn't respond, but he agreed, and it was nice to know Louis was on his side.

'I just need to survive,' he said.

'Is it that bad?' Louis knew little bits of what Lamont was involved in, and the deaths that surrounded him this year, but not much of any substance.

'I'll handle it. Watch the kids for now, especially Keyshawn. I don't want him internalising his pain.'

'Leave it to me, cuz. Nothing will happen to them.'

CHAPTER TWENTY-SEVEN
MONDAY 1 JUNE, 2015

THE DAYS FOLLOWING the execution of Delroy went well for Lennox. Led by Nicky Derrigan, his forces were pushing out numerous drug dealers with little resistance. The ruthless way he had dealt with the Williams' crew had left a fissure on the streets of Chapeltown, and no one wanted to get in his way.

Despite the successes, he had heard no response from Teflon or any of the other larger crews. Teflon had completely pulled his people back, and there were no signs of them selling any drugs, which was surprising. He brushed it off, however. He had shown him time and time again that he was superior, and would destroy him and his team if they stepped up. Teflon was soft at heart, and every time he had gone against Lennox, he had lost someone close to him. He would be silly to risk that again.

Lennox was firmly looking to the future. Soon, Chapeltown would be united under his control. To restock the war fund, he had raided Delroy's drug spots, planning to sell the product, along with what he had stolen from Lamont's team. It went against his credo, but he consoled himself with the fact he wasn't selling the drugs in Chapeltown.

Through Mark Patrick, he had arranged sales with several out-of-town buyers that would flood their own areas with the high-quality product. Sitting comfy in his safe house, he poured himself a drink with a smug smile on his face.

MACK SAT in his front room, glaring at a western on the TV and chain smoking. It was late evening. He had tried calling Lennox numerous times, but hadn't received a response, and it was making him antsy. He'd resented Delroy and his treatment of him over the years, culminating in him sharing information about his family, namely his daughter Alicia. He had expected Lennox to use her to lure out Delroy, but had been sickened when he murdered her. There was nothing to be done about it now. He had to think about his own future, and that meant getting the rest of the fortune Lennox had promised him for his involvement.

Once he got the funds, he was done with England. His family had land in St Kitts, and he would live like a king with the money he earned. Mack was so lost in his musings that when his door was kicked open, he didn't immediately react. By the time he'd made it to his feet, Shorty and K-Bar were in the room, dressed in all-black and armed with pistols, both trained on his head. He raised his hands, shivering with fear in the middle of his living room.

'Where's Lennox?' asked Shorty.

'I don't know!'

Shorty shook his head. K-Bar — usually the calm one — stepped forward, cracking him around the head with his gun. He crumpled to the floor as K-Bar stood over him, a murderous look in his eyes.

'You better talk, Mack. We know you set up Delroy. If you don't start talking, the beating is gonna be worse than the last one I gave you, and that's before we get into some special shit.'

Mack shifted back, terrified by Shorty's words.

'H-He threatened m-me. Said if I didn't go along with it, he would kill me,' he tried.

'He threatened all of us too,' replied Shorty. 'He took out people close to all of us, but we'd never back down from him. You sold out a

TARGET PART III

man that fed you for decades. If you hadn't been so shit with your money, you'd be retired now. Who did you deal with in Lennox's crew? There's no way he'd deal with a prick like you directly.'

'. . . Sinclair. This young crazy kid who works for Lennox. He made the offer and gave me a direct line to his boss.'

'Bet he's not taking your calls anymore now that you're useless, is he?' said K-Bar dryly. Mack pretended not to hear.

'I want all the information you have on the crew. Don't piss around either,' Shorty demanded. Mack didn't hesitate. He spilled information about potential hangouts, and descriptions of the people Sinclair was with. He even gave a description of the car he'd driven. K-Bar stored all the information in his phone.

'Guess we got what we came for,' he said to Shorty, who nodded.

'What happens to me now?' stammered Mack. His eyes widened when Shorty's finger tightened on the gun.

'This is for Del and Alicia.' He fired twice, bullets exploding into Mack's neck and cheek. Standing over Mack's prone frame, he fired twice more. They quickly left the house, jumping straight into the waiting car, which drove away at speed.

TERRY WAITED IN HIS AUDI. Maka had contacted him in a panic, saying he needed help after all the problems with the crew. Terry had arranged to meet with him, an oily smile on his face, as he plotted how he was going to profit from the situation. Maka told him Lennox had made his moves against the crew, robbing them of product, and murdering Teflon's sister, along with Delroy and his daughter. Terry had gleefully passed all the information onto Murphy, hoping it would keep him off his back.

Maka arrived a short while later. He looked harried, shiftily looking in all directions. Hastily greeting him, he got to the point.

'We're fucked. Supplier's cut us off after all the shit that's happened. Teflon's fucked off and left us in the lurch, and half the team is locked up. I need you to step up if you can handle it.'

'Course I can handle it, mate,' replied Terry, trying to keep his voice level. 'Where's Shorty and K-Bar?'

'Shorty's injured. One of Lennox's guys beat him badly. K-Bar's all depressed because Rika Jones got blasted, and he was loved up,' said Maka, his tone full of scorn. It surprised Terry. Maka was usually calm, but all the stress had seemingly gotten to him.

'Shit . . . you shoulda called me earlier, pal. I could have helped.'

'I know. It's been bad, though. Taken a while to get things relatively back in line. That's what I need you for.'

'Go on.'

'I've had to scrape a deal with some Slovenians. They've got links all over, but they've struggled to crack into the Hood.'

Terry nodded. 'I've heard of a few of those Russian lot trying to make moves. Do you want me to meet them?'

'Yes. We're likely to get ripped off, but see what you can do. I know you've wanted more responsibility for a while. This is your chance to be a player again, and show what you're made of.'

Terry grinned. 'I won't let you down, Maka. When's the meet?'

Maka handed Terry a piece of paper with the details.

'Everything is on there. Make sure you burn that paper too. Ring me after you're done, and we'll discuss next steps. Cool?'

'Leave it to me, mate.'

Terry watched him drive away, his grin widening. This was what he had been waiting for. He had Maka dependent on him, and had more titbits he could feed the police. Climbing into his ride, he motored away, already calling Murphy. Hopefully, this would keep him off his back.

CHAPTER TWENTY-EIGHT
TUESDAY 2 JUNE, 2015

TERRY ARRIVED at the spot where he was meeting the Slovenians just after ten in the evening. It was a house on Brownhill Crescent in Harehills. He hadn't told the police about the meeting. He wanted to use Maka a while longer before he gave him up. The information regarding Lennox and Teflon had been passed on to Murphy. It matched up with a lot of the talk going around the Hood regarding Lennox and his crusade against dealers. Terry hoped the police arrested them quickly, leaving the path free for him to keep climbing the ladder.

As he climbed from his car, he thought back to his initial arrest. He'd been caught red-handed doing a deal, and he'd thought his life was over. Now, through cunning and solid moves, he had made it work.

Knocking on the door, he planted a smile on his face when a woman answered. She wasn't the nicest, with slightly crossed eyes and crooked teeth. The body was ridiculous, however, and she wore a plunging top showcasing her tremendous cleavage. He forced his eyes back to hers.

'Hi love, I'm here to meet *Ivan*,' he said. She nodded and let him in, pointing to the room ahead. Terry entered with a stroll, turning up his nose at the sight of the living room. There were dirty plates on the flimsy coffee table, a small LCD television on a spindly stand in the middle of the room, and creaking floorboards that sank under the weight of Terry's feet. He glanced back at the woman, who was pointing to the next room. Hoping for her sake she wasn't wasting his time, he wrenched open the door and entered the kitchen, where he froze.

'Good to see you, Terry,' said K-Bar, his gun raised and pointed at Terry's chest.

'K, what's going on? What's all this?'

'Guess you could say we're tidying up,' replied K-Bar.

'I don't get you,' said Terry, feeling a bead of sweat at the top of his head. He needed to pick his words carefully here. As nice as K-Bar could be, he was deadly. Slowly, he raised his hands, trying to show K-Bar he wasn't a threat.

'Yeah, you do. *Informer.*'

Terry's blood ran cold as he realised instantly that the game was up. If they knew he was a police informant, there was utterly no way out.

'Listen,' he started, thinking on the spot, 'the Feds followed me here. You kill me, they're coming straight for you.'

K-Bar's smile both terrified and confused him.

'Wouldn't be the first time you've sent them after me, right? Was it you who told them about some of my other moves?'

Terry shook his head jerkily, nausea bubbling in his stomach.

'Please . . .' he started, only to be cut down by a single bullet to the forehead. Not even giving him a second glance, K-Bar left the house. The woman who had set Terry up was long gone, and there was nothing connecting her to the house.

Shorty waited for him in a car down the street.

'All done?' he asked. K-Bar nodded.

'Pity we can't take his car too. Fucking snitch.'

'It's done. I'll call Maka and let him know.'

TARGET PART III

SINCLAIR WAS next on the list. They tracked the car he was using to a spot in the heart of Miles Hill. Shorty had two men with him, named Kareem and Majid. Both men were strongly built and could handle themselves. They all wore masks to cover their faces and prevent detection. The driver kept the car running, and the trio hurried to the house. There was no time to worry about unlocking the door. Kareem kicked it in with ease and charged into the living room, gun raised.

Shorty and Majid hurried upstairs. Shorty took one room, Majid another. Bursting into the bedroom, Shorty found Sinclair shrugging off the woman he was with, trying to go for a butterfly knife that rested on the bedside table.

'Don't do it to yourself,' Shorty warned, ready to shoot if he moved. Sinclair looked like he was still thinking of going for it, but stopped moving. The woman he was with screamed as Majid entered the room, followed seconds later by Kareem.

'Oi, shut it, before I shut you up,' snapped Shorty. Trembling, she complied.

'What the fuck do you want?' If Sinclair was scared, he wasn't showing it. Lamont had mentioned the young assassin who had killed Akeem, but he had thought he was exaggerating. He looked around fourteen years old. He had no facial hair, a tapered fade, and a bony chest and skinny frame. It was hard to imagine him being able to lift a gun, let alone shoot it.

'Darling. I suggest you wait downstairs. Don't leave before I've spoken to you. My people are waiting outside,' Shorty told the woman. Unconcerned about her nakedness, she scuttled from the room.

'Get on with it then!' Sinclair was still showing no fear. Shorty smirked.

'You have to answer for what you did to Akeem.'

'Who the hell is Akeem?'

The men beside Shorty tensed, but Shorty ignored them for now.

'The man you shot on Chapeltown Road.'

'What about him?'

'This guy here,' Shorty motioned to Kareem. 'He's his brother.'

Sinclair shifted slightly in the bed. Other than his bottom lip quivering, he showed no reaction.

'This guy,' he motioned next to Majid, 'is a good friend. I'm gonna leave them to deal with you, while I speak to your pretty little girlfriend.'

The men advanced on Sinclair. As Shorty headed downstairs, he heard the first scream. The naked woman had done as ordered, sitting on the cherry red sofa, using a small throw pillow to cover her nakedness.

'Is this your house?' Shorty asked.

She shook her head.

'Get some clothes and go home. If I hear you've said a word about what happened here, I'm gonna come and find you. Write your name and address.'

After a few minutes, he called Kareem and Majid off. Both men looked like they wanted to do more damage, but they were on a tight schedule. Sinclair was left face-down on the bed, after being half-strangled, with wounds to his genitals, arms, and legs, and a large hole in the back of the head. It was a grisly revenge for Akeem's murder.

'I hope this makes things right,' said Shorty, after they had cleaned up and changed their clothes at a safe house in Scott Hall.

'It does,' replied Kareem. 'My brother was a soldier and knew the rules, but I'm glad we made it right.'

'Give Vincent my regards when you go back home,' said Shorty. 'Teflon's too.'

'We will. You need any more help up here?'

Shorty shook his head. 'We're nearly done, fam. Thanks for the offer.'

After slapping hands with both men, Shorty left to link with K-Bar and Lamont.

THE EXECUTIONS OF MACK, Terry Worthy, and Sinclair, was a coordinated effort that took place within 24 hours. Rather than resting on their laurels, the crew was committed to finishing Lennox. Teflon had put up twenty thousand pounds in reward money, wanting all addresses linked to Lennox and his men. His surveillance of the Jackie

TARGET PART III

Smart Court property had paid dividends when his men saw Mark Patrick show up to give orders to the men staying there. After a quick phone call, they had tailed him discretely to a spot on Archery Road.

Ten men were ready to rush the spot. They had no confirmation Lennox was there, but it was deemed to be worth the risk.

Lamont, K-Bar and Shorty were all present, armed and focused.

'He doesn't even have people watching the spot,' K-Bar remarked.

'He could have people watching from any of these houses. We go in quick and heavy, and we don't leave anyone alive,' said Lamont. K-Bar and Shorty both shared a look, grinning at him. They trusted his combat instincts much more now that they knew he had some kills under his belt.

'Quick and heavy is fine. Let's make it happen and finish this swiftly.'

'WHAT THE HELL are you trying to tell me?' Lennox snapped. He was with Derrigan and Mark Patrick, and neither had good things to say. Lennox had been at the house for the past few days, wanting to remain close to the action in the Hood. During that time, he'd added little touches to the spot, adding an X-Box, a widescreen television and games and DVDs to stave his boredom.

As they spoke, Derrigan kept glancing over at the console, clearly bored with the conversation. He had his feet up on the coffee table, hoping the others would stop talking soon.

'Teflon and his team are coming back on us,' said Mark. 'They've attacked a few spots, and they got Sinclair. Tortured him pretty badly before they killed him too.'

'I don't care about Sinclair,' said Lennox. 'He was a tool, and he outlived his usefulness. Mack is dead too, so I'm guessing they found out about him giving up Delroy.'

'What are we doing now, then?' Derrigan asked. Before Lennox could reply, gunfire ensued. Mark knocked over the coffee table, using it for quick cover as a group of men swarmed into the room. Mark saw K-Bar lining up a shot on Lennox, and let go a burst of shots. They all ripped into K-Bar, who did a stutter-step-like movement before falling backwards. Enraged, Shorty blasted Mark before he could move, four bullets putting him down for the count. Lennox scrambled away, with Derrigan watching his back. Lamont fired a shot at him, but it missed. He and Shorty exchanged a look and ran after Lennox, chasing him into the next room. Two goons waited for them. Shorty cut them down, but the distraction gave Lennox time to slip out of the door.

'Go!' Shorty shouted. 'I'll handle Derrigan.'

Nodding, Lamont ran after Lennox. Derrigan eyed Shorty, then smiled. Both men aimed their weapons at one another.

'Round 2 then?' he said. 'We never got to finish our fight.' He lowered his gun slightly, which was a fatal mistake. Shorty pumped the rest of his clip into him, sending him crashing into the wall.

'I don't have time for that shit,' he said to Derrigan's prone frame. He turned to one of the men who had followed him. 'Finish this piece of shit off.'

Running back through to the main room, Shorty hurried toward K-Bar, who was unmoving on the ground. Two of their goons were standing over him.

'K . . .' he whispered, knowing it was too late. His long-time friend and comrade was dead. Mark had clinically put him down. The bullets to the chest had finished him. Blinking away tears, Shorty took K-Bar's gloved hand in his own. 'I'm sorry, fam. You deserved better than this.'

After squeezing K-Bar's hand one last time, he hurried after Lamont.

LENNOX HURTLED from the house during the confusion. There had always been a chance of getting caught, but he had never actually expected it to happen. Somehow, Teflon had tracked him down and, from the sounds of things, wiped out his two remaining pillars in Derrigan and Mark Patrick. He was absolutely furious at the turn-around. This was his time. He'd murdered Delroy and his entire family to earn this, and yet Teflon had surprised him once again.

TARGET PART III

As he rounded the corner onto Blackman Lane, he heard footsteps following, slowly growing closer.

'Stop, Lennox.'

Lennox heard the click of a gun and complied, turning slowly to face Teflon. They stood in the middle of the quiet streets, staring one another down. It was the first time they had been face-to-face since their brief meeting in March. For a man he'd believed was steps away from a breakdown after his sister's death, Teflon looked remarkably composed. He stepped closer to Lennox, gun aimed at his chest. Lennox noticed his hands weren't shaking.

'Have you killed before?' he asked.

'Does it matter at this stage?' Teflon replied. 'You're finished.'

'You think?'

'The police are hitting several of your known spots. They want you for various murders, and we've taken out your main team. This has been a long time coming.'

Lennox found his anger growing in the face of his calm demeanour.

'You're nothing without your people, Teflon. Your bitch screamed for you before she died. Your sis and that old barber probably did the same, if they even got the chance. All deaths I orchestrated, because you weren't strong enough to stop me.'

Teflon nodded, seemingly in agreement, which was a shock. Lennox didn't like this side. They'd spoken on the phone when he'd given him Ryan Peters' location, and he'd sounded frustrated.

'The deaths hurt me. For too long, I forced myself into thinking having those feelings was a weakness. I envied you at one point, because you have no feelings, and you're truly ruthless. Now, I pity you. People don't weaken me. They strengthen me. My connections to people have kept me going, even when I thought it was money, or the power I had at my fingertips. In the end, power nor money stopped those close to me from losing their lives.'

Lennox shook his head, not wanting to listen to Teflon's redemption bullshit.

'You're not strong enough to be at the top. You don't have the stomach to do the things needed to lead.'

'I agree. It's a *strength* I don't want. I've been on borrowed time for too long.' His finger tightened on the gun.

Fear welled within Lennox, but was instantly quashed. He refused to be afraid of Teflon.

'No matter what happens here, you don't win. You can't walk off into the sunset with your bitch. I took her. I took your sister.'

'I'll never truly be over their losses, but I know I'll be okay,' Teflon's response again took him by surprise. 'Jenny loved me. She saw something in me, and we were happy for a time. I want to experience that same happiness again.'

Despite himself, Lennox snorted. Teflon smirked.

'I don't expect you to understand. Like I said, I pity you. You couldn't hold onto your woman without threatening her. I'm guessing your mum scarred you.'

Lennox froze. Then he roared and stepped toward Teflon, before coming to his senses and remembering the man was armed. He snarled, wanting to tear him apart.

'You—'

'She was a prostitute. You couldn't take that she cared about getting high more than she cared about you. You never had a role model, and it made you into some cold, unfeeling husk. Your plans failed. You can't have Chapeltown, because you're even worse for the community than I am. You don't care about anything but yourself.' He paused. 'I care more about them than I do myself. Never thought I would say that.'

'Fuck you,' Lennox spat. 'If you pull that trigger, you're truly no better than me, no matter what you say, or how you try to justify it.'

Teflon shook his head.

'I can honestly say I'm doing this not for revenge, but because it's the right thing for everyone else.'

The gun fired once, the bullet slamming into Lennox's stomach and sending him careening into a nearby wall. Aware they were out in the open, Teflon stood over him. Lennox coughed, blood dribbling from his mouth, his eyes dimming.

. . .

TARGET PART III

LAMONT WASN'T LEAVING it to chance. The final bullet smashed into Lennox's forehead.

He glanced down at the fallen criminal, the ramifications of what he had done washing over him for a second. He turned and saw Shorty nearby, gun by his side. The two friends shared a nod, acknowledging what had transpired.

'C'mon,' said Shorty. 'Let's get out of here. Someone will have called the Feds.'

Looking at Lennox's body one last time, Lamont followed Shorty away from the scene.

EPILOGUE
WEDNESDAY SEPTEMBER 9, 2015

'YOU NEED TO CHEER UP, MATE.'

Rigby let Murphy's words drift over him as always. They were on their way to a crime scene, and the March weather was particularly cold. Wind whipped through the open window on the passenger side door. Murphy embraced it, closing his eyes and breathing it in deeply. Rigby zipped his jacket up as far as it would go, shaking his head and muttering as he navigated a left turn.

'Seriously, it's been months,' Murphy continued, knowing he wouldn't reply. 'You can't dwell on things forever. I mean, we did bloody outstanding work. We smashed a few crime rings and locked up dozens of people. That's a win.'

'Teflon and Shorty got away. Worthy ended up dead, meaning they probably learned he was the grass.'

'Worthy was never the sharpest knife in the drawer, was he?' Murphy scoffed.

Rigby finally glared at his partner. 'That's a callous attitude to have. Even for a hard bastard like you.'

'I'm not wrong, though, am I? He was a screwup all of his life, and look where it got him. At least he tried to leave us a parting gift.'

TARGET PART III

'Even with his help, we failed. Teflon and Shorty got clear away.'

'Their crew is finished. Delroy's crew is finished. That's the two biggest crews right there. That's a win, so you need to shake the misery and move on.'

Rigby didn't reply. He wasn't sure he could do that. To him, it seemed like yesterday they had found the bodies of Lennox Thompson and several of his men. Rigby never had the chance to fully go after him for the murders he *knew* he had ordered, but the brass were happy. They had closed multiple murder cases, causing a significant dent in street traffic in and around Chapeltown.

Relations between the community and the police were thawing, but there was still work to be done. He wondered if Teflon was done for good, or if he would try to take advantage of the power vacuum the way other crews were attempting to, and become stronger than ever.

They were approaching the crime scene, though, and as Rigby brought the car to a halt, his mind shifted from Teflon as always. It was a new day, a new crime, and it demanded his full attention.

COSTA DE ORO, URUGUAY

'Gracey, let your dad hold the phone. You're shaking it!'

The smile on Lamont's face couldn't get any wider. He was on a beach on the other side of the world, talking to people he loved via FaceTime. Grace Turner's face took up most of the phone screen, but Lamont knew Amy and Shorty were with her. She had recovered well enough to go home, but was still taking a truckload of medication, and had weekly hospital trips for check-ups. Shorty and Amy were trying again, and though it was early days, from what he could see, they were doing well. They seemed more open with one another, which was good to see.

Shorty had followed Lamont's example, stepping away from the life of crime. He had saved his money over the past year, and wanted to set up his own business, but he wasn't sure what he wanted to do.

For now, he was content staying with Grace and catching up on the time he'd missed. There had been a few trips to Huddersfield, and a few awkward meetings between half-siblings, but it was all progress, and it all made Lamont smile every time he heard more about it.

The pair were still finding their way back to the level of brotherhood they once had, but they were taking steps to repair their relationship, one day at a time.

'Gracey, go get a drink with your mum; let me talk to Uncle L in peace.'

'Okay, daddy. Bye, Uncle L.'

'Talk to you soon, Gracey.'

Shorty took the phone and went to sit outside in Amy's back garden. There was a moment of silence between them, neither forcing any conversation.

'You look good, L,' Shorty finally said. 'Down there agrees with you, man. You look healthy.'

'I feel it,' Lamont admitted.

'Being away has done you the world of good.'

Lamont wiped his eye with his free hand. 'I still have a lot of work to do. It's hard sometimes, dealing with everything that's happened. Gets overwhelming. What I'm learning is that I need to accept the fact I'm not superman, and that it's okay to be down.'

Shorty didn't fully grasp what Lamont was saying. He still had issues communicating with Amy, resisting the urge to storm out when they argued, but like Lamont, he was learning to live with it. All that mattered to him was that Lamont finally looked like he was healing.

'I don't really get it, fam, but I'm glad that *you* get it.'

That was enough for Lamont. He wouldn't have been able to be so open with Shorty in the past. They were the best of friends, but hid parts of themselves from each other, allowing resentment to fester until frustrations overflowed. Now, their friendship had evolved. It wasn't as deep as it had been, but it was realer, and it was still developing.

'What's going on with Bianca and Keyshawn then?'

Lamont's stomach plummeted when Shorty mentioned Marika's kids. Thinking about her was hard, and it had taken some time for him to truly come to terms with the fact his little sister was gone. He pointed the blame at Lennox, but deep down, he still had some issues to work through with his guilt.

'When I'm back in the city, they will come with me. Bianca is happy. Hard to tell with Keyshawn.'

Lamont didn't have to say more. Shorty knew Keyshawn was like Lamont in temperament. They both internalised their pain, and Keyshawn was clearly feeling the pain of his mother's murder. He had lashed out at Lamont a few times, blaming him for what happened, but he always apologised. It would take time, but he would help him through it.

They would help each other through it.

'They're gonna be fine, L. You're gonna do good by them; give them what you never had.'

Lamont lowered his head for a moment, overcome by emotion. He and Shorty had never really spoken about his upbringing, and the influence his Aunt had on him after his parents died, but he was right. Lamont was new to parenting, but vowed to be there for both of them, and to raise them right.

'Thanks, Shorty.'

'Anytime, fam. I'm gonna see what those two are up to. I'll speak to you soon, though. If you don't come back to Leeds, we're coming down there to find you.'

Lamont chuckled. 'I'll hold you to that.'

The connection was cut, and Lamont put the phone down. Stretching, he stood up and looked over the balcony of his hotel. He had a gorgeous view of the pale sands, and the seas that were almost turquoise. At night, it was a place of wonder, with the music and dancing, and the carefree attitude of the locals. It made him feel tranquil, and without his responsibilities back home, he would give serious thought to living here. As he stood there in his light blue vest and khaki board shorts, he remembered a few years back, sitting in Jenny's back garden, speaking of a want to travel, having already purchased tickets to Uruguay.

Tickets that were never used.

For a fleeting moment, he wondered how things would have changed if they had made the trip, but he closed his eyes and took a deep breath. The pain would always be there. In spite of that, he would be okay.

Staring out at the lapping waves, Lamont felt a wave of contentment he never thought he deserved to feel, then looked up at the sky, closing his eyes with a small smile on his face.

DID YOU ENJOY THE READ?

And here we are! Thank you for reading the final book in the Target series!

AP is hands-down my favourite of my books, and definitely the one I wrote the quickest. The goal was simple: Bring it home and end it well, and I think I did it. I hope you loved Lamont's journey as much as I enjoyed writing it.

Please take a minute or two to help me by leaving a review – even if it's just a few lines. Reviews help massively with getting my books in front of new readers. I personally read every review and take all feedback on board.

To support me, please click the relevant link below:
    UK: http://www.amazon.co.uk/review/create-review?&asin=B08NZZXVY4
    US: http://www.amazon.com/review/create-review?&asin=B08NZZXVY4

DID YOU ENJOY THE READ?

Make sure you're following me on Amazon to keep up to date with my releases, or that you're signed up to my email list, and I'll see you at the next book!

GET A FREE NOVELLA

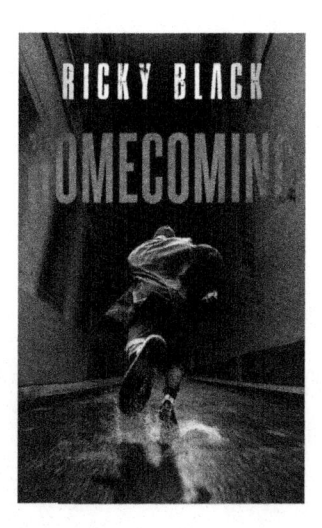

Building a relationship with my readers is one of the best things about writing. I'm first and foremost a fan of books, and getting to talk at length about them is a bonus.

If you sign up to the mailing list, you'll receive a copy of my novella Homecoming, absolutely free.

You can get this immediately here

ALSO BY RICKY BLACK

The Target Series:

Origins: The Road To Power

Target

Target Part 2: The Takedown

Target Part 3: Absolute Power

The Complete Target Collection

The Deeds Family Series:

Blood & Business

Good Deed, Bad Deeds

Deeds to the City

ABOUT RICKY BLACK

Ricky Black was born and raised in Chapeltown, Leeds. He began writing seriously in 2004, working on mainly crime pieces.

In 2016, he published the first of his crime series, Target, and has published seven more books since.

Visit https://rickyblackbooks.com for information regarding new releases and special offers and promotions.

To Marc.

When I was low and didn't want to finish, and wanted to write something else, you patiently rolled up your sleeves and kept me on track.

You're my brother, and I hope you see this and understand just how valuable you were, are, and will continue to be.

Copyright © 2021 by Ricky Black

All rights reserved.

No part of this book may be reproduced in any form or by any electronic or mechanical means, including information storage and retrieval systems, without written permission from the author, except for the use of brief quotations in a book review.

Printed in Great Britain
by Amazon